U0011396

一本突破中式英文盲點

掌握華人學英語
發音·文法·字彙關鍵

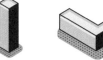

張西亞／著

Daniel Mark McMahon、吳娟／校訂

　　書如其名，寫這本書的初衷是針對中英文的差異，希望以中文的視角提供華人學英文時應該注意的地方。了解自己母語與外語之間思維、邏輯、結構等的差異，可以降低母語的干擾，對於學外語會有很大的幫助。因此，本書取材都盡量以此為原則，這是和一般英文學習書籍的一個很大的差異。同時，取材也注重貼近生活化的日常英語，以及流行的字詞。

　　學英文的方向最粗略的分類為：發音、文法、字彙。英語發音與文法字彙通常是涇渭分明，鮮少被同時納於一書，本書將兩者並陳，並且偶有交疊，可算是一個創新嘗試。

　　本書共分 11 章：發音篇 2 章（第 1、2 章）、文法篇 5 章（第 3、4、5、6、7 章）、字彙篇 2 章（第 8、9 章）、其他 2 章（第 10、11 章）。內容由淺入深，讀者可依自己的程度與興趣，選擇喜好的章節閱讀。建議初學者可以先讀第 1、3、4、5、8 章，再進入第 2、6、7、9、10、11 章。本書適合國中與高中的讀者作為英語輔助教材，也適合大學生與社會人士作為加強語文能力的工具。

　　學母語像是幼年成長的「禮物」，自然容易，得來全不費工夫。我們出生幾個月大開始牙牙學語，到 6 歲入學正式讀書前和大人溝通就已經毫無問題，通順流利，母語發音與基本文法已然到位。幼兒是怎麼習得母語的？語言學家有不同的學派理論，其中有些專家認為：嬰兒學母語的能力幾乎是「本能」。

　　然而，長大之後要學外語，已經深植我們血液之中的超強的母語卻反

而會變成干擾，越成年才學外語，干擾越大。更麻煩的是，干擾的來源，不僅僅是發音、文法、字彙等語言層面，更包括思維邏輯、文化習慣等各方面的影響。

「母語干擾」最可怕的地方是它會造成盲點，形成習慣，由盲點導致的錯誤並不是粗心、馬虎的問題，而是我們並不知道自己有錯。因此即使聽到、看到對的發音或文句，也很可能「聽而不聞，看而不見」，根本沒有感覺！

學習任何外語的最佳途徑就是從小在完整全面的外語環境中成長學習，自然地學會，甚至不必刻意去學發音與文法。但問題是，絕大多數的我們都沒有這樣的環境！超過了幼年關鍵吸收期，就很難自然地學會，需要下功夫，從基本動作開始學，打好基礎，才能逐步向上。

外語的難易取決於它與你的母語的距離，越近越容易學。中英文之間的距離相當遠，簡單地列出一些中英文的不同：

中文	英文
約 247 部首，立體組合	26 個字母，排列組合
表意文字，以字為主	表音文字，以音為主
24 個輔音，13 個元音	24 個子音，17 個母音（KK 音標）
聲調語言（聲調表示不同意義）（4 聲，一聲一字）	語調語言（聲調只表示不同語氣）重音語言
音節計時語言	重音計時語言
一單字一音節	單字多音節，有輕重音節
動詞無時態	動詞有時態
單字無性別	單字有性別
單字無複數形	單字有複數形
增加新字難	增加新字易
字難文法易	字易文法難
藝術性高	藝術性低

固有中華文化底蘊傳承；文字統一	受其他語言或文化影響極大，如法國、拉丁（羅馬）、希臘等等

　　中文的最早的來源是象形（六書：象形、指事、會意、形聲、轉注、假借），由部首組合堆疊，深具藝術性、文化性、歷史性。英文由 26 個字母組成，容易排列組合，再加上吸收融入了許多國家的語言，語音與文字都演變地相當複雜，也使得英文成為世界上大體公認的單字最多的語言。根據《牛津字典》（Oxford English Dictionary, 1989）的統計，英文有 171,476 在用單字（in common use），老舊不用的有 47,156 個。

　　英美有名的大字典（Merriam-Webster, Oxford 等）每年都還會增加成千上百的新字，近年最著名的如 selfie（自拍）、vape（吸電子菸）等，這兩個字都曾在字典的年度新字中名列前茅。

　　雖然字彙庫這麼龐大，幸運的是，常用到的單字只是很小的一部分，那麼，我們到底需要多少單字量才夠用呢？眾說紛紜，差別很大。提供以下的數字做為學習的參考：日常會話單字約 1,000 ～ 2,000 字；閱讀與書寫約 4,000 ～ 6,000 字；高階到流利約 8,000 ～ 10,000 字以上。一般高等教育程度的英語母語人士則約在 15,000 ～ 25,000 字以上。

　　另外，中英文在文法結構上的差異也很大，包括：

1. 中文重意合，英文重形合

   中文強調意義上的連貫，詞彙的連結靠語意，文句規則鬆散靈活。英文重形合，強調形式上的關連，句子結構嚴謹，連結規則鮮明。

2. 中文多短句，英文多長句

   中文語意大多透過小短句來表達。英文架構環環相扣，主從關係分明，透過連接詞可以衍生連結許多子句，文章常出現很長的句子，這時候需要知道文法的規則，將句子切割分解，才能閱讀愉快。

3. **中文多重複，英文多變化**

英文正式文章很講究表達方式（字詞、片語、子句）的變化：(1) 上下文不重複相同的字詞，盡量用其他同義字，(2) 文章不過度重複相同的句型，各種句型（簡單句、複合句、複雜句）需穿插運用。對我們來說，增加了讀寫的難度。

4. **中文先因後果，英文先果後因**

中文敘事的順序是先鋪陳好背景氛圍，再進入重點，重點在最後面。英文句子則相反，先講重點，再說細節。

由於英美兩國在近代史中長期國力強盛以及擴張的政策佈局，全世界以英語作為母語、或官方語言、或第二語言的國家已近百個，其他的國家中也有許多從小學或中學就開始教英文。另外，全球儲存的各類電子訊息中，英文的部分佔了至少 70%，可以說，英文已是母語之外的通用語言（global lingua franca）。

工欲善其事，必先利其器。學英文是隨時都離不開字典的，字典是最強的工具。美式線上字典中常受推薦的如 Merriam-Webster；英式如 Oxford 與 Cambridge。有的網站可連上許多字典，實用又方便，如 OneLook Dictionary Search 網站，只要鍵入一個單字，就有約 30 個各類的字典任你選擇。

許多英語書籍（包括本書）都會整理出許多學英文的規則，確實有助於學習，但也要切記：幾乎所有的規則都會有不少甚至有很多的例外！只要多加練習與運用，自然而然就能習慣與熟練。

最後要提醒：學發音，要用「心」聽；學文法，要用「心」看。學 speaking 要先「聽得懂」，聽得懂，才能講；學 writing 要先「看得懂」，看得懂，才能寫。

另外，學外語最難改的就是口音（accent）了，唐朝詩人賀知章 1500 年前在他膾炙人口的《回鄉偶書》中就告訴我們：少小離家老大回，鄉音

無改鬢毛衰⋯⋯。詩中的老者，少小離家，老大回鄉，但鄉音不改，根深蒂固。英語並非我們的母語，有點口音也是自然的，不必太過拘泥，只要盡力就夠了，更重要的是學好聽力、文法、詞彙，這樣，無論是講話或寫文章都能清楚通順地表達，就達到學語言的目的了！

本書最後的【附錄 1】是音標的說明。【附錄 2】是習題解答。

最後要感謝台北市閱讀寫作協會理事長汪詠黛和時報文化公司趙政岷董事長，以及相識半世紀的老友克思明（輔仁大學歷史學系教授，前文學院院長），在他們滿滿的信任奔走及慨然應允下，本書才得以完成與順利出版。也特別感謝 Daniel Mark McMahon（輔仁大學歷史學系教授，前清雲科技大學應用外語系教授）以 native speaker 的角度，給本書不少的寶貴指教與校訂。另外，吳娟（輔仁大學外語學院專任講師兼國際學生中心主任）慷慨地提供了專業的意見與校正，也在此一併致謝。最後，謝謝時報文化公司編輯團隊的熱忱盡責與製作水準，讓本書能如期圓滿地出版。

3.8 感嘆詞 169

CHAPTER 4　句子結構 ✚✚✚　170

4.1 基本分類 170

4.2 從屬子句 175

Part 3　字彙篇

CHAPTER 8　單字的形成方式 +++　231

☞ Part 4　其他篇

Part 1

→● 發音篇

　　雖然語言專家對母語的習得有不同的觀點，但如果說母語是幼兒成長的禮物，應不為過，因為它得來全不費功夫。我們從未學過發音時嘴形如何、舌頭擺哪等，但說母語時，各器官就自動就位、自然發生。但過了幼兒的關鍵吸收期，去學外語就完全不是那麼回事了！因為相關器官就不再聽話，不再自動就位。

　　學習任何事物（科技、運動等），一定都得從「基本動作」學起。英文最重要的基本動作是⑴發音：發音器官（主要包括唇、舌、顎、喉等）的位置與動作；⑵文法：包括詞類屬性、字詞順序、文句架構等。以中文發音來說，器官位置不對，就很難發出正確的音來。例如有的人會將「熱」發成「樂」，是因為ㄖ音的舌頭不碰觸上齒齦，如果舌碰齦，就發不出ㄖ音，而偏向ㄌ音了。由此可見發音器官的位置與動作對於發音是多麼重要了！

　　英語發音也是同樣的道理，器官的位置與動作決定一切的發音，以單字 Apple 中的 /æ/ 為例，舌頭要放很低，嘴要張很大，如果舌頭翹得很高，就發不出對的音來。又如 thing 中的 /θ/，舌頭要微微伸出兩齒之間，如果舌頭放在上齒之後或上齒齦，發出的音就會偏向 /t/。

　　學外語需要訓練嘴部肌肉新的運動方式，過了幼兒關鍵期，學新的運動方式最好能先了解發音器官的位置與動作！用母語中類似的發音去模仿外語是很自然、很有幫助的方式，但這終究還是「像不像」，而器官的位置與動作才是「對不對」。正確的基本動作只是第一步，學了基本動作不見得會成為高手，但至少可以放心地去練習了，此外還要再加上持久地多聽、多讀、多講，才能逐漸融入體內，讓發音器官慢慢形成一種不自覺的習慣（muscle memory）。

　　學發音，要用「心」聽，能夠「聽音」，才能夠「發音」！

CHAPTER 1

基本發音

　　首先要說明的是，作者與讀者溝通發音時，因為無法在書面上發出聲音來，必須採用某種音標符號才能溝通，所以本書採用了我們都比較熟悉的美式音標之一的 KK 音標（請參見附錄 1 的說明），但請注意，幾乎美國人都不知道什麼是 KK 音標！

　　事實上，每一本英美字典都有它自己的音標符號系統，每一本的符號設計都略有不同，甚至於連音標的數目也不同，這牽涉到編纂字典的語言專家對發音的認知與見解，多少各有主見，因此，表現方式也不盡相同。

　　每本字典都有各自不同的符號的原因在於：音標只是一種符號。英美發音不同就是英美發音不同的問題，不是音標的問題，無論使用什麼符號，都不影響發音的本身。舉個似遠實近的比方，莎士比亞的劇作《羅密歐與茱麗葉》中有句名言：

> A rose by any other name　玫瑰即使換名字
> would smell as sweet.　依然照舊吐芬芳

　　以中文來說，注音符號中的ㄅㄆㄇㄈ對等於漢語拼音中的 b p m f，但不管是用哪種符號，都不改其音！

　　以美式發音來說，Merriam-Webster 常受推薦。Cambridge Advanced Learner's Dictionary 將英式與美式兩種發音放在同一頁面，很好用。而 OneLook Dictionary Search 網站可點選約 30 個字典，非常方便。

　　KK 與現代美式英語發音略有歧異，需要特別注意，包括：

1. KK 將某些單字（如 lady, only, study）的尾音標註為短音 /ɪ/，但實際上美國人多發長音 /i/

2. KK 的長母音 /e/ 與 /o/（如 make /e/, boat /o/）為單母音符號，但這

兩個音在美國基本上都被發成相當於双母音的 /eɪ/ 與 /oʊ/

　　上述的第一項在現代英美字典中如 Merriam-Webster, Oxford, Cambridge，都標長音 /i/；而第二項在 Oxford, Cambridge 中都將双母音 /eɪ/ 與 /oʊ/ 標為美式發音。

　　而美國地大人多，不同區域當然會有不同腔調與發音，本書所謂的「美式」或「美國音」，只是指美國較通用的音。書中常說到「美國人」，也只是一種方便的說法，用來汎指以美式英語為母語的人士。同理也適用於本書中的「英式」、「英國音」、「英國人」。

　　美國主要的幼兒啟蒙發音教學法是 phonics（自然發音），教兒童們一些字母與發音的對應關係，幫助他們直覺發音（看到字母，發對應的音）。phonics 非常棒，如果熟悉規則（幾乎所有規則都有例外），有資料顯示準確度可達約 80%，很了不起，但是對於非母語的人，除非從小就已奠定良好的自然發音基礎，否則，還是有層層麻煩，包括 (1) 規則不少；(2) 有約 20% 的例外；(3) 美國人在教發音時，會引用簡單的字作為發音參考，如 a for apple, e for egg……，但 apple, egg 雖然簡單，其中的 a 和 e 到底怎麼發？對我們來說，可能都有問題。

　　英文屬於表音文字，這種文字最理想的狀況正如大文豪蕭伯納曾殷切期盼的語言系統：字母與聲音是一對一的對應，形音一致，可以聽音拼字，看字發音。可是，英語有 40 多個發音，如果要達到字母與聲音一對一的對應，就需要有 40 多個字母；然而事實上英文只有 26 個字母，達不到聽音拼字，看字發音。

　　由字母去猜讀音（read the spelling），常會出錯，所以有人說：學英文發音，要先用耳朵聽，不能只用眼睛看（what you see is not what they say），尤其是母音字母，每個字母都有太多的發音可能（子音字母與發音較為接近），以英文字母 a 為例，可能的發音大於 10 種，如：

apple	/æ/	image	/ɪ/
apron	/e/	many	/ɛ/
father	/ɑ/	America	/ə/
call	/ɔ/		

　　上述單字中的 a 都是「獨立」的，在這裡，獨立的定義是：它所屬的

音節中沒有其他母音字母，但其前後可能有子音字母。這樣的獨立 a 有 7 種發音，還不包括它與其他字母合在一起時的發音，如 ea, oa, ae, ai, au, aw 等。

　　一個字母就有這麼多發音，因此，新的單字一定要查字典或聽語音教學，找出正確的發音。如果不查字典或不用「心」聽，讓錯誤留在腦海，可能會造成自己永遠不知道的慣性，一旦如此，即使是很簡單的字，就算經常聽到別人正確的發音，也是聽而不聞，感覺不到自己的錯誤，連改正的機會都沒有了。

　　中文和英文在發音方面的比較，粗略來說：

1. 中文單字是單音節，重點在 4 個聲調的不同；英文單字是多音節，重點在母音、子音和重音的組合
2. 中文單字在整個句子中的聲調通常是較固定的；英文單字在句子中則隨重音與語調的不同而常常變化
3. 中文的聲調會改變字意；英文的語調會改變句意

　　主要的發音器官與位置包括：會動的器官如唇、舌、顎、喉等；不會動的位置如牙齒、上齒齦、硬顎、軟顎等。動作包括：嘴唇張闔、嘴巴大小、嘴形圓寬、舌頭高低前後、上下顎位置等。

　　我們比較不習慣發音的地方包括：

短母音	双母音
獨立子音	連續子音
無聲子音	重音音節
輕音	

　　除了上述單字的個別發音外，中英文最大的差別在於句子的語調與韻律。通常，中文比較被歸屬於 syllable-timed language （音節計時語言），這種語言的每個音節的發音長度基本上是一樣的（如法文、西班牙文等），語調幾乎一樣，沒有重音在哪的問題。一個句子的單字越多，唸起來的時間越長。

　　英文是 stress-timed language （重音計時語言），重音非常重要，韻律跟著重音走，整個句子的語調隨重音而變。句子中有的音節須讀的又重又長，有的又輕又短，完全視重音而定。讀句子的時間長短幾乎不是取決

於字數的多少，而是重音的多少。相較之下，英文像雲霄飛車，中文像平路公車。因此，絕不能以唸中文的方式去唸英文，也不能以聽中文的習慣去聽英文。

美式英語的演進方式和其他語言大體相同：取決於群體的接受度（約定俗成）；演進趨勢也和世界上所有其他的語言大體相同：發音越來越簡化，文法越來越弱化。

KK 音標有 41 個發音（詳見附錄 1 的說明），分為 17 個母音和 24 個子音。母音與子音的特性差異包括：

1. 子音靠器官碰觸或接近而發聲；母音無碰觸
2. 母音「主要」靠舌頭位置變換去發出不同音

母音是音節的核心，音節的定義包括：

1. 一個母音 + 前後有一個子音或多個子音
2. 一個獨立的母音

只有子音，無法形成音節，必須與母音搭配，音節由母音決定。通常，一個單字有幾個母音就有幾個音節，以下 7 個單字 takes, ahead, potatoes, elevator, congratulations, comparability, Americanization 依序有 1,2,3,4,5,6,7 個母音，因此，也是它們的音節數。

特別提醒：本書所說的母音或子音，指的是聲音（sound），而不是字母（letter），例如 strength 雖然有 8 個字母（7 個子音字母，1 個母音字母 e），卻只有 1 個音節，1 個母音 /ɛ/。

中英文子音的相似度較大（比母音大），而且，子音字母的發音可能較少（不像母音字母 a 有 10 多種發音的可能）。對我們來說，子音較容易學，因此，本書將先講子音，再談母音。

1.1　子音

基本上，發音時，氣流（air stream）由喉嚨流向口腔或鼻腔（只有 3

個子音是通過鼻腔）。發子音時，氣流會受到某些阻礙（器官相互碰觸或接近而阻擋了氣流）；發母音時，氣流則不受任何阻礙而通暢無阻地流向體外。

英文有 26 個字母，其中有 21 個代表子音的字母，這 21 個子音字母中有 17 個被直接轉用為子音的音標符號:/b, d, f, g, h, j, k, l, m, n, p, r, s, t, v, w, z/（有 4 個未被轉用：c, q, x, y）。而 KK 音標有 24 個子音發音，因此，尚須設計 7 個音標符號，它們是：/θ/, /ð/, /ʃ/, /ʒ/, /tʃ/, /dʒ/, /ŋ/。

如果比較子音與母音，子音較易於看字母辨音，聽音辨字母。中英文的子音相似度比較大，不少音可以用母語來模仿。

24 個子音中有 15 個是有聲子音（濁音，voiced consonants），9 個是無聲子音（清音，voiceless/unvoiced consonants）。15 個有聲子音是：/b/, /d/, /g/, /l/, /m/, /n/, /r/, /v/, /w/, /z/, /j/,/ŋ/, /ð/, /dʒ/, /tʃ/。9 個無聲子音是：/f/, /h/, /k/, /p/, /s/, /t/,/ʒ/, /θ/, /ʃ/。

清音或濁音是由喉嚨是否振動來決定的。清音（無聲）發音時，不振動；濁音（有聲）發音時，要振動。測試的方法是：用手觸摸喉嚨聲帶處，可以感覺到振動（有聲），或不振動（無聲）。

所有母音都是濁音；而子音則有些是清音，有些是濁音。

中文基本上大多是音節發音，少有單獨子音的情形，因此，對我們來說，如果是子音加母音（音節），很簡單；但是，如果子音單獨地出現，就會造成些麻煩（因為不習慣）。

在描述子音與母音之前，我們須先了解發音的「基本動作」：

a. 發聲方式→ 阻擋聲流的方式
b. 發音器官→ 器官及相關位置

小節【1.1.1.1】與【1.1.1.2】將介紹這兩個主宰發音的主要關鍵。

1.1.1 IPA 子音表

下表是參照 IPA（International Phonetic Alphabet）所列出的子音表。IPA 是一套現今全世界所有語言音標符號的國際標準，詳見附錄 1 中的說明。IPA 原表是所有普世語言都可用的，下表則是針對英語 KK 音標的子音而修訂的。

	1	2	3	4	5	6	7	8
停頓音（爆破音）	pb			td			kg	
鼻音	m			n			ŋ	
摩擦音		fv	θð	sz	ʃʒ			h
逼近音	(w)			r		j	w	
邊近音				l				

1.1.1.1 發聲方式

上表的直軸代表子音發聲的方式（Manner of Articulation）：

1. 停頓音 Stop（或 Plosive 爆破音）：

   氣流先被器官完全阻擋停頓，嘴內產生壓力，然後突然放開，氣流如爆破般發聲。

2. 鼻音（Nasal）：

   軟顎降至最低點，氣流向上通過鼻腔（不是口腔）。

3. 摩擦音（Fricative）：

   有兩個器官輕觸或極為接近，氣流通過時產生亂流，如磨擦發聲。這種音可以持續發聲一段時間。

4. 逼近音（Approximant）：

   器官接近，但不如磨擦音那麼接近，不產生亂流，在嘴內形成一個狹窄通道，聲帶發出的氣流由此通道流出。

5. 邊近音（Lateral approximant）：

   如同逼近音，但氣流通過舌頭的兩側。

上表共 22 個子音音標，都是單一符號，還有兩個子音未列出：/tʃ/ 和 /dʒ/，因為它們是用兩個符號來表示的。表中有 9 個音 /f v θ ð s z ʃ ʒ h/ 屬於摩擦音，這是最多的子音發音方式。

1.1.1.2 器官位置

上表的橫軸代表子音發音器官的位置（Place of Articulation）：

①双唇（Bilabial）：双唇微閉。

②唇齒（Labiodental）：上牙略碰下唇。

③齒間（Interdental）：舌頭置於兩齒間。

④上齒齦（Alveolar ridge）：舌尖輕觸上齒齦。

⑤上齒齦略向後方（Postalveolar）：舌尖靠近此處。

⑥硬顎（Palatal / hard palate）：舌尖靠近硬顎。

⑦軟顎（Velum / soft palate）：舌後方輕觸軟顎。

⑧聲門（Glottis）：喉嚨稍微縮緊。

上齒齦是子音最常用到的器官，上表有 7 個音 /t d n s z r l/ 的舌尖輕觸或靠近上齒齦（/r/ 不碰觸，其他 6 個則輕觸）。另外，/w/ 屬 velar 音，但因双唇也靠近縮小，所以也列於 bilabial 中。

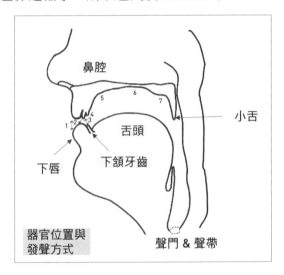

建議多用上表與上圖來練習子音的發音方式與器官位置，多做嘴部肌肉運動，相信絕對會有極大的助益和嶄新的體會。

1.1.2 配對的子音（無聲／有聲 pairs）

子音有個很重要的特性：24 個子音中大部分是成雙成對的。所謂的成雙成對是指兩個音的發音方式與器官位置完全一樣，只不過，一個無聲，一個有聲，相互對應如 sister sounds。這樣的配對（pairs）有 8 組，共 16 個子音，如下表：

無聲 / 有聲子音配對	
無聲	有聲

/p/	/b/
/t/	/d/
/k/	/g/
/s/	/z/
/f/	/v/
/θ/	/ð/
/ʃ/	/ʒ/
/tʃ/	/dʒ/

在這些無聲 / 有聲配對中，我們經常犯的錯誤是在該發有聲子音時，卻發成了無聲子音，尤其是在單字的字尾時，我們會較習慣錯發成無聲子音，例如：

有聲	錯發成	無聲
as /z/	→	ass /s/
of /v/	→	off /f /
breathe /ð/	→	breath /θ/

無聲與有聲的發音雖然差異很小，對母語是英語的人來說，卻是聽得出來的。對我們華人來說，最常出錯、最容易出錯的應該是將 /z/ 錯發成 /s/ 了！英文常有許多情況，單字的字尾會改變成 s 或 es（如複數的名詞以及第三人稱單數的動詞等），這時，發 /z/ 的機率要比發 /s/ 的機率大。

無聲子音中唯一不在上表中的是 /h/，它沒有對應的有聲子音。/h/ 是個摩擦音，喉嚨稍縮緊，氣流產生摩擦而發聲。發 /h/ 時的嘴形不一定，通常取決於其後的母音。

停頓音（Stop Sounds）

上述的 8 對子音（pairs）中，有 3 對是停頓音（塞音）：/p//b/、/t//d/、/k//g/，它們出現的機率極大，據統計，幾乎有 80% 的英文單字至少有 1 個 stop sound。它們的發音方式都是經由器官的接觸阻擋住氣流，剎那間先完全無聲，然後放開擋氣的器官，釋出氣流，爆破式地發聲（plosive），下表最右一行是擋氣的器官及位置：

無聲	有聲	發聲方式	擋住氣流的器官
/p/	/b/	plosive	閉雙唇
/t/	/d/	plosive	舌尖觸上齒齦
/k/	/g/	plosive	舌後方靠近軟顎

三個無聲 /p//t//k/ 被稱為送氣音 aspiration sounds，特色是很清楚的噴氣 puff of air。有個測試的方法是：將一張薄衛生紙放在嘴巴下方，發 /p//t//k/ 時，紙巾會明顯擺動。

美式發音中，/p//t//k/ 有時送氣（aspirate），有時不送氣：

1. 在單字的字首　→ 送氣，如 pie, toy, key

2. 在重音節的開頭　→ 送氣，如 o`ppose, po`tato, a`ccount

3. 在單字的字尾　→ 不送氣，如 lip, light, ink

4. 在 /s/ 之後　→ 不送氣，如 spend, stand, sky

接下來討論其他 5 組成雙成對的子音 pairs：

Pair：/s/ 和 /z/

/s/ /z/ 是磨擦音，舌尖碰上齒齦，兩齒輕觸，氣流經由舌尖通過輕觸的兩齒，摩擦出聲。/s/ 無聲，/z/ 有聲。

我們非常容易犯的錯誤是：看到字母 s 就慣性地發 /s/。但 s 非常多的時候是發 /z/ 的，這種錯發成 /s/ 的現象很普遍，更嚴重的是，如果沒注意的話，很容易會一直錯發而不自知！

要如何區分字母 s 到底要發無聲 /s/？還是有聲 /z/ 呢？讓我們先來討論一種最常用的字尾 s 的發音規則（final s pronunciation rules），這個規則僅適用於單字的字尾發生變化的時候，在什麼情況下單字字尾會發生變化而需要加 s（或 es, 's）呢？通常有下列幾種情形：

① 複數形 → 如 beds, oranges, pens

② 第三人稱單數動詞現在式 → 如 eats, goes, wishes

③ 所有格 possessives → 如 cat's, boy's, Aubrey's

④ 縮簡 contractions → 如 it's, he's, what's

上述字尾變化成 s 時，發音方式有三種：/s/、/z/、/ɪz/，如何分辨呢？大原則如下：

    ① 字尾 s 前面的音是無聲，那 s 就繼續發無聲 /s/

    ② 字尾 s 前面的音是有聲，那 s 就繼續發有聲 /z/

在實際上應用上，三種音 /s/、/z/、/ɪz/ 的發音如下：

1. 原字的尾音是無聲子音 → 發 /s/

books, hopes, laughs, starts

這些字原來的字尾音是無聲子音，加上的 /s/ 也無聲，連在一起發，較好唸。/ts/ 類似中文的「次」。

2. 原字的尾音是有聲子音，或是母音 → 發 /z/

a. 有聲子音之後：calls, comes, fans, jobs, yours

b. 母音之後：days, goes, says, shoes, Windows

這些字原來的字尾是有聲子音，加上的 /z/ 也有聲，連在一起，聲帶連續振動。/dz/ 類似中文的「字」。

3. 原字的尾音是 /s/, /z/, /ʃ/, /ʒ/, /tʃ/, /dʒ/ → 發 /ɪz/ 或 /əz/

這 6 個音被稱為絲絲音 sibilant sounds，如果要在字尾加上 /s/ 或 /z/ 音，會很困難或不可能，如 horse /hɔrs/，不可能直接加 /s/ 或 /z/，這時候，就得發 /ɪz/ 或輕音 /əz/，如：

buses /sɪz/	pauses /zɪz/	finishes /ʃɪz/	rouges /ʒɪz/
pluses /sɪz/	rises /zɪz/	teaches /tʃɪz/	bridges /dʒɪz/

上面的單字由於加了 /ɪz/（或 /əz/）音，都增加了一個音節。美式較偏向發 /əz/，英式發 /ɪz/。

有趣的是，名詞在改為複數時，加 s；而動詞則是在第三人稱單數時，加 s，感覺上正好相反！

特別提醒：上述規則僅適用於當字尾發生變化時的發音，如果單字的字尾本身就是 s（或 es, se），就不照上述規則了。譬如，his 與 this 中的 s 都在母音 /ɪ/ 之後，但發音是 his /z/, this /s/；base 與 rise 中的 se 都在母音之後，但發音是 base /s/, rise /z/。再如：

    發 /z/：always, as, Charles, does, has, his, is, James, lose, news, nose, rise, series, surprise, these, was, wise

　　發 /s/：axis, base, bus, case, course, dangerous, dose, dress, gas, horse, miss, promise, response, sense, tennis, this, vase, us, yes

　　如果 s 不在字尾，而在字中間，也沒有規則可循，舉幾個我們熟悉，但容易唸錯的字：Disney, president, San Jose, visa，這幾個橘色字體的 s 都讀作 /z/，不是 /s/。

　　有些源自希臘的名詞字尾是 sis，如 analysis, basis, crisis, diagnosis, emphasis, hypothesis, prognosis, synthesis, thesis，英式發 /sɪs/，美式較偏向發 /səs/，複數字尾改為 ses，發音為 /siz/。

　　如果將 /z/ 錯發成 /s/，有些字可能會變成完全不同的意思：

/z/	錯發成	/s/
advise /z/	→	advice /s/
bruise /z/	→	Bruce /s/
eyes /z/	→	ice /s/
lose /z/	→	loose /s/
peas /z/	→	peace /s/
plays /z/	→	place /s/
president /z/	→	precedent /s/
raise /z/	→	race /s/
spies /z/	→	spice /s/

　　另外，有些字，如果字母 s 在名詞或形容詞中，發 /s/；在動詞中，發 /z/，如：

	名詞	動詞
excuse		
house	/s/	/z/
use		

　　我們常會將英文發音對應到類似的中文發音，有時確有幫助，但也要小心。譬如，字母 c 的發音 /si/ 常被直接對應到中文的「西」，ABCD 錯發成「AB 西 D」，I see 錯發成「I 西」，或是 city 錯發成「西 ty」。事實上，/si/ 與「西」的發音是很不同的。

Pair：/f/ 和 /v/

　　/f/ /v/ 是磨擦音，上牙碰下唇內部，氣流由唇齒之間通過，產生摩擦音。/f/ 無聲，/v/ 有聲。發音要清楚，我們常把 five /v/ 唸錯成 fife /f/，是橫笛。

　　字母 f 的發音是 /f/，但是，of 中的字母 f 是發 /v/，這是唯一的一次。

Pair：/θ/ 和 /ð/

　　/θ/ /ð/ 是英語中很特別的音，大部分歐美語言都沒這兩個音，中文也沒有，是我們最容易發錯的音之一。/θ/ /ð/ 是磨擦音，/θ/ 無聲；/ð/ 有聲。舌尖放於兩牙間，氣流通過舌尖與上牙底之間。發音時，可清楚看到舌頭伸出（雖然只一點點），擺在兩牙之間，想起來或看起來都怪怪的，中文沒有將舌頭伸出齒外的發音，不習慣。但必須如此才會對，一般認為印度英語未將舌頭伸出，而是舌尖抵住牙齒，這樣就偏向 /t//d/ 了。這裡只是說明不同的器官位置會產生不同的發音，沒有語言之間優劣對錯的問題。

　　/θ/ 與 /ð/ 如何分辨呢？如下：

1. /θ/ 大多出現於 content words（內容字、實字）：

　　如：anthem, bath, earth, fifth, month, thank, think, worth

2. /ð/ 主要有兩種形式：

　　a. 多數出現於 function words（功能字、虛字）

　　　　如：that, the, these, there, they, this, though, thus, with

　　b. 少數介於兩個母音之間的時候

　　　　如：brother, either, father, mother, leather, other, weather

　　有關內容字與功能字的定義，將於【1.7】節中說明。英文單字中，以 thm 結尾的，應該不超過 10 個，如 algorithm, rhythm。thm 的發音是 /ðəm/，多了一個極弱的 /ə/，這樣比較容易發音，也間接符合了 /ð/ 介於兩個母音之間。

　　絕大多數的英文單字是內容字，而極少的內容字發 /ð/（如 bathe, breathe, clothe, smooth 等），然而，功能字由於文法的需要，出現的頻率極大（如 the, this, that），據統計，/ð/ 幾乎出現於 80% 以上的英文句子中，所以，大家還是得好好地練習 /ð/ 的發音。

Pair：/ʃ/ 和 /ʒ/

/ʃ/ /ʒ/ 是磨擦音，舌頭接近上齒齦稍後方，但不碰觸，氣流經過舌頭，再通過輕觸的兩齒，摩擦出聲。/ʃ/ 無聲，/ʒ/ 有聲。我們對 /ʒ/ 音較陌生，練習時，可先發 /ʃ/，再改為有聲，就對了。在日常生活的單字中，發 /ʒ/ 的不是很多，例如：azure, leisure, measure, pleasure, television, vision。英文中沒有以 /ʒ/ 開頭的單字（除了少數外來語，如源自法語的 genre）。

Pair：/tʃ/ 和 /dʒ/

子音中有兩個音是用兩個符號來表示的：/tʃ/ 和 /dʒ/，雖是兩個符號，卻是一個音素（phoneme）。如何發音呢？先擺好 /t/ 的位置，再發 /ʃ/，就會發出 /tʃ/；先擺好 /d/ 的位置，再發 /ʒ/，就會發出 /dʒ/。/tʃ/ 無聲，/dʒ/ 有聲。/t/ 和 /d/ 須先擋住氣；/ʃ/ 和 /ʒ/ 是摩擦出聲；因此，/tʃ/ 和 /dʒ/ 叫做擋擦音（affricate）。要注意這兩個音的嘴形不是圓的，如果未按照基本動作先將舌頭擺在上齒齦（發 /t/ 與 /d/ 的位置），嘴形就容易錯成圓形；反之，按基本動作先將舌頭擺在上齒齦，嘴形就不容易出錯。

絲絲音（Sibilant Sounds）

子音中有 3 對音 /s/ /z/、/ʃ/ /ʒ/、/tʃ/ /dʒ/ 被稱為絲絲音，它們發聲的主要特徵是雙齒輕觸，將氣流由舌頭推出，經摩擦產出絲絲的聲音，這種聲音如同我們要求別人安靜時的「shhhh」，這種音可以拉得很長。發聲時，/s/ 與 /z/ 舌頭碰上齒齦，/ʃ/ 與 /ʒ/ 的舌頭在上齒齦後方，而 /tʃ/ 與 /dʒ/ 則先將舌頭擺在停頓音（/t/, /d/）的位置，再發絲絲音（/ʃ/, /ʒ/）。前面說過，這 6 個音在 final s 字尾變化情況時，發音是 /ɪz/（或 /əz/），如 bridges, finishes。

1.1.3 不配對的子音

除了上述的成雙成對的子音（16 個，8 對），還有 8 個不成雙成對的單子音（7 個有聲，1 個無聲：/h/）。以下介紹這 7 個有聲單子音：/l/, /r/, /m/, /n/, /ŋ/, /j/, /w/。

單子音 /l/

所有子音中，/l/ 與 /r/ 可能是我們最大的罩門了。

首先是 /l/ 音，它可分為在母音之前的 l 音（light l 或 clear l），或是在母音之後的 l 音（dark l）。light l 音如 late, led, like, luck，這些音對我們來說，非常簡單，中文歌詞中常有「啦啦啦……」，或英文歌詞的「la la la ……」，發音時舌尖碰上齒齦。

dark l 音通常是在母音之後，如：cancel, email, palm, tell, Voldemort 等。這個音比較困難（中文沒有 dark l 音，不能靠母語去模仿），發音時，舌後方很緊，後縮靠近軟顎，所以又稱為 velarized l（舌根化 l），舌尖碰不碰到上齒齦都無所謂。我們常犯的錯誤是：錯用圓嘴形的 /r/ 或 /o/ 來模仿 dark l。一些簡單的日常用字如下表：

/l/	錯發成	/o/, /r/, /ɚ/
cancel	→	cancer /ɚ/
deal	→	dear /r/
file	→	fire /r/
hall	→	whore /r/
pool	→	poor /r/
tangle	→	tango /o/
temple	→	tempo /o/
wall	→	war /r/

cancel 錯發成 cancer 讓人以為是疾病，deal 錯發成 dear 會招人白眼，在辦公室大聲將 file 錯發成 fire 可能引發大誤會。

單子音 /r/

/r/ 音在世界上多數語言中都有類似的音。美式 /r/ 是逼近音，舌頭緊繃翹起，靠近上齒齦，但不接觸。首先，要特別注意，這個音常會被我們忽略而不發音，如下表：

	少了 /r/ 錯發成	
born	→	bone
corn	→	cone
order	→	odor

party	→	potty
storm	→	stone
torn	→	tone

雖然美式發音的趨勢是簡單化、方便化，有一些子音在口語中都被簡化了，但是，/r/ 音幾乎在任何情況下，都不可簡化，這可說是美式發音的一個重要特色，這個強音明顯地區別了美國音與英國音的不同。

/l/ 與 /r/ 有個相同點：發音時，氣流通過舌頭的兩側，像是液體，因此，它們又被叫做 liquid consonants。但是，/r/ 的嘴唇向外成圓形，/l/ 不是圓的。

發 /r/ 時，舌尖不能碰觸上齒齦，如果碰到了，發音就會偏向 /l/。舉個對應於中文的例子，夏天時，有些人會將「熱」說成「樂」，是因為舌碰齦，發不出ㄖ音，而誤發成ㄌ音了。其他的例子如：肉說成漏；乳說成魯等。

鼻音：單子音 /m/, /n/, /ŋ/

軟顎決定鼻音或非鼻音，當軟顎下垂，空氣向上通過鼻腔（不是口腔），成為鼻音。鼻音只有 3 個：/m/, /n/, /ŋ/。

以 /m/ 為例，雙唇要閉合，氣流由鼻腔流出，這個音看似很容易，我們卻常發錯，主要原因是忘了閉雙唇，要切記。

另外兩個鼻音 /n/ 與 /ŋ/ 也是容易混淆的發音，我們較習慣發 /n/，不習慣發 /ŋ/，許多該發 /ŋ/ 的音都被我們錯用 /n/ 取代了。發這兩音的關鍵在於：

① 發 /n/ 時，舌尖碰上齒齦
② 發 /ŋ/ 時，舌後方碰軟顎

/n/ 是英語中出現頻率最高的子音之一。/ŋ/ 從不在單字的字首。如果用中文發音來類比，那麼：

an 類似ㄢ；ang 類似ㄤ
en 類似ㄣ；eng 類似ㄥ
in 類似「因」；ing 類似「應」

有的人將通訊平台 LINE 這個字發成 LAI（賴），是因為 LINE 的字尾的 /n/，舌尖要輕觸上齒齦，如果發尾音時，舌未碰齦，將 /n/ 省掉了，就變成 LAI 了。其他如 nine 發成 nai；mine 發成 mai 等。

有的人「王」與「完」發音混淆，是因為「王」是舌後方碰軟顎（類似 /ŋ/），如果是舌尖碰上齒齦（類似 /n/），就發不出「王」，而變成「完」了。

/ŋ/ 大多以字母 ng 出現，這個發音比較複雜，大致如下：

1. ng 出現於字尾 → 發 /ŋ/

   如 bring, king, long, morning, nothing, ring, sing, thing
   acting, doing, exciting, going, interesting, stopping

2. ng 出現於字中 → 發 /ŋg/

   如 anger, angry, England, finger, jungle, longer, tangle
   例外：發 /ŋ/ hanger, length, ringer, singer, strength
   例外：發 /ng/ engage, vanguard
   例外：發 /ndʒ/ binge, change, danger, hinge, range
   　　　long 發音為 /lɔŋ/，longer 發 /lɔŋgɚ/，longest 發 /lɔŋgəst/。

3. nc, nk, nx → 發 /ŋk/

   nk：如 bank, drink, frank, sink, tank, think, thank
   　　ankle, banker, blanket, canker, sinker
   nc：如 anchor, distinction, function, uncle
   nx：如 anxious

單子音 /j/

/j/ 是硬顎逼近音，發音時，雙唇往後拉，舌頭向上隆起，與硬顎形成一個空間，氣流由此空間通過而發聲。

通常，/j/ 是以字母 y 出現，如 year, yellow, yesterday, yield, you, kayak。英文單字沒有以 /j/ 音結尾的。

我們常會被 year/jɪr/ 與 ear/ɪr/ 兩者的發音所困擾，這可以從舌頭的位置來區別，year/jɪr/ 要先將舌尖向後靠近硬顎（先在 /j/ 的位置），ear/ɪr/ 的舌頭則靠近嘴前方（/ɪ/ 的位置）。這是練習的方向。

單子音 /w/

/w/ 基本上是軟顎逼近音，發音時，雙唇靠近，因此，又有 bilabial 音的味道，嘴形是圓的，舌頭後縮，與嘴後上方軟顎形成一個空間，氣流由此空間通過，經雙唇流出而發聲。

有個說法：Kiss your W. Bite your V. 因為發 /w/ 時，雙唇是圓的，像 kiss；發 /v/ 時，上牙碰下唇內部，像 bite。

雖然字母 w 會出現在字尾，如 now /naʊ/, saw /sɔ/, snow /sno/ 等，但是，/w/ 音從不在字尾。這幾個單字中的尾母音是 /aʊ/, /ɔ/, /o/，都不發子音 /w/，但嘴形都與 /w/ 相似。

若單字以 wh 開頭，現代美語幾乎都發成 /w/（古式美語發 /hw/），如 what, when, where, which, why, whale, whether, while, white 等，但有少數字則發 /hw/，如 who, whom, whose 等。

1.1.4 單獨子音與連續子音

中文少有像英文中單獨發音的子音，因此，不習慣。當遇到單獨的子音時（尤其是無聲子音），有時會自行在其後加一個母音，唸成音節，例如 p, b, t, d, k, g 單獨出現時，常被錯發成 /pə/, /bə/, /tə/, /də/, /kə/, /gə/，或是 /pi/, /bi/ 等。單獨子音在字尾的如 beep, knife, teeth；單獨子音在字中間如 access, batman, eruption。近來常被作為例子的如：

> Skype 中的 pe 被唸錯成 /pi/　　→ 正確的音是 /p/
> YouTube 的 be 被唸錯成 /bi/　　→ 正確的音是 /b/

日本人更是不習慣單獨的子音，因為日語發音規則在單獨子音之後須跟著母音，因此，講英語時，beer 像 bi-lu、milk 像 mi-lu-ku、slipper 像 su-li-pa、stop 像 su-to-pu。義大利語也是如此，幾乎所有單字都以母音結尾。這裡只是指出不同的語言各有各的發音規則與習慣，沒有語言之間優劣對錯的問題。英語不僅有單獨子音，還常見連續的子音，更是中文沒有的概念，初學時會造成些困難。以字尾或字中連發兩個音為例，如 box, excuse, friends, Linux, smoked, sports, texture 等。

有時候會連發三個子音，如 Alps, asked, asks, crisps, desks, text, next, tempts。甚至還有連發四個子音的，如 texts。有些連續的英文子音即使對

native speakers 來說，都會有難度，如 sixth, months, strength，其中，sixth 曾被美國的一個新聞網站選為最難唸的英文單字的前十名。

★ 1.1.5 中文視角 – 子音

中英文在子音方面的差異不小，我們要特別注意的如：
1. 中文沒有的子音：/θ/, /ð/, /ʒ/, dark/l/
2. 英文有 8 個成雙成對的「無聲 - 有聲」子音 pairs
3. 中文極少有獨立的無聲子音，更沒有連續的獨立子音
4. /r/ 音幾乎在任何情況下，都不弱化，這是美式發音的特色

1.2　母音

每一個音節必有一個母音，它是音節的核心，沒有母音就不能形成音節。

KK 音標有 17 個母音，但英文 26 個字母中，只有 5 個代表母音的字母：a e i o u（and sometimes y）。5 個母音字母無法對應 17 個母音發音，這是英文音形不一致的主要原因。如果看到字中的母音字母（5 個），去猜測它的發音（17 個），是很不簡單的。

除了 5 個母音字母各被用來代表 1 個發音符號（/ɑ/, /e/, /i/, /o/, /u/）之外，還須設計 12 個不同的音標符號，它們是：/æ/, /ɛ/, /ɪ/, /ɔ/, /ʊ/, /ʌ/, /ə/, /ɚ/, /ɝ/, /aɪ/, /ɔɪ/, /aʊ/。

母音有長母音與短母音之分，美國人一般在自然發音法（phonics）教學時，通常是先教 5 個母音字母 a e i o u 的代表性的長母音與短母音，如：

母音字母	長母音	短母音
a	/e/	/æ/
e	/i/	/ɛ/
i	/aɪ/	/ɪ/
o	/o/	/ɑ/
u	/ju/	/ʌ/

上表並不是所有的母音發音。這 5 個母音字母（a, e, i, o, u）本身的讀音正好是長母音（/e/, /i/, /aɪ/, /o/, /ju/）的讀音，中文裡有和它們幾乎相同的發音，我們看到它們，倍感親切，常會直覺地發長母音。不幸的是，這很容易發錯音，因為當這 5 個字母在重音節時，常會發短母音。舉例來說，我們常用的一些單字如 after, Amazon, Apple, banana, Canada, congratulate, damage, example, fancy, family, happen, jacket, language, manner, perhaps, relax, salary, satisfy, understand，其中標示橘色的 a 都在重音節，都發短母音 /æ/，但常容易被錯發成長母音 /e/。

有些短母音在中文裡幾乎沒有完全相同的發音，我們較不會發短母音，但偏偏它們出現的頻率很高，是我們最大的罩門之一，需要特別注意。

相對於在重音節裡常發短母音，這 5 個母音字母在輕音節裡時，它們都有可能發同一個輕母音 /ə/（例如：a in ago, e in the, i in sanity, o in commercial, u in focus, 它們都發輕母音 /ə/），因此，/ə/ 是所有母音中出現頻率最高的。更重要的是，美式英語趨向於大量地將輕音節裡的母音弱化為 /ə/，然而，我們的英語教育中極少講到 /ə/，它也是我們的罩門之一。

1.2.1 IPA 母音圖

發母音的最主要關鍵是：舌頭在嘴中的位置。舌頭是人類最靈敏的器官之一，它主宰了母音的發音（當然，還需要唇、嘴形等的配合，引發口腔或鼻腔內不同的共鳴音波）。

子音發音的重點在於：阻擋聲流的發聲方式與相關器官的接觸，這些都可以相當明確地加以敘述。但是，母音發音時，沒有任何發音器官的阻擋（沒有器官接觸），幾乎全靠舌頭位置的變換來發聲，這就很難明確地描述了。所幸 IPA（詳見【附錄 1】中之說明）有很棒的關於母音發音位置的梯形圖，顯示了舌頭在嘴中的相對位置，是極為有用的發音輔助。

下圖是將 IPA 官方的母音梯形圖修改而成的，原來的 IPA 圖包含了世界上所有語言的母音，而這張圖僅留下了美式母音。如果你面對此頁面，將臉轉向左手邊，且與頁面平行，這個梯形圖就符合了嘴巴的形狀方位：左斜線代表嘴前方，右直線是嘴後方，上下橫線表示嘴的上下方。這樣很容易看出舌頭在嘴裡的相對位置。這張圖極具參考價值，建議讀者要確實記住，效用極大。

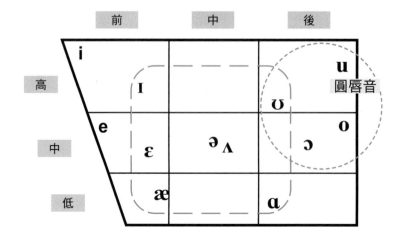

1.2.1.1　舌頭的位置決定發音

舌頭位置的變換決定了所有母音的發音（還得要嘴形等的配合），這看似簡單，但舌頭在一個嘴巴的空間中要擺在這麼多不同的位置，是需要學習的！上圖可分幾個角度來看母音的發音方式，包括：前後母音；舌頭上下；長短母音；嘴形圓否等，分述於下：

前、後母音

左方為前母音 front vowels，又稱為 bright vowels，因為聲音較為鮮明。發音時舌頭較靠嘴的前方，由上而下依次為：/i/, /ɪ/, /e/, /ɛ/, /æ/（/e/ 屬於双母音），/i/ 最高，/æ/ 最低。

右方為後母音 back vowels（dark vowels），舌頭往後，由上而下依次為：/u/, /ʊ/, /o/, /ɔ/, /ɑ/（/o/ 是双母音），/u/ 最高，/ɑ/ 最低。

舌頭上、下

音標符號越靠圖的上方，表示舌頭越在上方，嘴巴張得越小；音標符號越在下方，表示舌頭越靠下方，這時，嘴巴會自然地張得越大（兩者連動）。參照上圖，嘴巴張最大的是：前母音的 /æ/ 和後母音的 /ɑ/，下顎大墜，向兩邊咧開，相較之下，中文沒有像這樣大張其嘴的發音，不習慣；嘴巴開最小的是：前母音的 /i/ 和後母音的 /u/。

舌頭位置會影響聲頻：

> 舌頭越靠前、上方，口腔內共鳴的空間越小，聲音越尖；
>
> 舌頭越靠後、下方，口腔內共鳴的空間越大，聲音越低。

長、短母音

中間的方形虛線框中的 /ɪ/、/ɛ/、/æ/、/ɑ/、/ʊ/、/ʌ/、/ə/ 是短母音；方形虛線外圍部分的 /i/、/e/、/ɔ/、/o/、/u/ 是長母音。

嘴形圓否

圓形虛線框中的 /ʊ/、/ɔ/、/o/、/u/ 是圓唇音，通常，圓唇音都在嘴後方，越後方嘴越圓，這是所有語言都有的現象。

KK 音標有 17 個母音，14 個是單母音 monophthongs，另有 3 個是双母音 diphthongs（兩個單母音的組合）。上圖中有 12 個單母音，另外 2 個單母音：/ɚ/、/ɝ/ 都在 /ə/ 附近，它們被稱為 r-colored vowels（是美式英語的重要特徵之一），這兩個音是幾乎一樣的，/ɝ/ 用在重音節，/ɚ/ 在輕音節。發 /ə/ 時，舌在嘴的正中間，嘴巴半張。美式英語的 /ʌ/ 與 /ə/ 極類似，/ə/ 只出現在輕音節，/ʌ/ 通常在重音節。注意：美式 Merriam-Webster 線上字典將 /ʌ/ 與 /ə/ 都標示為 /ə/，完全不用 /ʌ/。

非常建議以 IPA 圖來多加練習發音的方式與器官的位置，相信對母音發音有極大的助益和嶄新的體會。再強調一次，對我們來說，如果不先對發音時的各器官的位置有些了解，而用中文的思維邏輯去模擬發音，這樣雖然也可達到一定程度，但可能還是會有無形的天花板。

母音發音最常以哪些字母出現呢？如下表：

母音	最常出現的字母	例子	其他出現的字母的例子
/i/	y	body	me, ski, tea, feed, yield
/ɪ/	i	big	here, manage, sync, dear, beer
/e/	a	make	main, may, eight, steak
/ɛ/	e	bed	any, head, friend, said
/æ/	a	cat	half, aunt
/u/	u	rule	fool, do, new, soup

/ʊ/	u	full	foot, wolf, could
/o/	o	go	snow, boat, soul, sew
/ɔ/	o	on	laud, call, dawn, bought, broad
/ɑ/	o	cop	father, calm
/ʌ/	u	gut	come, young, blood
/ɚ/	er	eager	comfort, yogurt, standard
/ɝ/	er	person	world, turn, girl, learn
/aɪ/	i	ice	style, tie, seismic
/aʊ/	ou	cloud	owl
/ɔɪ/	oi	oil	boy

1.2.2 短母音

本節介紹幾個常用的短母音 /æ/, /ɛ/, /ɪ/, /ɑ/, /ʊ/。

短母音 /æ/

/æ/ 是美式英語一個獨有的很特殊的音，世界上大多數的語言中沒有這個音，中文也沒有這樣嘴巴大張的發音，因此不太習慣。/æ/ 是前母音中嘴張最大、下顎最低（兩者自然連動）、舌頭最低的音，嘴咧向兩側。這個音絕大多數是以字母 a 出現，如：as, app, has，其他字如 laugh, plaid 等。

短母音 /ɛ/

發短母音 /ɛ/ 時，下顎微低，嘴巴略張，舌頭擺在前面中間略靠下。依據統計，/ɛ/ 這個發音大多數時候是以字母 e 出現，如 Hello，其他字母如 many, said。發音類似中文注音的「ㄝ」。

短母音 /ɪ/

短母音 /ɪ/，舌頭靠前上方，嘴巴張得很小。/ɪ/ 很多時候是以字母 i 出現，如 sit, Netflix，還有一部分以字母 e 出現，如 English，少數以其他字母出現的如 image。

短母音 /ɑ/

是後母音中嘴張最大、舌頭最低的音，嘴形不圓。常以字母 o 出現，如 Oscar, Apollo，其他字母如 father。

短母音 /ʊ/

短母音 /ʊ/，嘴巴張得很小，呈圓形，舌頭靠後上方。/ʊ/ 常以字母 u 出現，如 full，也常以字母 o 或字母 oo 出現，如：woman, good，其他字母如 would（與 wood 的發音相同）。

我們最困擾的長短音有 3 對：/e//ɛ/、/i//ɪ/、/u//ʊ/。在發音方法上要如何區別呢？相對性（如 /i/ vs. /ɪ/）原則如下：

> 長音的舌頭位置較高、嘴張得較小
> 短音的舌頭位置較低、嘴張得較大

知道發音器官的位置，不表示發音一定正確，但至少可以去練習基本動作了。不知道位置，很難發出對的音，舉例來說，如果舌頭翹得老高，是發不出 /æ/ 的。

1.2.3 母音字母 a e i o u 的發音

字母 a 的發音

字母 a 在單字中獨立出現時的發音多達 7 種（請參考【第 1 章 基本發音】中「獨立」的定義），如下表中標示橘色的字母 a：

母音字母 a		
發音音標	例子	
/æ/	apple	apps	have
/e/	apron	danger	haven
/ɑ/	father	wallet	spa
/ɔ/	call	talk	war
/ɪ/	beverage	climate	image
/ɛ/	any	many	scary
/ə/	America	MacArthur	vanilla

註：app 要連著唸，不可分成 a-p-p

我們慣性的錯誤是常看到字母 a 就發為長母音的 /e/，因此，有些短母音 /æ/ 被錯發成 /e/，例如 app 錯發成 ape；at 錯發成 ate；將 rap 錯發成 rape 等。單字中看到獨立字母 a（尤其是在重音節中），發 /æ/ 的機率非常大。

除了上述 7 種音，a 也常與其他母音字母一起發音，如：

	發音	例子
ae	/ɛ/	aesthetic
ai	/e/	main
	/ɛ/	said
au	/ɔ/	fault
ea	/i/	deal, freak, lean, pea
	/ɪ/	appear, dear, fear, hear
	/ɛ/	bread, heaven, Reagan
	/e/	break, great, steak
oa	/o/	coast

a 與其他的子音字母如 law 中的 aw，發 /ɔ/。say 中的 ay，發 /e/。要注意，says 中的 ay 則發 /ɛ/（said 中的 ai 也發 /ɛ/）。

特別提醒：KK 音標的 /e/，一般美國人發成相當於双母音的 /eɪ/。

光一個字母 a，就有這麼多的發音可能，對我們來說，確實是很大的困擾。在看到單字時，不會或不確定其中的 a 該怎麼唸時，最好的辦法就是：查字典！最好是英英字典！

字母 e 的發音

獨立字母 e 的發音通常有 5 種：

母音字母 e		
發音音標	例子	
/ɛ/	best	chef	Hello
/i/	even	evil	me
/ɪ/	expect	here	pretty
/e/	cafe	fete	resume
/ə/	camera	enemy	

　　我們慣性的錯誤是常看到字母 e 就發長母音的 /e/，因此，有些短母音 /ɛ/ 被錯發成 /e/，例如將 edge 錯發成 age；fell 錯發成 fail；get 錯發成 gate；let 錯發成 late；met 錯發成 mate；pepper 錯發成 paper；sell 錯發成 sail；tell 錯發成 tale 等。

　　除了上述 5 種發音，e 也常與其他母音字母合在一起發音（ea 已說明如前，故未列於下表中），例如：

	發音	例子
ee	/i/	eel, feed, meet, see
	/ɪ/	been, beer, career, deer, peer, pioneer
ei	/aɪ/	seismic
eu	/ju/	euphoria
ie	/ɛ/	friend

　　e 與其他子音字母結合如 grew 中的 ew，發音為 /u/；survey 中的 ey，發音為 /e/。

字母 i 的發音

　　獨立字母 i 的發音通常有 4 種：

母音字母 a		
發音音標	例子	
/aɪ/	bind	I've	grind
/ɪ/	kiss	tip
/i/	ski	tsunami
/ə/	animal	policy

　　我們慣性的錯誤是常看到字母 i 就發長母音的 /i/，因此，有不少短母音 /ɪ/ 被錯發成長母音 /i/，如 did 錯發成 deed；dip 錯發成 deep；fit 錯發成 feet；fill 錯發成 feel；hit 錯發成 heat；live 錯發成 leave；ship 錯發成 sheep；sit 錯發成 seat 等。

　　字母 i 也常與其他母音字母合在一起，如 ai, ie, ei 等，均已於字母 a, e 的例子中說明，不再贅述。

字母 o 的發音

獨立字母 o 發音通常有 6 種：

母音字母 o	
發音音標	例子
/ɑ/	Amazon, body, copy, Costco, hollow
/ɔ/	dog, log, lost
/o/	bovine, coma, donut, gross, slogan
/ʌ/	another, brother, company, mother, onion, stomach
/ə/	commercial, committee, computer, congratulations, consider, contain, Godiva, police, polite, together
/ʊ/	wolf

有些很常用的字，如 computer, congratulations, consider, police, polite, together，標示橘色的 o 都在輕音節，發音是 /ə/，不要錯發成 /ɑ/ /ɔ/ /o/ 等。

在美國，許多人已幾乎將 /ɑ/ 完全取代了 /ɔ/，如 coffee, comma, hot 等。但如果 /ɔ/ 之後是 /r/ 音，則還是發 /ɔr/，如 born, order, sword。

除了上述 6 種發音，o 也常與其他母音字母一起發音，如：

	發音	例子
oa	/o/	boat, coaster
	/ʊ/	cook, foot, look, poor
oo	/u/	cool, food, loom, pool
	/ʌ/	blood, flood
	/aʊ/	mouse
ou	/ʊ/	could, should would
oy	/ɔɪ/	boy

o 與其他子音字母結合如 low 中的 ow，發音為 /o/。

要注意：KK 音標的 /o/，一般美國音發成相當於双母音 /oʊ/。

字母 u 的發音

字母 u 的發音通常有 6 種：

母音字母 u			
發音音標	例子		
/ʌ/	us	buddy	
/u/	duke	super	Uber
/ju/	cute	humid	UBike
/ʊ/	bull	full	
/ɪ/	busy		
/ə/	focus		

　　當字母 u 的發音在 /u/ 與 /ju/ 之間時，美式發音傾向 /u/，例如：attitude, costume, due, nude, nuke, opportunity, produce, student, super, tube, Tuesday 等。英式發 /ju/。

　　除了 a e i o u 等 5 個母音字母之外，子音字母 y 有時也會發母音，如下：

/j/	yes	子音
/ɪ/	gym	母音
/aɪ/	byte	母音
/ə/	labyrinth	輕母音

双母音

　　KK 音標有 3 個双母音：/aɪ/, /ɔɪ/, /aʊ/，前面提過，KK 音標中的 /e/ 和 /o/，一般美國人也發成相當於双母音的：/e/ → /eɪ/；/o/ → /oʊ/。顧名思義，双母音是兩個母音的組合。發音時，兩個音都要發，所以聽起來會比單母音長一點。特別注意：舌頭一定會滑動（因為有兩個音），由第 1 個滑到第 2 個，通常，舌頭由下向上滑，顎由開到閉，嘴形由大變小。双母音通常由第 1 個音主控。

　　我們最常也最容易犯的錯誤包括：

　　　　1. 只發了第一個音，漏了第二個音
　　　　2. /eɪ/ 發成單母音；/oʊ/ 發成單母音

　　另外，双母音中的音與單母音中的音事實上都略有些微差異，例如，

/aɪ/ 中的 /a/ 發音時，舌頭比 /ɑ/ 稍前，這就是為什麼會標示為 /aɪ/，而不是 /ɑɪ/。

1.2.4 容易發錯的母音

以下僅歸納出幾個常見的系統性的錯誤傾向或慣性：

1. 將短母音錯發成長母音：

   a. 將短母音 /æ/ 錯發成長母音 /e/（橘色字母應發 /æ/）

      如：app, apple, at, dad, fat, have, man, mat, rap

   b. 將短母音 /ɛ/ 錯發成長母音 /e/（橘色字母應發 /ɛ/）

      如：bell, edge, fell, get, hell, let, pen, sell, tell

   c. 將短母音 /ɪ/ 錯發成長母音 /i/（橘色字母應發 /ɪ/）

      如：beer, did, dip, ill, fill, hit, lip, live, ship, sit

   d. 將短母音 /ɑ/ 錯發成長母音 /o/（橘色字母應發 /ɑ/）

      如：Apollo, comma, product, project, Oscar

   e. 將短母音 /ʊ/ 錯發成長母音 /u/（橘色字母應發 /ʊ/）

      如：book, cook, foot, good, poor, could, should

2. 將 /ʌ/ 錯發成 /ɑ/：（橘色字母應發 /ʌ/）：

      如：brother, mother, other, oven, Pizza Hut, nut, study

3. 將輕母音 /ə/ 錯發成其他音：（橘色字母應發 /ə/）

   a. 錯發成 /ɑ/

      如：commercial, complete, computer, consider

   b. 錯發成 /æ/

      如：England, Ireland, island, MacArthur, mechanism

   c. 錯發成 /o/

      如：innovation, police, polite

4. 將 /ɚ/ 錯發成其他音：（橘色字母應發 /ɚ/）

   a. 錯發成 /ɑr/

      如：attorney（/ɝ/: 在重音節），Edward, Harvard

         Leonard, Oscar, Richard, standard, vineyard

   b. 錯發成 /or/ 或 /ɔr/

      如：comfort, cupboard, error, information,

mirror, word, world, Oxford, Stanford

　　上述第 4 點所有單字中標示橘色的 ar 或 or 都在輕音節，都讀作 /ɚ/，但容易被錯發成 /ɑr/, /or/, /ɔr/。而其中有些人地物的名稱，很可能是受到中文音譯的誤導，例如：Oscar 中的 ar 發 /ɚ/ 被錯發成 /ɑr/，應該是音譯「奧斯卡」的誤導；Richard 中的 ar 發 /ɚ/ 被錯發成 /ɑr/，應該是音譯「理查」的誤導（但 Charlie 查理中的 ar 發 /ɑr/，它在重音節）。美國加州有不少城市的名字是當年西班牙時代留下來的，如 San Diego（聖地牙哥）、San Jose（聖荷西），其中的 a 是 /æ/，但常被錯發成 /e/，應是受到音譯「聖」的誤導。Amazon 發 /æməzɑn/，但字中的兩個 a 常被錯發成 /ɑ/，應是被音譯「亞馬遜」誤導了。

　　日常生活中有些字唸錯了（如將 at 錯發成 ate；pepper 錯發成 paper；look 錯發成 Luke），無傷大雅，但另有些字唸錯了，可能會造成誤會也不一定，如：

	錯發成	
ace /e/　王牌	→	ass /æ/　臀部
app /æ/　程式	→	ape /e/　猿
comma /ɑ/　逗號	→	coma /o/　昏迷
dad /æ/　爸爸	→	dead /ɛ/　死的
full /ʊ/　飽的	→	fool /u/　傻子
hat /æ/　帽子	→	hate /e/　憎恨
heaven /ɛ/　天堂	→	haven /e/　避風港
met /ɛ/　遇到	→	mate /e/　交配
order /ɔr/　秩序	→	odor /o/　臭氣
party /ɑr/　派對	→	potty /ɑ/　便壺
rap /æ/　說唱樂	→	rape /e/　強姦
rub /ʌ/　摩擦	→	rob /ɑ/　搶劫
wed /ɛ/　結婚	→	wade /e/　涉水

　　將 ace 錯發成 ass，或將 dad 發成 dead，很奇怪。吃飽飯時，將 full 錯發成 fool 可能發生衝突，如果將 met 發成 mate，後果更嚴重！聊天談到 rap 音樂時，如果將字母 a 發成長音，就變成 rape 了！

中英文在母音方面的差異不小，我們應特別注意的如：
1. 英文中的短母音是我們學習的罩門。
2. 中文沒有對應於英文短母音 /æ/ 與 /ɪ/ 的類似發音。
3. 我們看到母音字母（a e i o u）時，容易錯發成長母音。
4. 我們不習慣短母音，但偏偏它們出現的頻率很高。

1.3　不發音的字母

　　有的字母既然不發音（silent letters），為什麼要擺在單字裡？這問題連美國人都有困擾！簡單地說：最早期的英文拼字與發音是比較相符的，然而經過時間的演化以及吸收了大量的外來文字，例如 honest 這個字源自拉丁文 honestus，含有光榮的意思，經由法文，稍微變形後傳入英文的，而法文中字母 h 基本上是不發音。英國足球金童 Beckham 中的字母 h 也不發音。

　　有些不發音的字母被歸納成規則，例如：

① 字尾是 mb → b 不發音，如：bomb, climb, dumb, lamb
② 字尾是 mn → n 不發音，如：autumn, column, condemn, hymn
③ 字中有 bt → b 不發音，如：doubt, debt, subtle

　　下表是一些不發音（橘色字母）的例子：

不發音	例子
a	cocoa, logically, specifically（後兩者也可輕發 /ə/）
b	bomb, climb, doubt, debt, plumber, subtle
c	Connecticut, indict, muscle, scene, scissors
d	adjective, bridge, handkerchief, handsome, Wednesday
e	evening, every, everyone, fake, make
f	halfpenny（英式不發 f）
g	campaign, champagne, design, foreign, sign
h	Beckham, echo, ghost, honest, hour, rhyme, rhythm, Thames, Thomas, vehicle

i	business, fruit, tortoise
j	--
k	knee, kneel, knife, knight, knock, know
l	calf, chalk, could, folk, half, salmon, should, talk, walk, would, yolk
m	mnemonic
n	autumn, column, damn, hymn
o	leopard, people, subpoena
p	cupboard, pseudo, psycho, raspberry, receipt
q	--
r	iron
s	aisle, debris, Illinois, island, isle
t	Christmas, debut, depot, listen, mortgage, whistle
u	biscuit, build, gauge, guard, guess, guitar, tongue
v	--
w	answer, Greenwich, sword, two, wrap, wrong
x	prix, faux pas
y	--
z	rendezvous

1.4　重音 stress

　　英文單字發音最重要的關鍵應該是「重音」了，由於中文單字沒有重音的概念，使得它常常成為我們的單字發音的致命傷，甚至於比音標發音的本身還嚴重！重音擺錯了音節，不只是重音錯了而已，其他音節的發音很可能也會跟著錯。

　　重音的原則是：

　　　　1. 一個單字只有一個重音
　　　　2. 重音為王，輕音讓位
　　　　3. 重音在母音，不在子音
　　　　4. 重音是相對的，不是絕對的

重音節的母音不但要唸得高、長，通常還要將緊鄰的輕音節唸得低、短。pitch（音高）是重音最主要的特徵。

據統計，長度是二音節與三音節的名詞的重音大多數落在第一音節。下表的幾個常用專有名詞的重音在第一音節，我們常錯放在第二音節（` 為重音符號）：

重音應在 第一音節	重音誤放在 第二音節
`Amazon	A`mazon
`Android	An`droid
`Arabic	A`rabic
`Avatar	A`vatar
`Florida	Flo`rida
`Levi's	Le`vi's

其他第一音節的常用單字被錯發成第二音節的例子如（n. 名詞、a. 形容詞、n. 動詞等）：

重音應在 第一音節	重音誤放在 第二音節	意思
`adjective	ad`jective	n. 形容詞
`colleague	co`lleague	n. 同事
`diligent	di`ligent	a. 勤奮的
`exit	e`xit	v. 出去
`genome	ge`nome	n. 基因組
`illustrate	i`llustrate	v. 說明
`maintenance	main`tenance	n. 保養
`mechanism	me`chanism	n. 機制
`programmer	pro`grammer	n. 程式員
`processor	pro`cessor	n. 處理器
`purchase	pur`chase	n. v. 購買
`vibrate	vi`brate	v. 振動

錯發成第三音節，如：

重音應在 第一音節	重音誤放在 第三音節	意思
`architecture	archi`tecture	n. 建築
`elevator	ele`vator	n. 電梯
`escalator	esca`lator	n. 電扶梯
`generated	gene`rated	v. 產生
`innovative	inno`vative	a. 創新的
`operator	ope`rator	n. 操作者

一些其他常被錯發的例子如：

正確的重音	錯誤的重音	意思
ad`ministrator	adminis`trator	n. 管理人
after`noon	`afternoon	n. 下午
co`mmand	`command	n. v. 命令
de`monstrative	demons`trative	a. 示範的
em`ployer	employ`er	n. 雇主
Japa`nese	`Japanese	n. 日本人
my`self	`myself	pron. 我自己
per`cent	`percent	n. 百分比
re`frigerator	refrige`rator	n. 冰箱
re`quest	`request	n. v. 要求
re`spect	`respect	n. v. 敬重
re`view	`review	n. v. 複習
su`perlative	`superlative	a. 最高的

　　em`ployer 及 co`mmittee 的重音在第二音節，但可能受到 employ`ee 的重音在第三音節的影響，重音擺錯了！ employer 的重音也可以在第二音節。

　　二音節的單字如果可當名詞，也可當動詞，則名詞的重音在第一音節，動詞的重音在第二音節，如：

名詞	動詞
`addict 上癮者	a`ddict 上癮
`decrease 減少	de`crease 減少
`desert 荒漠	de`sert 遺棄
`increase 增加	in`crease 增加
`insult 侮辱	in`sult 侮辱
`object 物體	ob`ject 反對
`permit 許可證	per`mit 允許
`present 禮品	pre`sent 贈送
`produce 農產品	pro`duce 生產
`project 計畫	pro`ject 投射
`record 記錄	re`cord 記錄
`refund 退款	re`fund 退償
`refuse 垃圾	re`fuse 拒絕
`subject 主題	sub`ject 屈從

也有些双音節單字的名詞與動詞的重音相同，如 `capture, `comfort, con`trol, `process, re`ply, re`port, re`quest, re`spect 等，不要搞混了。

有些字的有不同重音的唸法，如 harassment, mustache 的重音在第一音節或第二音節，都有群眾。

有幾個可幫助記憶重音位置的「規則」（都可能有例外）如：

1. 字尾是 ion, ian, ic, ious → 重音通常在倒數第二音節

    如 do`nation, dis`cussion, poli`tician, `ethnic, de`licious

2. 字尾是 cy, ty, phy, gy, al → 重音通常在倒數第三音節

    如 `fluency, co`mmunity, bi`ography, `energy, i`dentical

四音節及以上的單字，重音大部分在中間的音節，不會在第一音節或最後，如 communi`cation, consci`entiousness, gene`rosity.

本節所述的是單字的重音，句子中的重音則將於【1.7節韻律】中討論。

★ 1.4.1 中文視角 – 重音

中文與英文在重音方面存在不小的差異，我們要特別注意的地方包括：

1. 中文是一個單字一個音節，沒有重音的問題。英文則截然不同，重音極為重要！
2. 重音擺錯了音節，不只是重音錯了而已，很可能也會影響其他音節的發音。
3. 二音節的單字如果可當名詞，也可當動詞，則名詞的重音在第一音節，動詞的重音在第二音節。也有一些例外。
4. 大多數 2 音節與 3 音節名詞的重音在第 1 音節。

1.5 輕音

輕母音 schwa /ə/ 是美式英語極重要的特徵，許多輕音節中的母音常發成 /ə/，這個音是所有發音中最「懶」、最不費力的，也是出現率最高的母音，它增加了說英語的流暢度與韻律感。

schwa 被稱為「央音」，因為發音時，舌頭正好在正中間（平常休息時的位置），嘴半張，由聲帶吐出氣即可，最輕鬆。/ə/ 只會出現在輕音節，要特別一提的是，所有五個母音字母 a e i o u 出現於輕音節時，都有可能發 /ə/！尤其是緊鄰重音節的母音字母，這也就是為什麼它是母音中出現頻率最高的音了！

母音字母（a e i o u）發 /ə/ 的例子如下表：

發音音標	Schwa /ə/ 例子（標示橘色的字母）
a	ago, America, Apollo, banana, sofa, salad, vanilla
e	camera, celebrate, enemy, even
i	animal, experiment, family, Florida, president, policy
o	commercial, computer, consider, police, polite, today
u	campus, focus, success, supply, support
	其他
io	nation, suspicion, vision

Big Mac 讀作 /mæk/。而 McDonald's 的重音在第二音節，第一音節的 Mc 發輕音 /mək/，我們容易被中譯「麥」當勞誤導。類似例子如 MacArthur, McCain, McCarthy，其中的 Mc 或 Mac 都讀作 /mək/，它們都在輕音節。

單字 man 讀作 /mæn/，但在 salesman 中讀作 /mən/；fast 讀作 /fæst/，在 breakfast 中讀作 /fəst/。它們都在輕音節。

以下 20 個國家的名字中各有一個 a，該如何發音？

> Bosnia, Brazil, China, Columbia, Cuba, Dominica, Ethiopia, Finland, Germany, India, Italy, Korea, Libya, Mongolia, Nigeria, Poland, Serbia, Slovenia, Switzerland, Syria

如果我們的用中文音譯的思維，這 20 個字母 a 幾乎都有可能被錯發成 /ɑ/（阿），事實上，它們全都發輕音 /ə/，特別重要的是：20 個 a 都在輕音音節。

以下 20 個單字都各有一個字母 o，每個都發 /ə/，同樣地，20 個 o 都在輕音節：

> atom, bacon, commercial, committee, computer, congratulations, consider, contain, dinosaur, domestic, freedom, Godiva, harmony, offend, parrot, police, polite, potassium, today, together

下面幾個字都與 photograph /ˈfotəgræf/ 同源，可以看出，重音節兩旁的母音（標示橘色的字母 o 或 a）都發輕音 /ə/：

pho`tography	/fəˈtɑgrəfɪ/
pho`tographer	/fəˈtɑgrəfɚ/
photo`graphic	/fotəˈgræfɪk/

一些其他的例子，專有名詞如 Aˈmerica, Goˈdiva，一般名詞如 aˈbility, aˈnalysis, baˈnana, caˈpacity, coˈrona, faˈcility, paˈjamas, vaˈnilla，每個字中緊鄰重音兩旁的母音都發 /ə/。

`telephone 與 teˈlephony 同源，這兩個字中的第一個 e，發音分別為 /ɛ/ 與 /ə/；然而，這兩個字中的第二個 e，則分別唸作 /ə/ 與 /ɛ/，顛倒過來了，原因是重音位置變換的影響。

有些音在英式英文中輕音節裡發短母音，但是，在美式英文中則偏向發 /ə/。特別是短母音 /ɪ/，如下面的標示橘色的字母發音：

basis, diligent, facet, liquid, notice, service, valid

★ 1.5.1 中文視角 – 輕音

中文與英文在輕音方面存在不小的差異，我們要特別注意的地方包括：

1. 輕母音 /ə/ 在美式發音中非常重要，可惜的是，這個音卻在華人的英語發音教育中嚴重地被忽略！
2. 五個母音字母 a e i o u 都有可能發 /ə/，尤其是緊鄰重音節旁的輕音節中的母音。
3. 重音與輕音是相伴隨的，重音是主角，輕音是反襯。既然重音要高、長，輕音就得低、短。
4. 美式英語有個很重要的趨勢：輕音節裡的母音被大量的 schwa 化（弱化），發 /ə/。另外，許多功能字在整個句子中也被 schwa 化，尤其是在連音（linking）時。

1.6　語調

中文是聲調語言，用聲調（tone）表達不同意義的單字。一個音節的 4 個聲調代表 4 種不同的字意，如媽、麻、馬、罵。

英語屬於語調語言，用語調（intonation）主導語意。語調指的是句子中音高的升降，句子的意思會因為語調而改變。例如：He's still on holiday，如果句尾的 holiday 尾音下降，是陳述句，表述一個訊息；如果 holiday 的尾音上升，則是疑問句，需要別人回答。單字 holiday 音高的升降轉折，會改變句意，但不會改變這個單字 holiday 的字意。英文句子中的單字音高不同時，那個單字的意義卻不變，和中文單字聲調的特性不同。

英語的語調有很多種，最普通、最重要的就是降調 falling intonation 和升調 rising intonation。降調通常用在陳述句、命令句以及 Wh 句（what, who, where, when, why, how），舉例：

> I am 6 feet tall.
>
> Come over here.
>
> What's your name?

　　第一句是陳述句，第二句是命令句，第三句是 "wh" 疑問句，都是在句尾（tall, here, name）語調下降。

　　升調則用在 Yes/No 疑問句（需要回答 Yes or No），如：

> Do you want some coffee?

　　這個問句尾端的 coffee 是升調。如果改成降調，就不像問句了，客人聽起來會覺得冷冷淡淡，感覺不到你的熱情。

　　有句話：It's not just what you say, it's how you say it. 同樣的句子，用不同的語調可以表達很不一樣的含意。

　　中文的語調通常沒有英文那麼的高低起伏，在不同類型的句子（陳述句、疑問句等）中，單字音調的變化也不那麼激烈。

1.7　韻律

> *Rhythm is something you either have or don't have, but when*
> *you have it, you have it all over.*　　　——Elvis Presley

　　英語屬於 stress-timed language，韻律 rhythm 是這類語言的音樂 musical flow。口語中有些字要 stress，有些字要 unstress，這樣才有韻律。

　　在說明韻律之前，需要先了解英文單分為兩大類：

　　1. content words（內容字、實字）

　　　　表達實質意義的字詞。包括：名詞、動詞、形容詞、副詞、疑問詞 WH words、否定詞等。

　　2. function words（功能字、虛字）

　　　　顯示文法功能的字詞。又稱為 grammar words，包括：冠詞、代名詞、介系詞、連接詞、助動詞等。

要注意：1. 代名詞（he, she, they, us 等）屬於功能字，因為對話双方都了解代名詞隱含的意思（它代替先行詞），所以它是舊資訊（英文的規則是新資訊要重讀，舊資訊則輕讀）。2. 否定詞屬於內容字，因為它比肯定詞更具資訊性，會影響句子的意義。3. 內容字可隨時增添新字，功能字則否，極少增加新字。

英語韻律的基本規則是：

1. 內容字要重讀

2. 功能字要輕讀

例句：He LIVES with his WIFE on a FARM in the VIllege.

句子中的 LIVES, WIFE, FARM, VIllege 是內容字，大寫代表重音，要重讀。而 He, with his, on a, in the 這些屬於功能字，要輕發。在 native speakers 的口語中，講得快時，甚至可以說只聽到這 4 個明顯的內容字。但即使我們只聽到 4 個內容字，也能了解基本概念。事實上，幼兒講話就是這樣，只講幾個重要的字，其他的模模糊糊，可是我們照樣聽得懂個大概。

句子讀起來的長短取決於內容字。功能字無論多少，因為輕、弱、短，都相對地不佔很多時間。再舉一例：

COWS EAT GRASS.
The COWS EAT the GRASS.
The COWS have been EAting the GRASS.

這三句雖然長短不同，但都只有 3 個內容字：COWS, EAT, GRASS，因此，講得很快時，會感覺時間長短相差不多。

另外，當連續幾個字都是內容字時（如第一句），字與字之間要稍微停頓（pause）。

中文屬於 syllable-timed language，講話時，每個字（音節）的長短及輕重都差不多，如果以這樣的思維去唸 The cows have been eating the grass，就會有 7 個字或 8 個音節的時間，這種 rhythm 和英文完全不同。英文重點完全放在內容字要 stress 上，對我們來說，聽起來高低起伏，像是雲霄飛車 roller coaster。

除了內容字與功能字的區別之外，如果在一個句子中，有要特別強調

的地方，就要 stress 那個重點。例如：He had a lot of money.。

如果我們將重音放在不同的字（將該字的 pitch 拉高），就可能特別強調不同的意思，有幾種可能：

1. Stress「had」
　　表示他「以前」很有錢，但是現在沒了

2. Stress「a lot of」
　　表示他以前「非常非常」有錢

3. Stress「money」
　　反諷他除了很有錢，沒別的

另外，句子中若含有對照比較的關係，也要 stress，如：

I didn't want a cappuccino; I wanted an espresso.

學好本章發音的基本動作，就足夠和美國人溝通了。

※ 練習題 – 發音 （請參考【附錄 2】的習題解答）

橘色字母的發音是否相同？

( )1.　　America　　　Amazon　　　(a) 相同　(b) 不同

( )2.　　apple　　　　make　　　　(a) 相同　(b) 不同

( )3.　　America　　　father　　　(a) 相同　(b) 不同

( )4.　　computer　　commercial　(a) 相同　(b) 不同

( )5.　　notice　　　innovation　(a) 相同　(b) 不同

( )6.　　image　　　imagine　　　(a) 相同　(b) 不同

( )7.　　polite　　　about　　　　(a) 相同　(b) 不同

( )8.　　Stanford　　Ford　　　　(a) 相同　(b) 不同

( )9.　　beer　　　　feel　　　　(a) 相同　(b) 不同

( )10.　said　　　　bed　　　　　(a) 相同　(b) 不同

( )11.　common　　command　　　(a) 相同　(b) 不同

( )12.　foot　　　　fool　　　　　(a) 相同　(b) 不同

( )13.　word　　　　world　　　　(a) 相同　(b) 不同

(　) 14.	saint	San Diego	(a) 相同	(b) 不同
(　) 15.	island	dreamland	(a) 相同	(b) 不同
(　) 16.	book	could	(a) 相同	(b) 不同
(　) 17.	faces	makes	(a) 相同	(b) 不同
(　) 18.	case	cause	(a) 相同	(b) 不同
(　) 19.	Skype	lip	(a) 相同	(b) 不同
(　) 20.	Chicago	China	(a) 相同	(b) 不同
(　) 21.	his	this	(a) 相同	(b) 不同
(　) 22.	says	heaven	(a) 相同	(b) 不同
(　) 23.	salad	salmon	(a) 相同	(b) 不同
(　) 24.	Christmas	investment	(a) 相同	(b) 不同
(　) 25.	they	breathe	(a) 相同	(b) 不同
(　) 26.	access	soccer	(a) 相同	(b) 不同
(　) 27.	does	dose	(a) 相同	(b) 不同
(　) 28.	azure	mirage	(a) 相同	(b) 不同
(　) 29.	speaks	speakers	(a) 相同	(b) 不同
(　) 30.	of	off	(a) 相同	(b) 不同
(　) 31.	danger	haven	(a) 相同	(b) 不同
(　) 32.	president	precedent	(a) 相同	(b) 不同
(　) 33.	brother	bother	(a) 相同	(b) 不同
(　) 34.	banker	uncle	(a) 相同	(b) 不同
(　) 35.	singer	engage	(a) 相同	(b) 不同
(　) 36.	eyes	ice	(a) 相同	(b) 不同
(　) 37.	great	grate	(a) 相同	(b) 不同
(　) 38.	app	ape	(a) 相同	(b) 不同
(　) 39.	dear	deal	(a) 相同	(b) 不同
(　) 40.	product	father	(a) 相同	(b) 不同
(　) 41.	at	ate	(a) 相同	(b) 不同
(　) 42.	Charlie	Richard	(a) 相同	(b) 不同
(　) 43.	Godiva	Apollo	(a) 相同	(b) 不同
(　) 44.	worth	with	(a) 相同	(b) 不同
(　) 45.	singer	finger	(a) 相同	(b) 不同

美式口語

　　美式口語往往在講話很快的時候，為了方便、快速、平順等原因，產生了許多發音的變化，特別是在朋友會話、音樂、電視電影、流行文化中，這些與我們在教科書上學的正規發音有很大的不同，對我們來說，聽與講都可能是大問題。

　　中文講得快的時候，基本上就是速度快慢的問題；而英文口語講快時，不只是速度快慢的問題，還有弱化、縮簡、連音、省音（本章都將略作說明）等的麻煩！

　　如果能長期在英語口語環境中學英語，當然是最好的。如果沒有這種環境，先去了解美式口語背後的邏輯，可以幫助你「聽」，聽得懂才較容易去學「講」。因此，本章簡略地整理歸納了一些口語發音的技巧與規則，提供參考。不過，最重要的是：先學好第 1 章的正規發音，就足夠溝通了，沒有問題了，可以先跳過第 2 章，日後如果真的有興趣和時間，再來讀本章。

2.1　各種變音

　　美式口語許多發音的變化，很難清楚地界定分類，但為了方便我們華人學習的目的，本書還是嘗試將各種變音分為幾類，簡略地加以整理，包括：weak form, contractions, connected speech 等，如下：

2.1.1　弱化發音（Weak Form）

　　美式口語的一個重點在於弱化發音，包括 (1) 輕音節的發音，(2) 功能字的發音，而絕大多數的弱化指的是 schwa 化（/ə/）。

功能字在口語中常有兩種發音方式：strong form 與 weak form。現今的大趨勢是：功能字被大量地弱化（schwa 化），僅有它們在被強調時，才會用 strong form。例子如下表：

	Strong	Weak			Strong	Weak
an	/æn/	/ən/	for		/fɔr/	/fə/
and	/ænd/	/ənd/	from		/frɑm/	/frəm/
are	/ɑr/	/ər/	of		/ɑv/	/əv/
as	/æz/	/əz/	that		/ðæt/	/ðət/
at	/æt/	/ət/	to		/tu/	/tə/
but	/bʌt/	/bət/	was		/wɑz/	/wəz/

weak form 可能有非常多發音，以 and 來說，可能的音包括：/ænd/, /ənd/, /ən/, /n̩d/, /n̩/，常會視說話的對象或需要而定。為了簡明起見，上表都僅列出一個作為參考。以整個句子為例：

What do you do at school?

3 個橘色的單字是功能字，都可以 weak form 發音：do /də/, you /jə/, at /ət/

What /dəjə/ do /ət/ school?

為什麼只有第一個 do 發輕音？因為它是助動詞（功能字）；第二個 do 則是主動詞（內容字）。內容字一般用 strong form。

中文句子中雖然單字沒有明顯的強與弱，一些虛詞也是發得很輕的，如：了、著、的、地、吧等助詞。

2.1.2 縮簡（Contractions）

本節所說的縮簡（contractions）是很廣義的，包括了一般我們熟悉的縮簡以及一些非正式的縮簡（informal contractions, relaxed contractions）等。我們熟悉的縮簡主要是代名詞與動詞或助動詞連在一起時的縮寫如：

	縮簡	發音
I am	I'm	/aɪm/

I would/had	I'd	/aɪd/
he is/has	he's	/hiz/
you have	you've	/juv/
she will	she'll	/ʃil/
they are	they're	/ðer/
how is	how's	/haʊz/
what is/has/does	what's	/wɑts/

　　apostrophe（'）表示有被省略的字母，要留意 she's 可表示 she is 或 she has；而 I'd 可表示 I had 或 I would。在讀音方面，I've 讀作 /aɪv/，they've 讀作 /ðev/，但 could've 則讀作 /kʊdəv/，這是因為 /v/ 的前面是子音 d，加個輕母音 /ə/ 就使得連音容易讀了。同樣的，I'd 讀作 /aɪd/，但 it'd 則讀作 /ɪtəd/。

　　助動詞 can /kæn/ 與 can't /kænt/ 的發音常易造成混淆，但在口語中，can 幾乎都輕發 /kən/，而 can't 發 /kænt/，從不發輕音，這使得它們很容易區別。

　　什麼時候在口語中不要用 contractions，要逐字發音呢？最常見的是在強調的語氣時，如：

　　　　I will do it. No matter what!

　　　　I have called several times.

　　另外，美式口語在快速對話時產生許多更輕鬆（relaxed）、更非正式的縮簡，其中很多是助動詞發音的簡化，僅簡單列出幾個例子如下：

Informal Contractions		
going to		gonna /gʌnə/*
want to		wanna /wɑnə/
got to		gotta /gɑtə/
have to		hafta /hæftə/
kind of		kinda /kaɪndə/
could have	could've /kʊdəv/	coulda /kʊdə/
should have	should've /ʃʊdəv/	shoulda /ʃʊdə/
would have	would've /wʊdəv/	woulda /wʊdə/

| must have | must've /mʌstəv/ | musta /mʌstə/ |

> * 注意，即使是同一個單字，英美字典中也可能有多種不同的發音，這不只是本節所說的口語化的縮簡字，也包括一般正式的單字。以 gonna 這個字的發音來說，在不同字典中可找到 /gənə/, /gʌnə/, /gɔnə/, /gɑnə/ 等不同的發音。

　　上述的各種縮簡在口語及一般書信中極為普遍，但在正式文章中，要謹慎使用，尤其忌諱非正式縮簡（informal contractions），如 gonna, wanna 等，也就是，嘴中說 gonna，筆下寫 going to。

2.1.3 連貫的說話方式（Connected Speech）

　　Connected Speech 是美式口語中極重要的成分，將話語連貫起來的最大原因是：減少發音器官位置的變更轉換，使得發音更平順與快速（美式口語的目的幾乎都如此）。前面說過，讀單字時，不可以 read the spelling，同樣的，在讀整個句子時，更是 what you see is not what they say。

　　Connected Speech 應該是我們不習慣美式口語的最大罩門，因為：中文一字一音節，字與字之間的區隔基本上清清楚楚，很少連音。

1. 連音（Linking or Catenation）

　　Linking 的產生主要是「前一個字的最後一個子音」與「後一個字的第一個音」連在一起唸，所產生的某種新的發音變化，幾種狀況如（劃底線的部分是連音）：

　　a. 連接 2 個相同的子音

　　　　單字的字尾是子音，而其後的音是相同的子音，可以連在一起，順著第一個子音，進入第二個子音，如 best time, big gift, both things, cheap places, feel like, good day, red dress, some more, stop playing, that time 等。有些時候雖然字母不一樣，但發音是一樣的，如：black coffee, enough for, look cool, nice sleep, quite tall。例外：/tʃ/ 和 /dʒ/，如 each choice, orange juice 都有兩個 /tʃ/ 或 /dʒ/，但不能連音，中間需有停頓，但可以縮短一些。

　　b. 連接 2 個 sister sounds

　　　　單字的最後是子音，而其後的音是 sister sounds（器官的位置與

動作相同的子音）時，將舌頭留在第一個子音的位置，直接去讀下個子音，聽起來就像是連在一起了，如 brea<u>the th</u>rough, chee<u>se s</u>andwich, dar<u>k g</u>reen, ha<u>ve f</u>un, jo<u>b p</u>osting, si<u>t d</u>own, slee<u>p b</u>etter, trie<u>d t</u>o, wha<u>t d</u>oes，這幾個 pairs：/p//b/, /k//g/, /s/ /z/, /t//d/, /θ//ð/ 都是 sister sounds。

c. 連接子音＋母音

單字的最後是子音，而其後的音是母音，就可以連發成一個音節，如 a<u>n a</u>pple, brea<u>k o</u>pen, do<u>es i</u>t, fa<u>ll o</u>n, kic<u>k i</u>t, nee<u>d i</u>t, sto<u>p i</u>t, that'<u>s i</u>t, tur<u>n o</u>ff, wa<u>ke u</u>p。日常例句：

Forge<u>t a</u>bout i<u>t</u>.

How'<u>s i</u>t going?

That's wha<u>t I</u> thought.

Wha<u>t a</u> mess!

What<u>'s u</u>p?

2. 省音（Elision）

Elision 是指在單字或句子中省略某個音，情況有很多種，僅舉數例如下：

a. schwa elision

average, broccoli, camera, chocolate, comfortable,

different, evening, every, family, favorite,

opera, restaurant, several, sophomore, vegetable

上述單字都是 3 音節或以上，標示橘色的字母原先讀作 /ə/ /ɚ/，它們都是重音節的鄰居，口語中被省略了。

b. t&d elision

單字：friendship, handsome, postman, sandwich, textbook

片語：hand bag, just said, last chance, most popular, next day

通常當 /t//d/ 介於兩個子音之間時，口語中被省略。

c. h elision

give her → /ˈgɪvə/, take him → /ˈtekɪm/, would he → /ˈwʊdɪ/

另外，有些省音甚至會反應在文字上面，如 iced cream 在文法上是對的，但 ice cream 甚至更普遍，或許是在口語進化的過程中，為了求快又

好唸，省掉了 d，而這又直接被用在文字上，就變成 ice cream 了。iced tea 與 ice tea 也是同樣的情況。

3. 插音（Intrusion）

　　Intrusion 是指當兩個母音連在一起時，比較不好唸，如果講得很快，非但不是省音，而是在兩個母音的中間插入一個 imaginary 子音（/j/、/w/、/r/），填補兩個連續母音之間縫隙，使得發音更順、更流暢（插入的子音要發的很弱很輕）。兩個母音的中間要插入哪個子音呢？原則是取決在前面的母音的舌頭位置及嘴形，插入類似動作的 /j/、或 /w/、或 /r/：

前面的母音是 /u/, /ʊ/, /aʊ/, /oʊ/	→ 插入 /w/
前面的母音是 /i/, /ɪ/, /aɪ/, /eɪ/, /ɔɪ/	→ 插入 /j/
前面的母音是 /ə/, /ɔ/	→ 插入 /r/

	加 /w/ /j/ /r/	
Do it!	插入 /w/	Do /ʷ/it!
go out	插入 /w/	go /ʷ/out
How are you?	插入 /w/	How /ʷ/are you?
buy it	插入 /j/	buy /ʲ/it
he asked	插入 /j/	he /ʲ/asked
father-in-law	插入 /r/	father-/ʳ/in-law
law and order	插入 /r/	law /ʳ/and order

　　上表中的 go out 插入 /w/ 是因為 go 的母音 /oʊ/ 的嘴形與 /w/ 的嘴形都是圓的，舌頭位置也相近，插入 /w/ 使得發音更順。同理，He asked 插入 /j/ 是因為 he 的母音 /i/ 的舌頭位置與 /j/ 的舌頭位置相近，也讓發音更順。

　　/j/ 與 /w/ 兩個音雖然屬於子音，但與母音很接近，所以又稱為半母音 semivowel。注音符號的「一」與「ㄨ」可作為輔音，也可以當元音，有點類似。

4. 變音（Changing Sounds）

　　Changing Sounds（又稱為 Assimilation）是指兩個鄰近的音產生發音

變化，而成為一個新的音。僅舉兩個例子：

> Can I get you anything? → Can I getcha/tʃə/ anything?
>
> Would you care to join us? → Wouldja/dʒə/ care to join us?

get you 轉成 getcha/tʃə/；Would you 轉成了 Wouldja/dʒə/。

中文也有類似的發音變化，譬如，我們會將「這樣子」說成「醬子」，甚或「醬」。另外，當兩個三聲的音連在一起時很不好唸，但將第一個字的三聲轉為二聲，就好唸多了！許多人會很自然地這麼說，卻不見得意識到他將三聲轉為二聲了！例如：

> 小姐、妳好、總統、老闆、水果、演講

有些疊字，我們會將第一個字轉為三聲，第二個字轉為二聲，例如：

> 爸爸、哥哥、妹妹

2.2 子音 /t/ 的 5 種發音

/t/ 是最常發的子音之一，它的發音方式五花八門，是變化最多、最有趣（最麻煩？）的一個子音，本節僅以 /t/ 為例子，讓讀者體會一下美式口語的特殊發音。/t/ 的發音方式包括：

1. True/t/ - 送氣 aspirated /t/：

    這是我們心目中的 /t/，是我們最習慣的發音。

    舌頭輕觸上齒齦，先擋住氣，再送氣，幾種狀況如下：

    單字的字首：take, tail, talk, tea, talk, tip

    重音節之首：ho`tel, re`turn, un`til

    此發音方式亦適用於 stop voiceless sounds：/p t k/

2. 不送氣 unaspirated /t/：

    雖不送氣，但器官要到位（舌尖輕觸上齒齦）。幾種情況：

    a. 在單字的字尾

        字尾：about, exit, jacket, light, ticket, update

    b. 緊跟在 /s/ 之後

        star, steak, step, style

此發音方式亦適用於 stop voiceless sounds：/p t k/

3. Flap t（或 Tap t，彈舌 t）：

　這是美式英語中最獨特的子音。我們有時候會感覺美國人講話時，某些 /t/ 怎聽起來像 /d/ 呢？事實上，大多數美國人確實將某些 /t/ 發成 voiced quick /d/。發音方式是將舌頭快速碰一下上齒齦（alveolar tap）。彈舌 t 發生在下列情形：

　a. /t/ 在兩個母音之間，且在輕音音節，如：

　　better, bottom, butter, city, computer, daughter, later

　　matter, metal, pretty, Saturday, water

　　連字如 a lot of, out of, what are, what about

　　注意：/t/ 在重音音節時不成立，如 attach /ə`tætʃ/

　b. /t/ 在 r 之後，母音之前，且在輕音音節，如：

　　dirty, forty, party, shorty, thirty

　c. /t/ 在母音之後，dark l 之前，如：

　　Beatles, bottle, brittle, capital, Seattle, subtle, title

4. Glottal t：

　/t/ 不吐氣，將氣快速鎖在聲門（glottis, 會感覺到肚子稍稍硬起來），停一剎那。這種發音方式發生在下列兩種情形：

　a. 緊隨重音節之後的輕音節中發 /tən/ 時

　　以 button /bʌtən/ 來說，先發 /bʌ/，將氣阻在聲門，再發 /n/（幾乎省略 /ə/），這時的 /n/ 就像是一個音節（syllabic ŋ）。/t/ 與 /n/ 的舌頭位置是一樣的，易於由 /t/ 轉為 /n/。例子：

　　　cotton, important, Manhattan, mountain, written

　b. /t/ 之後緊跟著子音時

　　batman, fitness, outside

　　eat something, hit me

　　此發音方式適用於 stop sounds：/p t k/，如：

　　　kick the ball, help me, keep going, stop sign

5. Vanishing t：

　如果符合兩個條件：(a) /t/ 在 /n/ 與母音（特別是 /ɚ/）中間

　　　　　　　　　　(b) /t/ 在輕音節

　　　　　　　　　→ 省略 /t/

如 center, internet, interview, printer, Santa, twenty, winter
/t/ 與 /n/ 的舌頭在同一位置，把 /t/ 發得極輕，幾乎省了。

如果我們發音時只用正規的第 1 項的 True/t/，不管其他的 Flap t、Glottal t 等等，是可以的，沒有任何問題的，別人都聽得懂，只是，聽起來較不 native 而已，這也沒什麼關係。

上述的五種 /t/ 唸法聽起來都略有差異，但它們都屬於同一個音素（phoneme）。雖然唸法不同，但不會改變單字的意思。

順便一提，以 Flap t 來說，美式口語會將 got to 簡化趨向唸成 godda、lot of 唸成 lodda、might have 唸成 mighda、out of 唸成 oudda、sort of 唸成 sorda 等等。英國人通常不發 Flap t。

/t/ 在英文中這麼常見而普遍，卻有這麼多的花樣，還真有些麻煩！尤其 Flap t 與 Glottal t 對我們來說，確實是有難度的。

母音的長短（Vowel Length）

另外，停頓音 /p//t//k/ 在單字的字尾不送氣，那麼，如何分辨 cup vs. cub; feet vs. feed; lack vs. lag 呢？這就要靠母音的長短（Vowel Length）幫助區分了，一個簡單的原則是：

　　1. 無聲子音之前的母音發得短
　　2. 有聲子音之前的母音發得長

這個原則使得字尾子音（有聲或無聲）的辨識較容易。以 feet/fit/ 與 feed/fid/ 為例，/i/ 在 feet 發音時間短，/i/ 在 feed 較長，這樣就可以區別這兩個字了。不僅停頓音如此，一些其他的子音也一樣，例如：/s/ 與 /z/，price 的 /aɪ/ 比 prize 的 /aɪ/ 短；又如 /f/ 與 /v/，/i/ 在 leaf 唸得短，在 leave 唸得長。很常用的 have /hæv/ 的母音 /æ/ 要唸得長，如果唸得短了，就會像 half /hæf/ 了。

總結

本章總結而論，美式口語的趨勢是弱化、縮簡、連音、省音等，目的是好唸平順以及快速省時，重點如：1. 能弱化就弱化（schwa 化 – 輕音節功能字）；2. 能縮簡就縮簡；3. 能連音就連音。

Part 2

 文法篇

　　glamour（魅力）這個字是由 grammar（文法）演化而來。中英文各有各的魅力，以文法架構來說，中文像流水，英文像竹節。中文有形無形、可收可放；英文節節相扣、結構嚴謹。

　　對於學習文法，有些學者主張自然學習法，有些則主張要先熟悉規則。建議：兩者都嘗試，找出適合自己的方式，很可能會是兩者相輔相成。

　　中文的邏輯思維常會造成學英文的干擾，建議：至少在學習英文時（上課或自修），即使短暫，也要盡力放空母語的思維，才能專心學他們的文法。

　　現代多數的語言專家認為語言規則是約定俗成（descriptive grammar）的，由大家講話與寫作的習慣中去歸納而得來，不是硬梆梆的規則（prescriptive grammar），但無論如何，還是有許多的邏輯、順序、規則（幾乎所有規則都有例外），和中文大不同。尤其對於非母語的我們來說，了解文法，對學英文一定有幫助。

　　如前言中所述，學外語最難改的就是口音（accent）。英語並非我們的母語，有點口音也是自然的，不必拘泥於口音，盡力就夠了，更重要的是學好聽力、文法、詞彙，講話或寫文章都能清楚通順地表達，就達到學語言的目的了！

　　文法是字詞文句連結組合時的規則，語言的根本大法。文法的好壞大致上決定了聽讀說寫的「內在程度」。

　　學文法的第一步是先了解各詞類的功能與角色。

8 大詞類

　　語言的文法結構基本上都呈現在各種詞類之間的關係與規則上。每種語言都有各自的特性，學語言一定要先分清該語言的詞類，才能了解字詞擺放的位置與彼此之間的關係，構造出合文法的句子。

　　英文有 8 類不同性質的單字，英文稱為 parts of speech。另一種講法，我們會更容易了解，叫做 word classes（單字分類），就是依照單字的「文法性質」，分為 8 類，各取一個名字。好比音樂的音符，如果想讀懂或譜寫音樂篇章（文句），一定得先學各種音符（字詞），然後按照邏輯與規則，將音符連結成一首音樂。

　　我們有時將 word 翻譯成「字」，有時又翻譯成「詞」。「字」或「詞」在討論英文時會有點模糊，因為「詞」在中文裡通常是兩個字 (或以上)，但也可以是一個字，而英文的 word 則是「單字」，多於一個字而不成句的叫 phrase(片語)。本書中不做嚴格區分，將「字」與「詞」互用。

8 大詞類及功能如下（極簡略的描述）：

詞類	功能
名詞　noun	→ 人、事、物等等的名稱
動詞　verb	→ 主詞執行的動作或狀態
代名詞　pronoun	→ 替代句子中提過的名詞
形容詞　adjective	→ 對名詞或代名詞的修飾
副詞　adverb	→ 最主要功能：修飾動詞
介系詞　preposition	→ 兩名詞之間的相互關係
連接詞　conjunction	→ 字、片語、子句接著劑
感嘆詞　interjection	→ 表達情緒或驚嘆的短詞

8 種詞類在句子中各自扮演不同的「角色」（主詞、受詞、修飾詞等）：

例句：**Tom bought a very good present for his mother.**

	詞類	角色
Tom	名詞	主詞
bought	動詞	動作
a	不定冠詞	限定詞，修飾詞
very	副詞	修飾詞
good	形容詞	修飾詞
present	名詞	直接受詞
for	介系詞	表達他母親與禮物的關係
his	代名詞	代替 Tom 的
mother	名詞	間接受詞

注意：上表中的名詞可作為主詞、直接受詞、與間接受詞；而形容詞、副詞、與冠詞都具有修飾的功能。

8 大詞類可分為內容字與功能字，內容字是表達實質意義的字詞（如 Tom, bought, very, good, present, mother），功能字則扮演文法角色（如 a, for, his）。內容字包含名詞、動詞、形容詞、副詞，這四類佔了英文單字的絕大部分（有統計稱大於 99%），單字中約 1/2 是名詞、約 1/4 形容詞、約 1/7 動詞，而且，理論上它們可以無限擴充，所有新字幾乎都是內容字。另一方面，功能字包含代名詞、連接詞、介系詞，雖然字數極少，但因為任何句子都需要功能字去符合文法規則或顯示字詞之間的關係，它們出現的頻率非常驚人，根據一些大型語料庫的統計，在句子中出現最多的前 10 名單字幾乎全是功能字，其中，the 是冠軍。

另外，內容字的作用限於單字本身的意義，用錯了就是錯一個字而已；功能字則扮演文法角色，它的作用超乎功能字的本身，用錯了，小則影響句子結構，大則影響意義。

8 個詞類中，僅有連接詞、介系詞、感嘆詞不會改變形式，其他 5 類都可能會隨著時態、性別、單複數、比較級等而變形。

能分清詞類，有助於正確使用字彙，是學文法最重要的起手式，也是大多數文法書將詞類分析置於書本最前面的原因。

中英文各詞類中差異性最大的就是動詞了。英文動詞的時態有 12 種之多，這還只是主動語態而已，尚須考慮相對應的被動語態。中文動詞是

沒有時態的，我們很不習慣這麼多的變化，因此最容易在動詞用法上出錯。何況，除了時態，動詞還會跟著數量及人稱而變化。不過，有些語言更複雜，不但動詞變化更多，甚至連形容詞、冠詞都可能跟著陰性、陽性、中性、單複數等而變化。英文在這方面算是簡單的了！

　　和中文差異性第二大的，應該算是連接詞了。英文重形合，利用連接詞明確嚴謹地定義句子的從屬關係，常有長句子出現；中文重意合，從屬關係大多由語意邏輯來協助結合，而不是連接詞，短句居多。了解連接詞對英文讀寫都有很大的幫助，如果以中文的心態來學英文，就不易體會了。

　　還有一個詞類也是我們不易掌握與運用的：小字小詞的介系詞，看似簡單，卻大多沒有一定的規則，需要時間去習慣。

3.1　動詞

　　任何語言的詞類中，最最重要的就是：名詞與動詞。因為，任何一個句子想表達的意義不外乎：主詞（某人、事、物）「做了什麼」或「是什麼狀態」，做了什麼可用「一般動詞」來表達，是什麼狀態可用「be 動詞」來表達。

　　名詞是句子的主角，動詞是句子的靈魂。一個完整的英文子句「必須有、也只能有一個」主要動詞 main verb，這是英文句子結構的重大要件，中文句子結構沒有這麼嚴格的概念。

3.1.1　動詞類別

　　動詞有很多種分類的方式，以我們學習文法特性的角度，有幾類動詞需要特別注意：

1. 動作動詞（action verb）
　　主詞執行某種動態的動作，可以隨時開始或停止
2. 非動作動詞（non-action verb）
　　非動作靜態或長期的狀態，不可隨時開始或停止
3. 聯繫動詞（linking verb）

作為主詞與其補語的聯繫

4. 瞬間動詞

動作在發生的那一剎那就完成了，不具持續性

3.1.1.1　動作動詞

動作動詞是我們最常見、最習慣的動詞。絕大多數的動詞屬於動作動詞（又叫 dynamic verb），如 ask, buy, drink, eat, jump, read, study, walk 等，是一種實質的動作，可隨時開始、隨時結束、可被看見。

3.1.1.2　非動作動詞

非動作動詞是不帶動作的動詞，因為不牽涉動作，又被稱作狀態動詞（stative verbs），或靜態動詞，它表達的是一種存在或狀態，包括：be 動詞、擁有（如 belong, have, own）、情感（如 hate, like, love）、心理（如 believe, forget, know, need, want）、意見（如 agree, approve, prefer）、感官（如 feel, hear, see, smell, taste）。

非動作動詞在文法上最重要的特性是：不可以用進行式。因為它所表達是一種狀態或靜態，不是可以隨時開始或停止的動作，不能用進行式來表達，如：

I am loving her.	→ 錯
I love her.	→ 對
He is having a luxury car.	→ 錯
He has a luxury car.	→ 對
The Alexa is costing $129.	→ 錯
The Alexa costs $129.	→ 對
I have been knowing him since I was 12.	→ 錯
I have known him since I was 12.	→ 對
We used to drink coffee, but now we're preferring boba tea.	→ 錯
We used to drink coffee, but now we prefer boba tea.	→ 對

注意：有一些動詞有時是動作動詞，有時又可作為非動作動詞，包括

feel, have, think, love，如：

> I am having dinner.
>
> I have two sons.

第一句的 having 是動作動詞（吃），可用進行式；第二句的 have 是非動作動詞（擁有），不可用進行式，不可以寫成 I am having two sons。又如：

> What are you thinking about?
>
> What do you think of the #MeToo movement?

第一句中的 thinking 是動作動詞（想），可用進行式；第二句的 think 是非動作動詞（想法、意見），不可用進行式。再如：

> Mom is tasting the soup to see if it needs salt.
>
> This beef tastes like chicken.

第一句的 tasting 是動作動詞（試嚐），可用進行式；第二句的 tastes 是非動作動詞（嚐起來的感覺），不可用進行式。

順便一提，McDonald's 有句時髦而且深入人心的廣告詞：

> I'm lovin' it.

這是一句大家公認的非常成功的廣告標語，但以文法來說，是錯誤的，或許也正因為如此（文法錯誤），才更吸引人！

3.1.1.3　連綴動詞

有一類的動詞叫連綴動詞（linking verb），功能是聯繫主詞與其補語（complement），用補語來表達主詞的特徵、性質、狀況等，一般而言，連綴動詞也都屬於狀態動詞；反之則不盡然。最常見的如 be（is, was, has been……）, become, appear, grow, prove, remain, seem, turn 等，還有感官動詞如 feel, look, smell, sound, taste。

依照文法規則，連綴動詞與一般動詞的最大差異是：

連綴動詞之後要跟形容詞　→用來描述主詞

而一般動詞之後要跟副詞　→用來修飾動詞

連綴動詞句型如：

主詞＋連綴動詞＋主詞補語

補語可以是形容詞、名詞、或介系詞等；但不能用副詞。如：

Barry still looks great.

Maurice was a musician and songwriter.

Robin was at his best when he performed I Started A Joke.

上述三個句子不是表達 Barry, Maurice, Robin 在做什麼動作，而是提供主詞的補充訊息，表示他們是什麼，或什麼狀態，三個動詞 looks, was, was 都是連綴動詞；三個主詞補語：great 是形容詞，musician and songwriter 是名詞片語，at his best 是介系詞片語。

再舉兩個例句：

I feel bad about the mistake.	→ feel 是連綴，bad 是形容詞
The team played badly last night.	→ played 是動作，badly 是副詞

另外，要特別留意：有些動詞可以是動作動詞，也可以是連綴動詞。例如：

The cake tasted good.	→ tasted 是連綴動詞
He tasted the cake.	→ tasted 是動作動詞
The dog smelled bad.	→ smelled 是連綴動詞
The dog smelled him all over.	→ smelled 是動作動詞

中文有時在主詞與補語之間不需要連綴動詞，如：淑芬好美，家豪很酷。這兩句話主詞與補語之間沒有連綴動詞。英文則很嚴謹，一定要有連綴動詞。

如何判定連綴動詞呢？有個簡單的測試方法：將連綴動詞用 be 動詞取代，如果詞意仍符合邏輯，它就是連綴動詞，反之則不是。如：

His cap looked good.

He looked at the sky.

如果以 was 取代 looked：

His cap was good.

He was at the sky.

第一句詞意符合邏輯，looked 是連綴動詞；第二句不合邏輯，looked 不是連綴動詞。

狀態動詞與連綴動詞有什麼分別？大體上：

1. 狀態動詞（非動作）描述的是主詞的狀態，而非動作。我們在文法上要特別注意的重點在於狀態動詞不能用進行式。

2. 連綴動詞的功能是聯繫主詞和其補語。文法重點在於連綴動詞之後跟著的是形容詞（或名詞、介系詞片語等），但不能跟副詞。連綴動詞屬於狀態動詞；反之則不盡然。

3.1.1.4 瞬間動詞

大部分的動作動詞可以描述具持續性的動作，如 play, work 等。有部分的動詞則描述動作在發生那一剎那就結束了、完成了，不具持續性，這類動詞叫瞬間動詞，例如 arrive, begin, come, die, enter, finish, give, lend, marry, open, receive, start。

瞬間動詞的文法重點是：

1. 可以使用完成式

2. 不可使用表示「一段時間」的副詞片語

She has arrived at the airport for 2 hours.	→ 錯
The meeting has started for a little while.	→ 錯
How long have you bought your house?	→ 錯

上三句的 has arrived, has started, have bought 都是瞬間動詞的完成式，它們不可用表示「一段時間」的副詞片語：for 2 hours, for a little while, How long。或可依序改為如下的例子：

She has arrived at the airport.

　或 She arrived at the airport 2 hours ago.

The meeting has started.

　或 The meeting started a little while ago.

How long have you had your house?

形容一個過世很久了，可以說 He has died；但不能說 He has died for a long time. 如果想表達類似的意義，可以說：

He has been dead for a long time.

完成式 has been dead 表示一種持續性狀態（從過去到現在），可以用「一段時間」的 for a long time。

3.1.2 時態

動詞的時態 tense 可分為時間 time 和狀態 aspect。時間指的是過去、現在、未來 3 種；狀態則表述某個動詞的執行狀況，例如：正在進行中或是已經完成了等，分為 4 種，如下：

簡單狀態	simple
進行狀態	continuous（or progressive）
完成狀態	perfect
完成進行狀態	perfect continuous

3.1.2.1 時態的種類與意涵

時間有 3 種，狀態有 4 種，3 與 4 相乘，有 12 種可能，也就是說，有 12 種時態的主動語態表達句型（尚須考慮被動語態），如下表：

狀態　　時間	Time	Active Voice（主動） Passive Voice（被動）
簡單	現在	I do it. It is done.
	過去	I did it. It was done.
	未來	I will do it. It will be done.
	現在	I have done it. It has been done.

完成	過去	I had done it. It had been done.
	未來	It will have been done.
進行	現在	I am doing it. It is being done.
	過去	I was doing it. It was being done.
	未來	I will be doing it. （被動式少見）
完成進行	現在	I have been doing it. （被動式少見）
	過去	I had been doing it. （被動式少見）
	未來	t will be being done. （被動式少見）

這 12 種時態句子的在文法上的意涵與例句表列如下：

句型		意涵與例句
現在	簡單	現時的情況，事實，習慣、經常性、重複性的事件 He is an English teacher.（現時的情況） Water boils at 100 degrees Celsius.（事實） My mom usually shops on Saturdays.（習慣） 常用副詞（頻率）如：always, every day, often, rarely, sometimes 等
	進行	正在發生（進行中）的事件，且尚未完成，可能持續短暫的一段時間 He is currently writing a new textbook. They are still waiting for our reply. Right now, he is visiting his girlfriend and singing songs to her. 常用副詞如：at the moment, at present, now, right now 等
	完成	作為過去已發生的事件與現在的連結；過去已完成並對現在有影響（如經驗），完成的時間點不重要，句中沒有特定時間點 He has already written ten books. 常用副詞如：already, before, never, yet, since, so far 等（不確定時間點）

	完成進行	過去某時間點已發生，而且持續到現在／未來的事件 He has been writing novels since he was 25. 常用副詞如：for 2 months, since 1990 等 重點：強調持續一段時間
過去	簡單	過去某特定時間點發生的已完成的事件，與現在無關 通常會明確標明事件發生的時間（也可能隱含而不明示） They played badminton last Friday. 常用副詞如：ago, yesterday, last week, in 2018 等
	進行	過去某特定時間點正在進行中的（較長的）事件 句子可能會有另一（較短的）事件插入打岔 I was taking a shower when the doorbell rang. While I was taking a shower, the doorbell rang. 較早的用過去進行式（taking a shower），是背景（較長） 較晚的用過去式（the doorbell rang），是 interruption（較短） 通常，When ＋過去式；而 While ＋過去進行式 常用副詞如：at this time yesterday, when he arrived 等 ＊如果兩件事同時持續進行，可用兩個過去進行式： My wife was eating dinner while I was watching TV.
	完成	在過去某時間點之前已經完成的事件。句子中常描述兩個事件： 較早的用過去完成式，較晚的用過去式 The movie had already started when we got to the theater. 較早－電影已開始；較晚－趕到電影院 常用副詞如：before he came, when she called 等
	完成進行	在過去某特定時間點之前已進行一段時間，並且持續的進行事件 （和過去完成式類似，句子中常有兩個事件） He had been writing that book for a few months when he became ill. 較早的事件用過去完成進行式（寫書），是背景 較晚的事件用過去式（生病），是表達重點 常用副詞如：for a few months 等
	簡單	未來可能的事、預測、事實、服務、承諾等 I don't think he'll come tonight.（預測） Hold on. I'll put you through.（服務） The sun will rise tomorrow.（事實） 常用副詞如：in a few minutes, tomorrow, next week 等

未來	進行	未來某特定時間點將發生（進行中）的事件 He will be doing his homework tonight. I will be studying when you arrive. 句子中有未來時間點（tonight, when you arrive） 常用副詞如：tomorrow at 8 o'clock, at this time tomorrow 等
	完成	在未來某時間點（行動）之前將已完成的事件 He will have done his homework by the time we arrive. 先發生的用未來完成式（will have done his homework） 後發生的用現在簡單式（we arrive） 常用副詞如：by the time 等
	完成進行	在未來某時間點之前已進行一段時間，並會持續進行的事件 He will have been watching TV for 3 hours by the time his mom returns. 先發生的用未來完成進行式（will have been watching TV） 後發生的用現在簡單式（his mom returns） 常用副詞如：for 3 hours, by the time 等

　　上表充分顯示了英文對於事件發生的時間與次序的嚴謹邏輯，我們在運用這些句型之前，首先要瞭解：每一種句型都明示或隱含一個特定的時間參考點（現在、過去、未來），每個發生的事件都按照這個參考點來安排發生的順序，並依照事件之間彼此的相互關係決定執行的狀態（簡單、進行、完成、完成進行）。簡言之，要寫出正確的時態，最重要的原則是先決定：

　　　　1. 各事件發生的時間（現在、過去、未來）及先後順序
　　　　2. 各事件的執行狀態（簡單、進行、完成、完成進行）

　　中文動詞只有一個時態，不會變，事件發生的順序和狀態都可用一些助詞（副詞、介詞等）來輔助說明，例如，「正」表示進行式，「已」或「了」表示完成式。
　　中文的習慣與思維造成了我們在學英文時，最先學會現在簡單式，然後是：過去簡單式、未來簡單式、以及現在進行式等，這些是我們能直接吸收的簡單句型，其他的句型則最好先了解英文文法相關的規則，才容易

吸收。

3.1.2.2　各種句型時態對比

　　中英文動詞存在如此鉅大的差異，以下將針對一些容易混淆的時態句型，用對照的方式，舉些例子相互比較，說明差異：

1. 現在簡單式 vs. 現在進行式：

　　我們的思維常將現在簡單式想做僅限於表達現在的情況，但現在簡單式不只是現在的情況，也能表示事實、習慣、經常性、長期性等等，都超越了僅僅是「現在的情況」，如 The moon orbits the earth. 是從以前到未來的永恆狀況；現在進行式則表示進行中短暫的事件（就在講話當下），如：

The phone rings.	→電話會響（功能）
The phone is ringing.	→電話正響（暫時）

He lives in Syria.	→隱含長期性
At present, he is living in Syria.	→短期暫住

Look, it snows.	→錯誤
Look, it's snowing.	→正確（暫時）

We build a pavilion in the garden.	→不妥
We are building (or built, have built) a pavilion in the garden.	

She works for a cosmetics company. This month, she's working on the new line of face masks.	→ works（長期）；working（短暫）

2. 現在完成式 vs. 現在完成進行式：

　　a. 現在完成式表示已做完的事，而現在完成進行式表示尚未完成的行動，如：

Joey has eaten the hot dogs and buns.	→已吃完，時間不重要
Joey has been eating the hot dogs and buns.	→可能未吃完，在繼續

b. 現在完成式表達數量或頻率，現在完成進行式表達時程長度：

Kyle has played video games 20 times this week.	→ 20 次
Kyle has been playing Fortnite since 8:00.	→從 8 點到現在

c. 現在完成進行式也可表示和現在相關的剛完成的事件：

You're out of breath. Have you been running?	→剛剛跑完
It's been raining so the pavement is wet.	→從 8 點到現在

3. 過去簡單式 vs. 現在完成式：

a. 兩者的意義與用法常易混淆。由於中文的關係，我們較習慣前者，而不太會用後者。過去簡單式表示過去的事件，與現在無關，句子中常會標明過去某特定時間點。現在完成式則表示對現在有影響的已完成的事件，發生的時間不重要，句子中通常沒有特定時間點，如：

I studied eight pages last night.	→ 昨天晚上讀了 8 頁
I've already studied eight pages.	→ 讀了 8 頁，時候不重要

I have graduated from college in 2018.	→ 錯誤
I graduated from college in 2018.	→ 正確

b. 現在完成式隱含過去某事件的影響持續到現在，是與現在的一種連結；過去簡單式則表示已過去了，不再繼續，如：

Mozart wrote more than 600 pieces of music.	→過去了，不繼續
Elton John has written many songs.	→可能會繼續寫

He worked for Netflix.	→ 已離開 Netflix
He has worked for Netflix for two years.	→ 還在 Netflix

c. 現在完成式可與尚未結束的特定時間連用，而過去簡單式則與過去的特定時間連用，如：

I didn't see him this afternoon.	→下午未見到，現已是晚上
I haven't seen him this afternoon.	→仍是下午，還有機會見到

Last year, he visited me twice.	→去年已過去，他來了兩次
This year, he has visited me twice.	→仍是今年，可能還會再來

4. 過去簡單式 vs. 過去完成式：

a. 過去完成式常不單獨出現。句子常會有兩個事件，顯示發生時間的先後，先發生的事件用過去完成式，表達「過去的過去」，後發生的事件用過去簡單式，如：

The concert had started when he arrived.	→ 音樂會已開始，他才到
When the concert ended, he had left.	→ 音樂會結束，他已先走

b. 當句子中有 time words（如 before, after, by the time）時，事件發生的順序非常明顯，可用過去簡單式代替過去完成式。下面第 1,3 句文法上較清晰，但也可以用第 2,4 句：

By the time we got to the theater, the movie had started.

By the time we got to the theater, the movie started.

They restarted the volleyball match as soon as the rain had stopped.

They restarted the volleyball match as soon as the rain stopped.

c. 過去完成式表示已經在過去某時間完成的事件，如下句用 had dreamed，因為昨天已買了一輛超跑：

I bought a Lamborghini yesterday. For my whole life, I had always dreamed of owning a super sports car.

5. 未來簡單式 vs. 現在簡單式：

由於中文的思維，我們常會錯用現在式來表達未來，如：

I see you tomorrow.	→ 錯誤
I'll see you tomorrow.	→ 正確

I buy it if you give me some discount.	→ 錯誤
I'll buy it if you give me some discount.	→ 正確

6. 未來簡單式除了 will（shall）之外，還有三種表達方式：

　　a. be going to 句型 - 基於某些證據的預測，表達確定性

　　　It'll probably rain this afternoon.

　　　Look at those black clouds. It's going to rain any minute.

　　　第一句表示可能性，第二句則是基於事實的預測。另外，will
　　　常用來表達在對話當下（at the time of speaking）的臨時決定；
　　　而 be going to 則是說話前已先決定要做某事：

| I am thirsty. I think I'll buy some juice. | → 臨時決定 |
| I'm going to ask Amber out this evening. | → 說話前已決定 |

　　b. 現在進行式句型（be Ving）- 已確定安排好要做某事

　　　They are getting married next month.

　　　I'm having dinner with my parent tonight.

　　c. 現在簡單式句型 - 安排好的日程表、進度、時程

　　　The plane arrives at 14:00 tomorrow.

　　　The restaurant opens at 5 PM tonight.

　　　The concert starts next Saturday at 19:00.

7. 未來式的句型中若有兩個子句：

　　主要子句要用未來式，而以 time words（如 when, if, after, before,
until, as soon as）開頭的子句要用現在簡單式：

　　　When he graduates, he'll look for a job.

　　　He is going to move after he graduates.

8. 在「未來某特定時間點」要做的事情：

　　應該用未來進行式，由於中文的習慣，我們常容易錯用了未來簡單式，
下例的 this evening 是未來的特定時間點：

| I will watch TV when you call this evening. | → 錯誤 |
| I will be watching TV when you call this evening. | → 正確 |

9. 進行式的句子通常都會標明「特定時間點」：

以下例句中的橘色字代表「特定時間點」：

He is flying to Kenya at this moment.

He was flying to Kenya at this time yesterday.

He will be flying to Kenya at this time tomorrow.

10 現在完成式 vs. 過去完成式 vs. 未來完成式：

現在完成式的參考時間點是「現在」，過去完成式的參考時間點是「過去某特定時間點」，未來完成式的參考時間點是「未來某特定時間點」，如：

I've been to Uruguay three times.	→ 現在完成
I had been to Uruguay twice by the time I was 10.	→ 過去完成
I'll have been to Uruguay four times by next June.	→ 未來完成

3.1.3 時態變化

任何一個動詞都有 5 種形式：原式、過去式、現在分詞、過去分詞、第三人稱單數。動詞的時態變化大體上分為規則性變化與不規則性變化，如下表的例子：

	原式	過去式	過去分詞	現在分詞	第三人稱單數
規則	play	played	played	playing	plays
不規則	go	went	gone	going	goes
	read	read	read	reading	reads
	run	ran	run	running	runs

規則變化動詞的過去式與過去分詞的字尾都是 ed（如上表的 play）；不規則變化動詞則非如此（如上表的 go）。

在動詞的 5 種形式中，有些有 5 種不同的寫法，如 go, went, gone, going, goes；有些則少於 5 種，如 play 有 4 種寫法，read 有 3 種。只有一個動詞（be）例外，它有 8 個形式：be, am, is, are, was, were, being, been。

中文的動詞只有一個形式，因此，我們常會抱怨英文動詞有這麼多的

變化。不過，比上不足，比下有餘，有些語言的動詞甚至有幾十種變化（如義大利文），學英文可算是幸福的了！

3.1.3.1　規則動詞（過去式與過去分詞）

1. 字尾＋ ed

    start → started　　　 wish → wished

2. 字尾是 e，加 d

    smile → smiled　　　 hope → hoped

3. 單音節單字，字尾是 CVC（最後 3 個字母，C: 子音字母，V: 母音字母），則重複字尾的子音字母，再加 ed

    stop → stopped　　　 hop → hopped

4. 多音節單字，字尾是 CVC

    a. 重音在最後，重複字尾，再加 ed

    control → controlled　　 refer → referred

    b. 重音不在最後，只加 ed

    cancel → canceled　　 travel → traveled

    英式：cancelled, travelled

5. 字尾是「子音字母＋ y」，去除 y，加 ied

    cry → cried　　　 satisfy → satisfied

3.1.3.2　不規則動詞（過去式與過去分詞）

不規則動詞很多，僅舉些日常的例子如下表：

原式	過去式	過去分詞	註
bet	bet	bet	
bind	bound	bound	綁
bound	bounded	bounded	彈回
cast	cast	cast	
cost	cost	cost	
dive	dived, dove	dived	
dream	dreamed, dreamt	dreamed, dreamt	
find	found	found	發現
found	founded	founded	創立

freeze	froze	frozen	
grind	ground	ground	磨碎
ground	grounded	grounded	擱淺
get	got	got, gotten	
hang	hung	hung	吊物
hang	hanged	hanged	吊人
hurt	hurt	hurt	
lay	laid	laid	放置
lie	lay	lain	躺
lie	lied	lied	說謊
light	lit, lighted	lit, lighted	
set	set	set	
shine	shined	shined	擦亮
shine	shone	shone	照耀
sink	sank, sunk	sunk	
spring	sprang, sprung	sprung	
wake	woke, waked	woken, woke, waked	
wind	wound	wound	捲
wound	wounded	wounded	受傷

　　順便一提，上述兩節的過去式與過去分詞，當字尾是加 ed 而且 e 也要發音時（如 ended, started），美式發音偏向輕音 /əd/，英式發 /ɪd/。

3.1.3.3 動詞的進行式

　　1. 字尾＋ ing

　　　clean → cleaning　　　wish → wishing

　　2. 尾是 e，去除 e，然後加 ing

　　　give → giving　　　hope → hoping

　　3. 單音節單字，字尾是 CVC（最後 3 個字母，C: 子音字母，V: 母音字母），則重複字尾的子音字母，再加 ing

　　　cut → cutting　　　hop → hopping

　　4. 多音節單字，字尾是 CVC

a. 重音在最後，重複字尾，再加 ing

control → controlling　　refer → referring

b. 重音不在最後，只加 ing

cancel → canceling　　travel → traveling

英式：cancelling, travelling

5. 字尾是「ie」, 改為 y, 再加 ing

die → dying　　lie → lying

3.1.4 助動詞

主要動詞是動作的執行者（actor），而助動詞（auxiliary/helping verb）則是幫助動詞來表達人稱、時態、語態（voice）、語氣（mood）等，只具有文法上的功能。

do, be, have 是最常見的助動詞。do 出現於簡單式；be 出現於進行式；have 用於完成式。它們都具有雙重身分，既可當助動詞，也可當動詞，例如：

What do you do?

He is just being funny.

Have you had lunch?

第一句中的第一個 do 是助動詞，第二個 do 是動詞現在式；第二句的 is 是助動詞，being 是動詞現在進行式；第三句的 Have 是助動詞，had 是動詞完成式。中文也有類似狀況（可當助動詞，也可當動詞），如：我要手機，句中的「要」是動詞；而我要買手機，句中的「要」是表示意願的助動詞。

在 Yes/No 簡短問句的回答時，要用助動詞，而非主要動詞，如：Do you play rugby? 以中文的思維，可能會回答：Yes, I play.（我打），英文則不能這樣回答，要說：Yes, I do.

3.1.4.1 情態助動詞

有一類助動詞叫：情態助動詞 modal auxiliary verbs，共 9 個：can, could, may, might, must, shall, should, will, would 等。它們能幫助動詞表

達許多情態，例如：是否有能力（can）、是否准許（may）、是否必須（must）、是否應該（should）、是否必然（can't）、可能性（might）、做建議（could）、表示承諾（will）等。

1. 表達「能力」：

「能力」：can 表示現在或未來，could 表示過去，如：

Clark can speak Kryptonian fluently.

Tony can fix his super suit tomorrow morning.

Peter couldn't climb walls like a spider when he was a kid.

「能力」也可以用片語 be able to 來表達，如：

Bruce is able to do incredible things, yet he has no superpowers.

2. 表達「請求許可」：

「請求許可」可以用 may, could, can，如：

May I help you?

Could I please have a glass of beer?

Can I borrow your pen for a minute?

may 是請求許可很正式的用法，日常生活少用；最常用的是 can；could 比較婉轉。美國小孩如果問媽媽：Can I go out? 會被媽媽糾正為：May I go out? 但長大以後，大家都說：Can I ...? 如果在朋友間用 May I ...? 反而會讓人覺得做作或反諷。

雖然使用 can 已是非正式英語的普遍趨勢，但是，在正式英文中，還是用 may 與 could 比較適當。這種用法時，could 沒有過去式的意義。

請求許可也可以用 would 或 will：Would you do me a favor? 或 Will you do me a favor?

如果是表達「不允許」，則可用 cannot 或 can't，如 You can't park your car here.

3. 表達「是否應該」

「是否應該」可以用 should 或 must，如：

You should go and see a doctor.

You must be at your desk by 9 AM.

should 表示忠告，而 must 則是一種責任與義務。

4. 表達「現在或未來可能性」

「現在或未來可能性」通常可以用 may, might, could。注意：might 和 could 在形式上是過去式，但卻可以表示現在或未來的可能，對我們來說，會有些困惑，不習慣。如：

If we don't hurry, we could be late.

Be careful of the dog. It might bite you.

It's raining here, but it may be sunny there.

這三個助動詞的意義基本上沒什麼區別。美式英語的 may 較正式，而 could 和 might 則較通用。（註：may be 是助動詞＋動詞；maybe 是副詞）。

「非常可能」可以用 must 或 should，如：

He didn't eat any of the meat. He must be a vegetarian or vegan.

If they take the car, they should arrive by eleven.

「非常不可能」可用 can't，如：It can't be true.

5. 表達「過去的可能性」：

討論完「現在或未來的可能性」，那如何表達「過去的可能性」呢？答案是：用情態助動詞＋ have（完成式）來表達，這也是我們中文思維要注意的地方，如：

What was that noise? I suppose it could have been the wind.

I might have left my keys here this morning. Have you seen them?

Aurora looks tired today. She may not have slept well last night.

You shouldn't have shouted at her. It really upset her.

The students did well on the test. They must have studied hard.

6. 表達「過去未做的想像情境」：

有些情態助動詞可用來表示過去未做的想像情境（past modals of lost opportunities），包括 should have, could have 和 would have，都用來表達對過去未做某事的後悔（regret）。這種完成式的語法又是我們比較不習慣的。

「過去未做的想像情境」和「過去的可能性」是不同的：

a.「過去未做的想像情境」：你知道過去未發生
b.「過去的可能性」：你不確定過去發生了沒有

首先，考慮 should, could, would 的定義，大略的規則是：

should	給別人建議（是忠告的性質）
could	表示可能性
would	表示一種想像的結果

You should get some rest.

Maybe I could live in this country in the future.

I would help you if I had more time.

上述的大略規則應用到完成式時，則大體上：

should have：過去應做而未做（對過去的批評）

could have：過去能做而未做（當初的可能性）

would have：過去想做而未做（想像的狀況）

Maybe I didn't treat you

Quite as good as I should have

Maybe I didn't love you

Quite as often as I could have

Little things I should have said and done

I just never took the time

You were always on my mind …

—— Elvis Presley (lyrics from "Always On My Mind")

從上述對各類型的情態助動詞的討論可以看出每一個情態助動詞都可能表達好幾種意思，以 can 為例：

能力	If you think you can do it, you can.
可能性	Learning a language can be a real challenge.
請求許可	Can I borrow your eraser?

助動詞必須和動詞一同出現，這樣的組合稱作動詞片語 verb phrase，一個主要動詞前可有多個助動詞，如：

> 1 個助動詞：is eating
> 2 個助動詞：will be running
> 3 個助動詞：might have been waiting

總結而論，情態助動詞的一些特性包括：
> 1. 情態助動詞的後面必定是原式動詞或完成式
> 2. 情態助動詞不因主詞的人稱（I, you, they, it…）而變化
> 3. 特殊語法：用過去式表達現在或未來的可能（如 could）
> 4. 特殊語法：用完成式表達過去的可能（如 must have）
> 5. 特殊語法：過去未做的想像情境（如 would have）

3.1.5 及物與不及物動詞

見文思義，及物動詞（transitive verb）必有受詞（動詞的接受者），如 bring, buy, offer, send 等。不及物動詞（intransitive verb）則沒有受詞，如 appear, arrive, belong, consist, depend, emerge, exist, occur, remain, result 等。例句：

> We raise the flag when the sun rises, and we lower it when the sun goes down.

上句可以看出 raise 以及 rise 的區別，raise 是及物動詞，其後有受詞 the flag；rise 是不及物動詞，其後沒受詞。順便一提，這兩個字也都可以當名詞，美式的「加薪」是 pay raise，英式則用 pay rise。

動詞最普遍的狀況是：既可當及物動詞，又可當不及物動詞，視用法而定。如 climb, grow, sit, study 等，例句如下：

> Close your eyes. Love will come your way.　　→ Close 是及物動詞
>
> The gym closes at 10 PM.　　　　　　　　→ Close 是不及物動詞

有些不及物動詞可與介系詞搭配，如 listen to, wait for，這時候的功能就類同於及物動詞，在介系詞之後加受詞，如：

> Listen to the radio.
>
> Wait for me.

中式思維可能會將「聽收音機」譯成 listen the radio；「等我」會翻成 Wait me 或 Wait me a minute，都是錯誤地在不及物動詞之後漏掉了介系詞。其他的例子如 laugh at, look at 等。

3.1.6 準動詞

如前所述，英文文法有個重大原則：一個句子只能有一個主要動詞；一個句子也只能有一個時態（主要動詞的時態）；主要動詞也必須與主詞的人稱及數目相符。這類受限於時態、人稱、數目等而變化的動詞在文法中稱作受限動詞（finite verbs）。

相對於受限動詞，有另一類的形式叫做不受限動詞（non-finite verbs），它只有一個形式，不受限於時態、人稱、及數目等。又稱為準動詞（verbal）。

中文句子可以有連續的動詞，如「我喜歡吃水果」，這句子中的兩個動詞「喜歡」與「吃」連在一起，如以中文思維直譯，可能是 I enjoy eat fruit. 這樣的句子在英文中是絕對不行的，必須寫成：I enjoy eating fruit，只能有一個主動詞（enjoy），其他具動作含意的字詞須改為準動詞（eating）。準動詞的特徵是：無論主詞與主動詞如何改變，準動詞都不變。如：

> I love traveling.
>
> He loves traveling.
>
> They loved traveling.

　　主動詞在變（love, loves, loved），主詞也在變（I, He, They），但準動詞 traveling 都不變，也就是：一個句子只能有一個時態（主動詞的時態）。

　　準動詞這個字的意思是「由動詞衍伸出來的」，但要特別注意：它不是動詞！而是具有動詞含意的名詞、形容詞或副詞。verbals 有三大類：動名詞、分詞、不定詞（這三類準動詞都不會因主動詞改變而產生詞類變化）：

準動詞	形式	詞性
gerund（動名詞）	V ＋ ing	名詞
participle（分詞）	現在分詞或過去分詞	形容詞
infinitive（不定詞）	to ＋動詞原式	名詞、形容詞、副詞

　　下面三個例句中劃底線的是主動詞（受限動詞），依序是 loves, pretend, afford。橘色單字（準動詞）則依序是動名詞 playing、分詞 Smiling、不定詞 to eat：

> Jeremy <u>loves</u> playing basketball.
> Smiling faces sometimes <u>pretend</u> to be your friend.
> I can't <u>afford</u> to eat out tonight.

　　以下三節分別對動名詞、分詞、不定詞加以說明。

3.1.6.1　動名詞

　　動名詞是英文 gerund 的翻譯，它由動詞加 ing 形成。對我們來說，gerund 是生字一個，沒什麼感覺；中文的名詞則翻譯得十分貼切，它隱含動作（動詞）的意義，而文法功能卻是個名詞，或可稱為 verbal noun。動名詞可以：

> 1. 作為主詞
> 2. 作為補語
> 3. 作為動詞之後的受詞
> 4. 作為介系詞之後的受詞

Learning **never exhausts the mind.**	→ 作為主詞
Seeing **is** believing.	→ 作為補語

Love means never having to say you're sorry.	→ 動詞 means 的受詞
How can you stop the sun from shining?	→ 介系詞 from 的受詞

常有人會問：動名詞之前應該用所有格還是受格呢？在 formal writing 中，所有格才符合文法，如下例中的 his 與 your：

The teacher didn't like his giggling in the class.

I appreciate your taking the time to help me.

但在口語以及非正式寫作中，也有人用受格，如：

The teacher didn't like him giggling in the class.

I appreciate you taking the time to help me.

3.1.6.2 分詞

作為 verbal 功能的分詞有現在分詞與過去分詞，雖具有動詞含意，但文法上是形容詞：

Barking dogs seldom bite.	→ 現在分詞當形容詞
Rats desert a sinking ship.	→ 現在分詞當形容詞
Forbidden fruit is the sweetest.	→ 過去分詞當形容詞
One volunteer is worth two pressed men.	→ 過去分詞當形容詞
The girls sitting by the road were gossiping.	→ 現在分詞片語
Discouraged by the low pay, he quit his job.	→ 過去分詞片語

要注意當動詞字尾加 ing 時，有三種文法作用：

1. 進行式
2. 動名詞
3. 分詞

Bahrainis had been diving for pearls for thousands of years.

Pearl diving was occurring in Bahrain as far back as 5000 years.

Surrounded by azure waters, Bahrain offers a variety of diving tours.

While diving, a Bahraini began to feel exhausted and air starved.

第一句的 had been diving 是過去完成進行式；第二句的 diving 是動名詞；第三句的 diving 是現在分詞用做形容詞；第四句的 diving 是分詞片語中的現在分詞。

CHAPTER 3 8 大詞類

3.1.6.3　不定詞

不定詞（to＋原式動詞）的文法功能：

     1. 作為主詞（名詞）

     2. 作為受詞（名詞）

     3. 作為補語（名詞）

     4. 作為形容詞

     5. 作為副詞

To be or not to be, that is the question.	→ 主詞（名詞）
Women like to be a man's last romance.	→ 受詞（名詞）
My advice is to file a complaint at once.	→ 補語（名詞）
That was the game to watch.	→ 形容詞
Are you old enough to drive?	→ 副詞

3.1.6.4　不定詞與分詞的時序

不定詞或分詞本身是不具時態的（任何一個句子的時態完全由主要動詞決定），通常它們的時態隱含在它們與主要動詞的對比之上，如何界定它們與主要動詞發生的先後順序呢？原則是：

     1. 現在式不定詞 → 發生在主要動詞之同時或之後

       例句：Coach Popovich is eager to try out his new drills.

       現在式不定詞（to try）發生在主動詞（is）之後

     2. 完成式不定詞 → 發生在主要動詞之前

       例句：He always regrets to have lost that opportunity.

       完成式不定詞（to have lost）發生在主動詞（regrets）之前

     3. 現在分詞 → 發生在主要動詞之同時

例句：Walking in the park, she met many old friends.

現在分詞（Walking）表示和主動詞（met）同時發生。

4. 現在完成分詞 → 發生在主要動詞之前

例句：Having climbed the mountain, she felt a sense of achievement.

現在完成式分詞（Having climbed）發生在主動詞（felt）之前。

3.1.6.5 不定詞與動名詞的抉擇

什麼時候用不定詞？什麼時候用動名詞？很容易搞混。有幾個原則性的模式如下：

1. 在形容詞之後，通常用不定詞
2. 在名詞之後，通常用不定詞
3. 在主詞的位置，通常用動名詞
4. 在介系詞之後，用動名詞

依照上面的順序，舉 4 個例句如下：

It is not rude to leave（a meeting if it is failing to serve a useful purpose）, it is rude to make someone stay and waste their time.

——Elon Musk

My view is there's no bad time to innovate.　　　——Jeff Bezos

Figuring out what the next big trend is tells us what we should focus on.　　　——Mark Zuckerberg

People will always try to stop you from doing the right thing if it is unconventional.　　　——Warren Buffett

第一句的 rude 是形容詞，其後跟不定詞 to leave 與 to make；第二句的 bad time 是名詞片語，跟不定詞 to innovate；第三句的 Figuring out what the next big trend is 在主詞位置，是動名詞片語；第四句的 from 是介系詞，其後跟動名詞 doing。

上面的模式介紹了名詞、形容詞、介系詞的後面通常加不定詞還是動名詞，但最麻煩的是：動詞之後要加不定詞？還是動名詞？基本上有 4 種狀況：

1. 有些動詞習慣上加不定詞
2. 有些動詞習慣上加動名詞
3. 有些動詞可加不定詞，也可加動名詞，意思幾近相同
4. 有些動詞可加不定詞，也可加動名詞，但意思不一樣

　　這些分類都是語言上的習慣，基本上沒什麼大道理（語言不都是如此？），需多加練習，才能養成習慣上的直覺。分述如下：

有些動詞習慣上加不定詞，有些動詞習慣上加動名詞

這兩種狀況可以用下表舉些例子：

加不定詞的動詞	加動名詞的動詞
afford	admit
ask	avoid
choose	consider
decide	deny
fail	dislike
get	enjoy
hope	fancy
need	imagine
offer	mind
prefer	miss
promise	risk
refuse	（can't） stand

Pele wanted to play soccer.

Messi enjoys playing soccer.

動詞 wanted 要加不定詞，enjoys 要加動名詞。

有些動詞可加不定詞，也可加動名詞，意思幾近相同

這類動詞如 begin, continue, hate, like, love, prefer, start：

Ronaldo loves working out. 　→相似於　Ronaldo loves to work out.

Neymar likes rolling around. →相似於 Neymar likes to roll around.

有些動詞可加不定詞，也可加動名詞，但意思不一樣

這類動詞如 forget, remember, stop, try 等，以 forget 為例：

I'll never forget meeting her for the first time.

Don't forget to meet her at 3 o'clock this afternoon.

第一句用動名詞 meeting，表示不會忘記第一次遇見她（已見過她了）。第二句用 to meet，則是不要忘了和她下午見面（還不到見面的時間，是個提醒）。remember 與 forget 用法類似：

Do you remember dancing with me on our first date?

Remember to do your homework.

第一句 remember + gerund 表示一種記憶。第二句 to do 是一種 reminder，提醒別人要記得做功課。舉一個 stop 的例子：

He decided to stop vaping.

He stopped to smoke.

第一句用動名詞 vaping，表示要戒掉抽電子菸。第二句用 to smoke，表示他停下手邊的事情去抽菸。舉一個 try 的例子：

If your girlfriend is angry at you, try giving her flowers.

He tried to finish the work ahead of time.

try doing 表示嘗試另一種方法（通常是一種建議）。try to 表示努力去做（通常是較困難的事，不見得成功）。

如果你實在無法決定在動詞之後該用不定詞或動名詞？站在機率的角度，建議選擇不定詞，對的機率較大。

如果以時間性來看，不定詞與動名詞可大略區分為：

Infinitive　→ 將要或繼續發生的事情

Gerund　→ 已經發生過的事情

例如：

> Nice to meet you.
> Nice meeting you.

第一句可以在你被介紹給第一次見面的新朋友時說（聚會開始時）；第二句則用在聚會結束時道別。

順便一提，當別人說：(It's) nice to meet you. 時，按照中文思維，我們會回答：Me too. 這是錯誤的。因為句子的虛主詞是 It，正確的回答是 (It's) nice to meet you, too. 或者省略成 You too. 但前者比較禮貌，後者是較隨便的說法。

3.1.7 使役動詞

使役動詞（causative verbs）是很常用到的動詞，顧名思義，它的意思就是「叫某人去做某事」，包含：命令、要求、允許、說服、幫忙等，一般常用的有 make, have, let, get 和 help。使役動詞的句型有兩種：

> 主詞＋使役動詞＋受詞＋原形動詞（V）
> 主詞＋使役動詞＋受詞＋ infinitive form（to ＋ V）

詳細規則如下表：

使役動詞	＋動詞原式 或＋不定詞	使役動詞的意義
make		force/require
have	＋動詞原式	ask/request
let		allow/permit
get	＋不定詞	convince/encourage
help	兩者都可以	aid/assist

make, have, get 都有「叫某人做某事」的意思，make 最強（強制），have 其次（支使），get 最低（說服）。另外，let 是允許的意思，help 是幫助。使役動詞之後要加動詞原式的例句如：

> My mom always made me make my bed when I was a child.

I'll have my assistant call you to schedule the appointment.

I don't let my kid watch violent and scary movies.

上面句子中使役動詞（made, have, let）之後的 make, call, watch 都是動詞原式。另外舉 get, help 的例子：

I got the mechanic to check my brakes.

Could you help me (to) carry my bags?

get 的後面跟不定詞 to check。而 help 可以跟 carry，也可以 to carry，不過，用動詞原式最普遍。

至於是否可用 help + Ving？答案是不行的，但是，有種句型是 cannot help + Ving，例如貓王的唱過的知名老歌 Can't Help Falling In Love，意思是「忍不住」、「不得不」。另一種類似寫法是 can't help but，可是後面要加動詞原式，如 I can't help but think about you.

使役動詞中的 have, get 也可以用於被動態（passive voice），句型是：

主詞＋使役動詞＋受詞＋ past participle

例如下兩句中的 broken, cut 都是過去分詞：

I got my heart broken.

I had my hair cut at a barbershop.

3.1.8 條件句

條件句（conditional sentences）是英文的一種特殊文法，用兩個子句（條件子句＋結果子句）來表述真實或假想情況下，可能產生的結果。條件子句設定真實或假想的條件（condition），是從屬子句，一般以 if 開頭；結果子句陳述在設定條件下可能的結果（result），是主要子句。這句型類似於中文的「如果……，就……」。

條件句的基本句型有 4 種：

Conditional 0：Fact

條件子句：If + Present Simple（現在簡單式）
結果子句：Present Simple（現在簡單式）

If ice melts, it becomes water.
I have to have a visa if I go to your country.

Conditional 0 表示事實（fact, habit）。條件與結果都是事實。也可用 when 代替 if，如 When you shop online, you save time.

Conditional 1：Real（present or future）

條件子句：If + Present Simple（現在簡單式）
結果子句：Future Simple（未來簡單式）

If Samuel wins the lottery, he will buy a Ferrari.
I will eat popcorn if I go to the movies.

Conditional 1 表示現在或未來可能發生的事（probable, real）。條件與結果都是可能的。通常 will 只用在結果子句中。

Conditional 2：Unreal（present or future）

條件子句：If + Past Simple（過去簡單式）
結果子句：would ＋原形動詞

If I were a king, you would be my queen.
You would get wet if it rained.

Conditional 2 是假設狀況（unreal/imaginary），與現在事實不符，這是英文的特殊語法。條件子句用過去式，卻是現在式的意義，我們不習慣；結果子句則須用 would（could, might）助動詞。第一句的意思是：如果我是國王，妳就是皇后。但這只是假想，真實狀況是：I am not a king, so you are not the queen. 第二句的意思是：如果下雨，你衣服會濕。但事實上

沒下雨，你沒濕。通常 would 只能在結果子句中。

Conditional 3：Unreal（past）

> 條件子句：If + Past Perfect（過去完成式）
> 結果子句：would + Present Perfect（現在完成式）

> He would have passed the exam if he had studied harder,
> If I had known you were coming, I would have cooked wagyu steak.

Conditional 3 是與過去事實不符的狀況（unreal/imaginary）。這也是特殊語法。條件子句用過去完成式，卻表達與過去事實不符的假想，我們也不習慣；結果子句得用 would 助動詞。上面第一句的意思是：他如果用功，過去就會通過考試了，但事實是他過去不用功，所以被當了。第二句是馬後砲。同樣地，通常 would 只能在結果子句中。

條件句的特殊語法需要注意的地方包括：

1. Conditional 0：事實的。中文思維容易接受這種句法與時態
2. Conditional 1：可能的。中文思維容易接受這種句法與時態
3. Conditional 2：不符現在事實的假想。我們不習慣用<u>過去式</u>表達與<u>現在</u>事實不符的特殊文法
4. Conditional 3：不符過去事實的假想。我們不習慣<u>過去完成式</u>表達與<u>過去</u>事實不符的特殊文法

條件句的動詞時態如果搞混了，就不合文法了，例如：

> How much would it be if I pay cash?

這句話不合文法規則，可改為：

How much will it be if I pay cash?	→ Conditional 1
How much would it be if I paid cash?	→ Conditional 2

3.1.9　假設語氣

語氣（mood）是句子感情的顯現，動詞是傳達語氣是最重要的媒介。英文語氣的分類如下：

陳述語氣	indicative mood
祈使語氣	imperative mood
假設語氣	subjunctive mood

陳述語氣

陳述一個事實、想法、或問題等，這是最常用的一般句型。陳述語氣的動詞端視時間、狀態等而定，如：

He was looking online for a solution to his homework problem.

Have you finished your homework?

祈使語氣

向受話者提出請求、指示、命令、忠告等，這種語氣全都用動詞原形，而主詞一般是 you，通常不說出來：

Hurry up!

Please leave.

Come and join us.

Stop fidgeting. Sit still.

Don't smoke in this building.

假設語氣

是很特殊的句型，這種句型必須使用特定的、不同於一般文法規則的「假設語氣動詞」，要特別小心。透過假設語氣動詞，主要表達：（1）重要或緊急事件（2）建議、希望、要求（3）和事實相反的情況（4）其他等。這種語法現在已經很少見，但還是會出現在正式英文中。

假設語氣動詞只准許兩種時態：（1）原式動詞（2）過去式動詞。以下依這兩種時態類別將假設語氣的各種句型略作說明：

1. 假設語氣動詞 = 原式動詞

a. （形容詞＋原式動詞）的句型 → 表達重要、緊急等

形容詞如 crucial, essential, important, necessary, vital

> It is essential that all passengers remain seated during the flight.
>
> It is extremely important that everyone follow the guidelines.
>
> It was vital that they be warned of the risks.

上述形容詞之後的子句中的假設語氣動詞 remain, follow, be 都用原式。口語和非正式英文中可省略 that。

b. （主要動詞＋原式動詞）的句型 → 用在建議、要求等

主要動詞如 suggest, advise, demand, propose, recommend

> My mom insists that I be home before midnight.
>
> Her mom suggested that she get a summer job.
>
> We demanded that he apologize.

同樣地，這種句型中的名詞子句的假設語氣動詞是動詞原式 be, get, apologize。口語和非正式英文中可省略 that。

英國人在上述 a,b 兩類句子較喜歡用 should 如：

> We demanded that he should apologize.
>
> It was vital they should be warned of the risks.

其實，should 正是假設語氣句型的真正意義：建議別人「應該」如何如何，只是在美式英語中被省略掉了。

c. 固定用語

> God bless you.
>
> Long live the king.
>
> Heaven forbid（anything bad happen to you）

bless, live, forbid 都是動詞原式。

2. 假設語氣動詞 = 過去式動詞

a. If 句型

例句：If I were in your shoes, I would seek legal advice.

If I were in your shoes 是假設語氣，這與【3.1.8】節條件句

Conditional 2 中的 If 條件子句相同，表示與現在事實相反，假設語氣動詞用過去式 were。

b. Wish

用在當你的夢想或希望與事實不同的時候，例如：

　　I wish（that）I were rich. →但我不富有

這種句型（主詞＋ wish ＋名詞子句）很常見，類似的如 if only, would rather 等。

be 動詞在上述兩種句型（If, Wish）中，無論主詞是 I, you, he, it, they，假設語氣動詞都要用過去式 were。然而，在現代口語以及非正式場合，規則就沒那麼嚴謹，如下例中的 wasn't：

Success makes so many people hate you. I wish it wasn't that way.

　　　　　　　　　　　　　　　　　──Marilyn Monroe

另外，wish 表達「不可能」，但是，hope 則表達「可能」：

　　I hope（that）you pass the test.

這句話是希望你考試過關，是可能的情況（子句中的動詞亦可以用未來式）。hope 也可用來表達希望過去可能發生的情況，如 I hope he passed the test. 過去式 passed 表示他已考完試，但是，你不知道他是否通過了考試。

另一種 wish 的常見用法是：「祝福」，這與上述句型完全不同。差異在於：上述句型是 unreal 的遙想，而「祝福」的話語是 real，是可以實現的。句型及例子如下：

　　主詞＋動詞（ wish ）＋受詞＋祝福語（名詞片語）

　　I wish you a healthy, peaceful, and prosperous new year!

　　We wish you lots of success and happiness in your new job!

這種「祝福」句型常見的錯誤如：

　　I wish you ~~have~~ a Merry Christmas!

要注意在受詞（you）之後的祝福語是名詞片語，需刪除動詞

have。或者，也可寫成 I hope you have a Merry Christmas.

c. It's（high）time

表示做某事的時間到了，而且，現在才做已經晚了，如：

It's time you went to bed.

假設語氣動詞是過去式 went，表示現在你該睡了，而且，已經過了該睡的時間了，可加 high 做強調語氣。如果想說現在是上床的好時間（沒有過該睡的時間），那可以用：

It's time（for you）to go to bed.

3.1.10 片語動詞

片語動詞（phrasal verb）是一種習慣用語，是兩個字（少數是三個字）的組合，由一個動詞加上介系詞或是副詞所組成，可以看作是一個動詞。如下表：

片語動詞	非片語同義詞
call off	cancel
figure out	understand
give up	stop
hand in	submit
look into	investigate
make up for	compensate
put off	postpone
turn in	submit

片語動詞較為 informal, relaxed，在日常會話中極為普遍，但在正式寫作中，則多用單一動詞（如上表右列）。

片語動詞可能有多重意義，以 pick up 為例，意思包括：

John picked up a hitch-hiker.	→ 搭載
Paul picked up Spanish really quickly.	→ 學會
Ringo picked up the tab for this birthday party.	→ 付帳
George's luck has picked up.	→ 改好

片語動詞的意思有時與兩個字個別的原意相符，但也常與兩字個別的原意不同，而具有特別的新意，如：

He took off his shoes.	→ 脫掉。原意
The plane took off.	→ 起飛。新意
Turn up the volume on the radio.	→ 轉大。原意
Something unexpected has turned up.	→ 出現。新意

當片語動詞的受詞是代名詞（如 it, he, them），它只能跟在動詞之後，如 give it up，不能說 give up it。

有些片語動詞如果直接連起來，詞性就改變了，意思也有可能變了，如（下表的字詞都可能有很多個意思，這裡僅取其一，以便作為比較）：

片語動詞	意思	名詞	意思
break down	故障	breakdown	故障
make up	補償	makeup	化妝品
turn out	出席	turnout	出席人數
work out	健身	workout	健身

make up 雖然也有動詞化妝的意思，但極少人這樣用，通常化妝是：put on makeup, wear makeup, apply makeup 等。也有人將 makeup 寫作 make-up。

★ 3.1.11 中文視角 – 動詞

中英文的動詞有極大的差異，要特別注意的地方包括：

1. 英文動詞最多可有 5 種寫法（see, saw, seen, seeing, sees）；中文動詞只有一個形式。
2. 英文一個子句只能有一個主動詞，其他的動詞須轉成準動詞，才能入句；中文句子可能會有多個動詞。
3. 條件句有嚴謹的文法規則（句型、時態等）；中文的條件句是以「假如」、「如果」來表示。
4. 條件句用過去式動詞表達與現在或未來事實不符；用過去完成式表達與過去事實不符。這是中文思維不易理解的。

( ) 1. Iron Man is a 2008 American superhero film _____ on the Marvel Comics character of the same name.

(a) based   (b) base   (c) basing

( ) 2. Black Lightning is a fictional superhero _____ in American comic books published by DC Comics.

(a) appearing   (b) appear   (c) appeared

( ) 3. Gwyneth _____ been sleeping since 2 o'clock.

(a) was   (b) has   (c) had

( ) 4. Charlize has just _____ her rehearsal.

(a)been finishing   (b) finished   (c) had finished

( ) 5. I _____ that man.

(a)have been knowing   (b) had been knowning   (c) know

( ) 6. Scarlett _____ a yellow sports car.

(a)is having   (b) has been having   (c) has

( ) 7. Sigourney _____ from college in 1972.

(a) graduated   (b) has graduated   (c) had graduated

( ) 8. Look, _____.

(a) it's snowing   (b) it snows   (c) it snowed

( ) 9. Megan_____ a car 3 months ago.

(a) has bought   (b) bought   (c) buys

( ) 10. I _____ her when she was in college.

(a) have met   (b) met   (c) meet

( ) 11. If I _____ rich, I would travel a lot.

(a)was   (b) would be   (c) were

( ) 12. Had I known her name, I _____ introduced you to her.

(a) would   (b) had   (c) would have

( ) 13. Saoirse would have passed her exam if she _____ harder.

(a) had worked   (b) would work   (c) would have worked

( ) 14. If it hadn't snowed, her flight _____ not have been cancelled.

(a) might   (b) may   (c) had

( ) 15. I was beginning to get a headache. I _____ take a break.

    (a) have to   (b) had to   (c) must

( ) 16. If Melissa _____ the money, she would have bought a Bentley.

    (a) had   (b) had had   (c) would have had

( ) 17. Emma really dislikes _____ interrupted.

    (a) to be   (b) be   (c) being

( ) 18. Anne is not used to _____ late.

    (a) work   (b) have worked   (c) working

( ) 19. Meryl chose to _____ at home.

    (a) stay   (b) have stayed   (d) staying

( ) 20. Please remember _____ your seat belt.

    (a) to fasten   (b) fasten   (d) fastening

( ) 21. Sandra said she was at the party, but I don't remember _____ her.

    (a) to see   (b) seeing   (c) having seen

( ) 22. I'll never forget _____ the beautiful scenery.

    (a) to see   (b) seeing   (c) having seen

( ) 23. Britney pleaded guilty to _____ a false statement to the court.

    (a) make   (b) have made   (c) making

( ) 24. We love life, not because we are used to _____ but because we are used to _____.

    (a) live, love   (b) have lived, have loved   (c) living, loving

( ) 25. They're entitled to _____ some compensation.

    (a) receiving   (b) receive   (c) have received

( ) 26. You are the one that _____ what to do.

    (a) knows   (b) know   (c) have known

( ) 27. I'll have my assistant _____ you tomorrow.

    (a) to call   (b) call   (c) called

( ) 28. Sometimes she makes me _____ to scream.

    (a) to want   (b) want   (c) wanted

( ) 29. The boss doesn't let us _____ work early.

    (a) to leave   (b) leaving   (c) leave

( ) 30. I'll follow him wherever he _____.

(a)will go   (b) go   (c) goes

( ) 31. By noon yesterday, we _____ waiting for 4 hours.

(a) had been   (b) have been   (c) were

( ) 32. It has _____ three times this month.

(a) rained   (b)been raining   (c) rain

( ) 33. I managed _____ in touch with her.

(a) get   (b) to get   (c) getting

( ) 34. The doctor advised the patient not _____ fatty food.

(a) eat   (b) to eat   (c) eating

( ) 35. They suggested he _____ a car.

(a) rented   (b) to rent   (c) rent

( ) 36. I recommend _____ your sleeping habits.

(a) change   (b) to change   (c) changing

( ) 37. Olivia _____ going out to eat.

(a) suggested   (b) suggest   (c) advise

( ) 38. I would suggest he _____ to the hospital.

(a) go   (b) goes   (c) went

( ) 39. All the stories you told me, I _____ before.

(a) heard   (b) had heard   (c) has heard

( ) 40. The museum stood where the cinema _____ .

(a) was   (b) had been   (c) has been

( ) 41. He had me _____ that.

(a) did   (b) does   (c) do

( ) 42. I'll go crazy if that dog _____ stop barking.

(a) won't   (b) hasn't   (c) doesn't

( ) 43. They _____ worked for hours, so they decided to take a break.

(a) had   (b) has   (c) had been

( ) 44. They _____ some help.

(a) need   (b) are needing   (c) have needing

( ) 45. I will _____ to work this time tomorrow.

(a) drive   (b) be driving   (c) have driven

( ) 46. He will have done his homework by the time we _____ .

(a) are arriving　(b) arrive　(c) have arrived

(　) 47. The show will ＿＿ by 9:30 PM.

(a) end　(b) be ending　(c) have ended

(　) 48. We ＿＿ to Cairo at this time yesterday.

(a) flew　(b) had flown　(c) were flying

(　) 49. We were playing poker when she ＿＿.

(a) arrived　(b) had arrived　(c) were arriving

(　) 50. She had slept a little before the phone ＿＿.

(a) rang　(b) had rung　(c) was ringing

(　) 51. The plane ＿＿ by the time we got to the airport.

(a) left　(b) had left　(c) were leaving

(　) 52. He ＿＿ there for more than two hours when she finally arrived.

(a) waited　(b) had been waiting　(c) had waited

(　) 53. I'm going to have a shower as soon as I ＿＿ home.

(a) got　(b) will get　(c) get

(　) 54. Since that incident, I ＿＿ my friend's advice.

(a) follow　(b) followed　(c) have followed

(　) 55. Would you mind if I ＿＿work an hour early today?

(a) left　(b) leave　(c) will leave

(　) 56. Well, I think I'd rather ＿＿ an action movie.

(a) see　(b) to see　(c) seeing

(　) 57. Please don't make so much noise. I ＿＿ to work.

(a) try　(b) am trying　(c) will try

(　) 58. Where have you been? I ＿＿ looking for you for hours.

(a) had been　(b) have been　(c) was

(　) 59. Would you mind ＿＿ me a hand?

(a) give　(b) to give　(c) giving

(　) 60. I ＿＿ married next month.

(a) am　(b) get　(c) will get

(　) 61. It is important that everyone ＿＿ calm.

(a) remain　(b) remains　(c) will remain

(　) 62. I have never been here ＿＿.

(a) before   (b) ago   (c) yesterday

(　) 63. God ____ his parents should ever find out.

(a) forbids   (b) forbid   (c) will forbid

(　) 64. I ____ anything I can for you.

(a) do   (b) will do   (c) did

(　) 65. It's time you ____ to bed.

(a) go   (b) will go   (c) went

(　) 66. What was that noise? I suppose it ____ the wind.

(a) could be   (b) could have   (c) could have been

(　) 67. The students did well on the test. They ____ studied hard.

(a) must have   (b) must   (c) must be

(　) 68. She couldn't get her car ____ this morning.

(a) to start   (b) start   (c) started

(　) 69. I wish I ____ have to go to school tomorrow.

(a) don't   (b) didn't   (c) won't

(　) 70. If you can't reach me by mail, try ____ me instead

(a) to call   (b) calling   (c) to have called

(　) 71. I wish you ____ happy New Year!

(a) have   (b) have a   (c) a

(　) 72. He ____ watching TV for 3 hours by the time his mom returns.

(a) will be   (b) will have   (c) will have been

(　) 73. The smartphone ____ since the 1990s.

(a) has been around   (b) has started   (c) has been starting

(　) 74. Michael Jackson ____ for more than 10 years.

(a) has been dead   (b) has died   (c) was died

(　) 75. They ____ a house next to mine.

(a) build   (b) are building   (c) builds

(　) 76. Laurent ____ already speak 4 languages when he was 9.

(a) would   (b) could   (c) should

(　) 77. ____ you mind lending me some money?

(a) Should   (b) Could   (c) Would

(　) 78. ____ you like some tea?

(a) Should　(b) Could　(c) Would

（　）79. You are coughing. You ＿＿ go and see a doctor.

(a) should　(b) could　(c) would

（　）80. You ＿＿ study harder if you want to pass the exam.

(a) should　(b) could　(c) would

3.2　名詞

名詞（noun）的拉丁字源的意思是「name」：表示人物、地方、動物、事情、感覺、想法等等的名稱。名詞是句子的主角，它的屬性與特質在中文與英文中的差別不像動詞那麼大。名詞的主要文法功能包括：

1. 作為執行動詞的主詞	Billie won the award.
2. 作為及物動詞的受詞	Many people love Taylor.
3. 作為主詞補語	Ed is a songwriting beast.
4. 作為受詞補語	Katie named her daughter Suri.
5. 作為介系詞的受詞	Bruno wrote it for other singers.
6. 作為同位語（appositive）	I bought an album, Thriller.

名詞數量極大，約佔英文 1/2 的字彙。最簡單的分類如下：

普通名詞（Common Nouns）
專有名詞（Proper Nouns）

3.2.1　普通名詞／專有名詞

普通名詞是指一般人、物、事的名稱（general names）；專有名詞是指特定的人、物、事的名稱（specific names），專有名詞的第一個字母須大寫。一些例子如下表：

Common Nouns	Proper Nouns
woman	Adele, Madonna
dog	Goofy, Snoopy
company	Acer, Alibaba
basketball team	Lakers, Warriors
day	Friday, Saturday
city	Casablanca, Gotham
soda	Coke, Pepsi
disease	Parkinson's disease
war	World War II

Coke, Pepsi 不可數，但在餐廳點中點飲料時，可以說 a Coke，等同於 a glass of Coke（類似情形如不可數名詞 coffee 也可用 a coffee 表示 a cup of coffee）。

3.2.2 單數／複數

名詞由單數改為複數時，字尾的變化歸納如下：
1. 字尾＋ s
   例如：book → books　　cup → cups
2. 字尾是 ch, sh, s z, j, x，加 es
   例如：bus → buses　　couch → couches
3. 字尾是「子音字母＋ y」，去除 y，加 ies
   例如：baby → babies　　country → countries
4. 字尾是 f 或 fe，去除 f 或 fe，加 ves
   例如：calf → calves　　wife → wives
5. 字尾是 o，加 s
   例如：volcano → volcanos　　zoo → zoos
   例外：potatoes, tomatoes

除了上述的規則變化外，還有些不規則的變化，如：
6. 改變母音

foot → feet; mouse → mice; tooth → teeth; goose → geese

7. 字尾改成 ren 或 en

child → children; ox → oxen

8. 單複數同形

buffalo, cattle, deer, fish, means, sheep, species

9. 複合名詞，改主要字

son-in-law → sons-in-law; passer-by → passers-by

girl-friend → girl-friends; maid-servant → maid-servants

兩字都改：man-servant → men-servants; woman-doctor → women-doctors

10. 拉丁與希臘字源

axis → axes; crisis → crises; datum → data; focus → foci

3.2.3 可數／不可數

如果以「是否可以計數」的角度來將名詞分類，可分為可數（countable）與不可數（uncountable）兩大類。可數名詞是指可分離的個體，可以獨立計數；反之，不易區分界限的，則是不可數名詞。如：

可數名詞	不可數名詞
apologies, buses, caps, cell phones, headaches, ideas, months, photos, pizzas, plazas, sofas, teachers, times, valleys, watches, wolves, writers	advice, air, alphabet, baggage, bread, cheese, coffee, equipment, furniture, love, news, popcorn, power, rice, sugar, stuff, tea, wealth

我們須注意可數與不可數名詞在文法上的區分是：

1. 單數的可數名詞須加冠詞；不可數名詞不可加不定冠詞
2. 可數名詞加單數或複數動詞；不可數名詞必加單數動詞

其中，我們較容易犯的錯誤包括：

Thanks for giving me useful advices.

　　訂正：advice 不可數，須改為 advice

That's an interesting information.

　　訂正：information 不可數，須將不定冠詞 an 刪除

The good news are you don't have to pay for it!

　　訂正：news 不可數，須將複數動詞 are 改為單數動詞 is

I've loved pop music ever since I was child.

　　訂正：child 可數單數，須加冠詞 a child

It was tough decision to make.

　　訂正：decision 可數單數，須加冠詞，如 a tough decision

　　注意：不可用數目計數（uncountable）的東西仍然是可量測的（measurable），我們可以用相關量詞來形容，例如：我們不能說 a water，但可以說 a drop of water。其他如 a gust of wind, a bit of advice, a piece of equipment, two pieces of furniture, three packets of ketchup, four pieces of news 等，或者是 any salt, some syrup, little money, much time 等。

　　有些可數／不可數名詞與我們的中文思維有些出入，如：

assignments 可數	但	homework 不可數
bags 可數	但	baggage 不可數
ideas 可數	但	advice 不可數
messages 可數	但	information 不可數
sofas 可數	但	furniture 不可數

　　有些單字有時可數，有時不可數，常見的如：

How many times do I have to tell you?	→ 次數（可數）
How time flies!	→ 時光（不可數）
On the second floor were two large rooms.	→ 房間（可數）
There's no room for the furniture.	→ 空間（不可數）
The dish had a very delicious taste.	→ 嚐味道（可數）

She has good taste in clothes.	→ 品味（不可數）
Dan taught English at a small college.	→ 大學（可數）
Do you go to college?	→ 上大學（不可數）

可數名詞與不可數名詞各有屬於自己的量詞（quantifiers），用來表示計量單位，如：

可數量詞	不可數量詞
a few	a little
a number of	an amount of
few	little
fewer	less
many	much

How many papayas do you have?	→ 可數
How much money do you have?	→ 不可數
I have a few papayas for you.	→ 可數
I have a little money.	→ 不可數

few 和 little 表示「少」，是負面的；a few 和 a little 表示「一些」，相對為正面。

fewer 和 less 的分別看似很簡單，但有時在美國也會混淆，有些超級市場的快速結帳通道常掛著一個牌子，上面寫著 x items or less，可是，items 是可數的，文法上應該用 fewer。

數量單位如 an amount of, a number of, a quantity of 的用法要注意。an amount of 僅可跟不可數名詞；a number of 僅可跟可數名詞；a quantity of 可跟可數或不可數名詞，用於無生命的東西。一些例句如下：

Cycling gives an enormous amount of pleasure to many people.

A large number of cows were infected.

A large quantity of water is stored in the reservoir.

另外，有些量詞兩者都適用，如：

可數量詞	不可數量詞
a lot of（problems）	a lot of（stress）
plenty of（flowers）	plenty of（sunshine）
any（questions）	any（money）
some（cups）	some（coffee）
no（lightbulbs）	no（light）

　　有些物品因為具有兩個部分，都以複數形式出現，例如 binoculars, contact lenses, glasses, goggles, headphones, jeans, pants, pliers, scissors, shorts, pajamas（上衣與褲子）等。這些名詞都要跟複數動詞，如 Her shorts are too short。它們的數量單位是 pair，不能說 I wore a jean. 要說 I wore jeans 或者 I wore a pair of jeans。如果是多數，則用 two pairs of goggles, three pairs of scissors 等。要注意文法規則 a pair of 須加單數動詞，如：

> My pair of shoes is worn out.
>
> My shoes are worn out.
>
> A pair of scissors is on the desk.
>
> Two pairs of scissors are on the desk.

　　還有些名詞看似多數（以 s 結尾），實際上是單數意義，動詞用單數，如 athletics, billiards, diabetes, economics, ethics, measles, news, physics, rabies, The Netherlands, The Philippines 等。電影、電視、書籍、公司名稱如以 s 結尾，也是用單數動詞，如：

> The Netherlands is famous for windmills and tulips.
>
> Athletics refers to track and field sports such as running.
>
> Ghostbusters was a big hit in the 80s.
>
> Romeo and Juliet is a tragedy written by William Shakespeare.
>
> Starbucks was founded in Seattle in 1971.

　　而有些以 s 結尾的名詞，如 series, species 等，可以是單數（a species of bird），也可是多數（many species of birds）。

　　有些名詞看似單數（如 cattle, fish, police, people），卻是複數意義，必須用複數動詞，如下句中的 say 與 are：

People say that police are blocking off the street for sobriety tests.

fish, people 也可表示一個特定群體，這時可單可複，如下句中的 fishes（多個物種），a ...... people（一個民族）：

Researchers found many kinds of fishes off the coast of Namibia.

They are a welcoming and hospitable people.

另外，有些名詞的複數形可以是完全不同的意思，如風俗 custom, 關稅 customs；擔保（品）security, 證券 securities；字母 letter, 學問 letters；分鐘 minute, 會議紀錄 minutes 等等。

3.2.4 集體名詞

集體名詞（collective nouns）是英文名詞的一個特色，是指一群人或物的集合體，日常的例子如：audience, committee, class, family, government, staff, team 等。

集體名詞在文法上的重點是：可以用它表示整個集合體，這時要用單數動詞；也可以表示集體中的所有成員，這時用複數動詞。在句子中要跟什麼樣的動詞？單數或複數？並沒有絕對的規則，通常取決定於你想說的情況是什麼。

例句：My family lives in Moscow.

His family are all doctors.

第一句表示整個家，第二句強調每個成員。以集體名詞的基本結構而言，美式偏向單數動詞，英式則偏向複數，如：

The government is reluctant to alter its economic policy.　→ 美式

The government are reluctant to alter its economic policy.　→ 英式

如想表達集體名詞中的一個成員，需要加上一個可數的單位名詞，如下例中的 police officer 或 staff member（staffer）：

Do you know Shaquille is a police?　→ 錯

Do you know Shaquille is a police officer?　→ 對

She is a staff at Facebook.	→ 錯
She is a staff member at Facebook.	→ 對

What was it like being a junior faculty there?	→ 錯
What was it like being a junior faculty member there?	→ 對

　　集體名詞常被用作群體量詞，來描述一群人、動物、或其他，例如 a team of players 中的集體名詞 team。下表列出一些常見的群體量詞（斜體字）：

人	動物	其他
an army of soldiers	a flock of birds	a bouquet of flowers
a board of directors	a herd of cattle	a bunch of grapes
a choir of singers	a pack of wolves	a cloud of dust
a crowd of fans	a pride of lions	a collection of stamps
a panel of experts	a school of fish	a galaxy of stars
a staff of employees	a swarm of bees	a wealth of information

　　A band of musicians is coming this afternoon.

　　A pack of wolves runs through the woods.

　　上兩句的兩個主詞是 A band of musicians 和 A pack of wolves，而其中真正的主詞是 A band 以及 A pack，因此，動詞都是用單數。

3.2.5　所有格

　　單數名詞改為所有格 possessive 時，基本上只要加上 's 就可以了，如 a cat's, Jackson's, everyone's, someone else's 等。

　　複數名詞的所有格，如果字尾是 s，加撇號「'」（apostrophe）即可，如 two weeks' notice, three months' rent, ladies' night 等。如果字尾不是字母 s，則加 's，如 children's, women's, mice's 等。

　　複合名詞所有格的撇號加在最後的單字，如 Notre Dame's, daughters-in-law's, editor-in-chief's。不定代名詞所有格如 each other's, anybody's, someone's。

　　如果多個名詞共同擁有某些事物時，應在最後的名詞加 's，如 Thor and Cap's friendship；Spock, James, and Leonard's starship 等。如果是各自擁有，每個都須加 's，如 Beyonce's and Jay Z's music 等。

　　非生物名詞的所有格可以用 of 的模式來表達，有時會比較順，如 the bottom of the page（代替 the page's bottom）；the capital of Madagascar（代替 Madagascar's capital）……。

3.2.6　名詞作為同位語

　　同位語（appositive，原意為並列的、並置的）是用一個名詞（片語）、名詞子句緊跟著一個先行的名詞，定義或描述這個名詞，例如：

> Jennifer Lawrence, the popular actress, is also known as an advocate for feminism.

　　同位語 the popular actress 前後都加上了逗號，是非限定性語法（請參考【4.2.1.1】節）。再舉一個限定語法的同位語的例子：

> I like the famous actress Angelina Jolie who is probably known just as much for her off-screen persona.

　　這句的同位語是 Angelina Jolie，是必要的資訊，因為 famous actress 很多，如果未限定，就不知道講的是誰。

　　有時候，同位語也可放置於它所修飾的名詞之前，如下例中的同位語 A fabulous singer-songwriter：

> A fabulous singer-songwriter, Taylor Swift started her career at the age of 14.

3.3　代名詞

　　pronoun（代名詞）源自拉丁文，意思是「pro + noun」，pro 在此表示 in place of（代替）。代名詞功能正如其名：用來代替名詞，減少不斷

使用相同的話語，增加文句的通順與自然。例如：

Romeo works with Juliet.

Romeo likes working with Juliet.

Romeo and Juliet do many things together.

聽起來實在不太順，Romeo 和 Juliet 這兩個名字用了太多次，如果改為下面的句子就很順了：

Romeo works with Juliet.

He likes working with her.

They do many things together.

在用代名詞之前，必須先清楚它所代替的名詞（先行詞 antecedent）是什麼，在第一句話（Romeo works with Juliet.）說完後，He, her, They 這三個代名詞所代替的先行詞就非常清楚了。當然，代名詞的單複數及性別等都要和先行詞相符（agree）。

如同名詞一樣，代名詞可以當主詞，也可以當受詞，上面的例子中，He 與 They 是主詞，her 是受詞。

3.3.1 代名詞的分類

代名詞包括：人稱代名詞、所有代名詞、反身代名詞、指示代名詞、不定代名詞、疑問代名詞、關係代名詞等。

人稱代名詞（personal pronoun）

人稱代名詞用來代替人或物，如 I, we, you, they, me, us, them, it 等。需要注意在句子中，代名詞是主格或受格。如果句子中包括別人與你，禮貌上要將別人放置於前：

Roger and I practice tennis together very often.

I suggest you, Rafael, and I get together for coffee after the game.

Coach B asked Novak and me to be more focused in the match.

如果是主格，代名詞的次序為 you, he, I。如果是受格，次序是 you,

him, me。複數時，主格依 we, you, they 排列，受格則是 us, you, them。

所有格代名詞（possessive pronoun）

　　所有格表示所有權，即 ownership/possession。所有格代名詞的功能可分為兩類，第一類置於名詞之前，文法功能類似形容詞，如 my, your, his, their, its 等，或稱為所有格形容詞，例句：

　　　　"My turn," Cori shouted to her teammate.

　　　　Serena and Venus are sisters, and their parents were their coaches.

　　第二類像名詞，如 mine, yours, theirs 等。例句：

　　　　Naomi's car is a lot faster than mine.

　　　　The world is yours, embrace it.

　　mine 取代了 my car，就不必再用一次名詞 car 這個字了。

　　所有格代名詞有個常犯的錯誤是多加了撇號（'），例如所有代名詞 its 常被寫成 it's，事實上，it's = it is/it has；theirs 常被寫成 their's，而 there's = there is/there has；whose 常被寫成 who's，而 who's = who is/who has。

反身代名詞（reflexive pronoun）

　　反身代名詞有 8 個：myself, yourself, himself, herself, itself, ourselves, yourselves, themselves，沒有其他的寫法了。

　　使用反身代名詞的規則是：當句子中的主詞與受詞是同一人時，受詞須用反身代名詞：

　　　　Why do some people talk to themselves?

　　　　Thank you. I really enjoyed myself.

　　　　History repeats itself.

　　反身代名詞也可用於強調，例如：

　　　　Did you yourself make the cake?

　　　　I spoke to Muhammad Ali himself.

上述 yourself, himself 都是強調的作用，如果將它們刪除，只是減輕語氣，不會改變句子的主要意義。

指示代名詞（demonstrative pronoun）

指示代名詞用以指明句子中特定的人或事物，有 this, these, that, those，其中，this 和 these 是指時間或空間上較近的，that 和 those 則指時間或空間上較遠的。例句：

This is our house, and that is Oprah's house over there.

上句中的 This 與 that 是名詞。它們也常被用作形容詞，例如在 this class, these books 中，修飾主詞 class 和 books。

疑問代名詞（interrogative pronoun）

疑問代名詞的定義是帶領問句（開頭語）的代名詞：who, whom, what, which, whose（whoever, whomever, whatever, whichever 也可以）。它們在問句中的角色是主詞、受詞、或所有格。如：

Who told you?	→ who 主詞
Who（m） did you tell?	→ who（m） 受詞
Whose car is this?	→ whose 所有格

而當 where, when, why, how 用作疑問句開頭語時，它們是副詞，如 Why did you do that? 和 Where did you go? 中的 Why 與 Where 的功能是修飾動詞（它們不具備代名詞的功能：主詞、受詞、所有格）。

另外，在現代英文中，尤其是口語（或非正式文章），無論是主詞或受詞，都可以用 who。單字 whom 正在消失中！但是，在介系詞之後時基本上還是用 whom。

不定代名詞（indefinite pronoun）

不定代名詞指的是不特定的人、事、物。我們常碰到的問題是不定代名詞應該用單數？還是複數？以這個角度來看，不定代名詞可分為三類，如下：

1. 單數的不定代名詞，用單數動詞，如：

each, every, much, little, less, either, neither, one, another, anyone, everybody, something, nobody, nothing

Every people need to pay attention to the traffic signs.	→ 錯
Every person needs to pay attention to the traffic signs.	→ 對

One of my friends are an NBA player.	→ 錯
One of my friends is an NBA player.	→ 對

Neither of the two FIFA teams were able to score a goal.	→ 錯
Neither of the two FIFA teams was able to score a goal.	→ 對

2. 複數的不定代名詞，用複數動詞，如：

both, few, fewer, many, several

Many have tried, but few have succeeded.

Fewer than 7% of asylum seekers are accepted as political refugees.

3. 可單可複的不定代名詞，如 all, any, some，端視後面所跟的是可數名詞還是不可數名詞，如：

All cats love milk.	→ cats 複數
All information is confidential.	→ information 不可數

Some roses were still blooming.	→ roses 複數
Some of the money was stolen.	→ money 不可數

Are there any new video games?	→ games 複數
There wasn't any sugar left.	→ sugar 不可數

　　some 與 any 都代表「一些」。some 多用在肯定句，any 用在疑問句與否定句（或含有否定詞，如 never, hardly, scarcely）。然而，當 any 的意思為無論什麼都可以（it doesn't matter which one）時，它的意思就像 every，出現於肯定句，如：

You can take any bus.

She goes out with any boy who asks her.

疑問句一般用 any，如 Do you have any money? 但當我們比較期望肯定的答案，例如提供服務或提出要求時，則用 some：

Would you like some coffee?

Can I have some sugar?

關係代名詞（relative pronoun）

代名詞中和中文思維差異最大的就是關係代名詞了。常用的關係代名詞有：

who	whom	which
that	whose	

關係代名詞一定緊跟在先行詞（名詞）之後，具有 3 個功能：

1. 修飾它前面的名詞
2. 引領子句與它所修飾的名詞連結起來
3. 在子句中擔任主詞、受詞、所有格的角色

關係代名詞帶領的子句叫做關係子句（或稱為形容詞子句，因為子句有形容詞的功能）。表示人的時候，可以用 who, that, whom；表示事或物的時候，可以用 which, that；表示所有格時，用 whose。如下面的例句：

The man who called yesterday wants to buy the house.

The car, which was a yellow Porsche, swerved into the ditch.

The doctor that I was hoping to see wasn't on duty.

He complained to the neighbor whose dog bit him.

Don't use any words whose meanings you don't know well.

第一句的 who 代表 man，它引導其後的子句去修飾 man，同時在子句中擔任主詞。第二句的 which 代表 car，引導子句修飾 car，也在子句中當主詞。第三句的 that 指 doctor，引導子句修飾 doctor，並在子句中當受詞。第四、五句的 whose 是所有格，其後必跟著名詞，whose 的用法上不限於人或動物，也可以是事物，如第五句的 whose 指的是 words。

如果關係代名詞的先行詞為下列情況時，通常用 that：

1. 最高級

She is the most eloquent speaker that I have ever heard.

2. 一些代名詞，如 all, any, no, only, same

This is the same car that we were in last night.

3. 疑問代名詞，如 what, which, who

What is the problem that worries you the most?

4. 序數，如 first, second

He was the first boy that ever kissed her.

5. 「人與物」或「人與動物」

The boy and his dog that trespassed in our yard were yelled at.

關係代名詞的在句子架構上非常重要，因此，第 4 章的【4.2.1.1】節將再做詳細說明。

3.3.2 代名詞的主格與受格

代名詞代替名詞，因此，它可擔任名詞的功能與角色。代名詞可以當主詞、受詞、補語等，如：

She is a teacher.	→ She 主詞（主格）
The winners were Jeremy and I.	→ I 補語（主格）
They elected him their mayor.	→ him 直接受詞（受格）
I sent her a postcard.	→ her 間接受詞（受格）
Donald blamed everything on his sisters, brothers, and me.	→ me 介系詞受詞（受格）

當主詞或受詞是多個字詞組成的複合詞（如最後一句的 his sisters, brothers, and me）時，容易看不清應該用主格或受格，有個方法是：將複合詞的詞組拿掉，只留下代名詞 me，如 Donald blamed everything on me. 這樣就明白 me 是介系詞 on 的受詞。

有時候，主格與受格的角色會改變整個句子的意思，如：

She loves you more than I.

She loves you more than me.

第一句的 I 是主格，隱含 She loves you more than I（love you）– 她愛你甚於我愛你。第二句 me 是受格，隱含 She loves you more than（she loves）me – 她愛你甚於她愛我。

3.3.3 代名詞與先行詞

在寫作時，代名詞所代替的先行詞是什麼，一定要清楚明白，否則，句意會隱晦不明，如：

Mario was speaking to Luigi, and he looked very happy.

句子中的 he 代表誰？是 Mario 還是 Luigi？雖然基本規則是代名詞指最近的先行詞（he 指 Luigi），但是，這個句子應可寫得更清楚，改法很多，如果是指 Luigi，可寫成：

Mario was speaking to Luigi, who looked very happy.

如果是 Mario，可以改為：

Mario, who looked very happy, was speaking to Luigi.

再舉一例：

Although Dan works at the pizza shop, he never eats them himself.

上句的代名詞 them 沒有先行詞（雖然我們知道 them 是表示 pizzas，但文法不對），可以改成：

Although Dan works at the pizza shop, he never eats pizzas himself.

另外，在性別、人稱、數目上，代名詞必須得和先行詞相符（agree），如：

If a student fails a course, they must take the course again.

這句話的先行詞（a student）與代名詞（they）不符，可改為：

If a student fails a course, he or she must take the course again.

he or she 是現代英文中尊重性別的寫法，但如果文章中太多的 he or she 會顯得累贅，改善的方式之一是使用多數形態：

> If students fail a course, they must take the course again.

英文許多單字偏重男性，如 mankind, manpower, chairman, freshman 等，字中都有個「man」；相對的中文是人類、人力、主席、大一生，沒有性別的暗示，比較平等。

3.3.4　虛主詞

英文句子架構的基本規則是「句子必須有主詞，主詞在動詞之前」。有些句子在語意上不需要主詞，如中文「下雨了」，但英文還是得要虛主詞「It is raining.」，句中的 It 是虛主詞（dummy subject）。虛主詞本身不具任何意義，只是為了履行英文語法必須有主詞的規則，用 it 作為主詞的替代品。there 也可作為虛主詞，如：

> There are three posters in his room.
> There wasn't enough money to buy an electric car.

上兩句的 there 是虛主詞，替代真主詞，置於動詞之前。真主詞是 three posters 和 enough money，這時，動詞要與真主詞相符合，第一句的動詞用多數的 are，第二句是單數 wasn't。

一個句子的主詞如果相當冗長，會顯得頭重腳輕，如句子 That you finally got a wonderful job offer at Google is great. 的主詞太長（That you finally got a wonderful job offer at Google），可以用虛主詞（it）的架構將主詞延後，讀起來比較順：

> It is great that you finally got a wonderful job offer at Google.

真主詞是不定詞片語時，也可以用虛主詞句型，如：

| It is great to see you. | → To see you is great. | 真主詞 To see you |
| It is better to be early. | → To be early is better. | 真主詞 To be early |

it 常用來表達時間、天氣、溫度、距離等，如：It's 10:40 p.m.；It's hot.；It's late.；It's nice.

　　it 也可以當作虛受詞。下句中的真受詞是 that they've never stopped arguing about politics. 這時的 it 是真受詞的先行詞：

　　　　I find it amazing that they've never stopped arguing about politics.

※ 練習題 – 名詞與代名詞（請參考【附錄 2】的習題解答）

( ) 1. Listening to soft music and drinking a glass of wine ＿＿ me fall asleep.

　　(a) helps　(b) has helped　(c) help

( ) 2. Celine and ＿＿＿ are going to a conference.

　　(a) I　(b) me　(c) myself

( ) 3. Students who cheat on exams cheat ＿＿＿ .

　　(a) Himself　(b) themselves　(c) theirselves

( ) 4. The manager, along with three assistants, ＿＿＿ angry about the schedule change.

　　(a) am　(b) are　(c) is

( ) 5. It is I who ＿＿＿ sorry.

　　(a) am　(b) are　(c) is

( ) 6. Neither of the two teams ＿＿＿ in the NBA finals.

　　(a) were　(b) was　(c) has

( ) 7. One of my friends ＿＿＿ an MLB player.

　　(a) am　(b) are　(c) is

( ) 8. Each of the 100 houses ＿＿＿ damaged in the earthquake.

　　(a) was　(b) were　(c) has

( ) 9. I'd like to buy that videogame, but I don't have ＿＿＿ money.

　　(a) some　(b) any　(c) fewer

( ) 10. All but one ＿＿＿ rescued from the shipwreck.

　　(a) has　(b) was　(c) were

( ) 11. ＿＿＿ morning I woke up late.

(a) This　(b) Today　(c) Today's

（　　） 12. The book which I borrowed, _____ you may have read, is entitled 'A Higher Loyalty.'

(a) what　(b) which　(c) that

（　　） 13. J.K. Rowling, all of _____ books are popular, is a great writer.

(a) who　(b) which　(c) whose

（　　） 14. The library where we met, _____ I always borrow books, is the largest in the city.

(a) where　(b) which　(c) that

（　　） 15. Katy has two mobile phones, one of _____ is broken.

(a) that　(b) which　(c) what

（　　） 16. Mariah has two brothers, both of _____ smoke.

(a) which　(b) who　(c) whom

（　　） 17. I have no idea _____ you're talking about.

(a) what　(b) which　(c) that

（　　） 18. I drink _____ tea than you.

(a) little　(b) less　(c) fewer

（　　） 19. There are _____ trees in my city than those in your city.

(a) little　(b) less　(c) fewer

（　　） 20. You look worried. _____ there something wrong?

(a) Is　(b) Are　(c) Have

（　　） 21. She got me _____ a contract.

(a) sign　(b) to sign　(c) signing

（　　） 22. _____ I saw on TV shocked me.

(a) Which　(b) Where　(c) What

（　　） 23. These are the people _____ helped me.

(a) that　(b) which　(c) whose

（　　） 24. I can't figure out _____ you're doing it.

(a) which　(b) why　(c) what

（　　） 25. This is the kind of music _____ he is interested.

(a) what　(b) which　(c) in which

（　　） 26. This is the desk _____ which I put my correction fluid.

(a) on   (b) in   (c) at

(　) 27. The team won a silver medal, _____ they were very proud.

(a) which   (b) of which   (c) in which

(　) 28. Could I give you a piece of _____ ?

(a) recommendation   (b) advise   (c) advice

(　) 29. The president nominated Melody and _____ to serve on the committee.

(a) me   (b) I   (c) mine

(　) 30. This is a secret between _____ .

(a) he and I   (b) him and me   (c) him and I

(　) 31. For more info, please feel free to write to _____ .

(a) myself   (b) I   (c) me

(　) 32. We must be quick. We have _____ time.

(a) little   (b) a little   (c) a few

(　) 33. This park is not an interesting place to visit, so _____ tourists come here.

(a) little   (b) few   (c) a few

(　) 34. Listen carefully. I'm going to give you _____ advice.

(a) few   (b) little   (c) a little

(　) 35. This is a very boring place to live. There's _____ to do.

(a) little   (b) a little   (c) a few

(　) 36. "Have you ever been to Congo?" Yes, I've been there _____ times.

(a) few   (b) a few   (c) a little

(　) 37. Ahmad, as well as Mehrdad and Mehran, _____ to visit Tunisia.

(a) plan   (b) have planned   (c) plans

(　) 38. Eighty kilometers _____ not such a long distance.

(a) is   (b) are   (c) have been

(　) 39. A Tale of Two Cities is one of _____ great novels.

(a) Dickens   (b) Dickens's   (c) Dicken's

(　) 40. What criteria _____ used for assessing a student's ability?

(a) is   (b) has   (c) are

3.4　形容詞

　　形容詞（adjective）用來修飾名詞或代名詞，提供有關它們的一些訊息，雖然不是句子的核心，但可以較精確豐富地描述人事物的特質。形容詞在英文單字中數量僅次於名詞（名詞約 1/2，形容詞約 1/4）。

3.4.1　形容詞的位置

　　英文與中文的形容詞的差別不像動詞那麼大，中文的形容詞通常是兩個字，再加上「的」，置於名詞之前，例如：美麗的、迷人的、可愛的。英文形容詞（單詞）最常見的位置也是在名詞之前，如 young lady, lovely smile, honored guest 等。

　　有些固定的片語將形容詞置於名詞之後，如 Attorney General, court martial, heir apparent 等。

　　當形容詞修飾不定代名詞時（如 everything, nothing, somebody, anywhere），需後置，如：

> She was looking for something inexpensive.
>
> I would like to go somewhere quiet.

　　有些形容詞如與另一個最高級形容詞同時修飾一個名詞，通常後置，如 the best restaurant available, the worst conditions imaginable。

　　有些形容詞可在名詞之前或之後，意思可能不一樣，如：

a responsible person	→ 可信賴的人
the person responsible	→ 負責人
Is there any cost involved?	→ 涉及到的
It is a long and involved story.	→ 複雜的

　　形容詞的另一大角色是作為主詞補語（如下例的 awesome, awful, upset），這樣的句型中，形容詞擺在連綴動詞（如下例的 is, smells, looked）之後：

> The car is awesome.
>
> The skunk smells awful.

She looked upset.

前一節中的指示代名詞（this, that, these, those）如果置於名詞之前，功能就像形容詞一樣，所以又稱為指示形容詞，如：

Even smart people fall for this phishing scam.
Those jeans make your legs look so long.

the ＋形容詞

有些形容詞前面可加上 the 來泛指某個類型的群體，如：

the disabled	殘障人士
the old	老人
the poor	窮人
the rich	有錢人

這樣的寫法，雖然看起來沒有名詞（只有 the + adjective），但卻代表具有複數意義（動詞要用複數形）的某種群體，是名詞的性質。有個英文諺語後來成為一首英文歌的歌名叫做：

When the going gets tough, the tough get going.

簡單地翻譯，就是：艱困生頑強。the going（指外在艱困的環境）是單數，動詞用 gets；the tough（the ＋形容詞）代表群體（指的是堅強的人），是複數，動詞用 get。

有的形容詞雖然只有細微差異，但意思差很大，如：

advance 預先的 例：an advance payment	advanced 高階的 例：an advanced course
alone 獨自的 例：She was all alone.	lonely 孤獨的 例：a lonely feeling
classical 古典的 例：classical music	classic 經典的，一流的 例：a classic car
economical 節省的，實惠的 例：an economical car	economic 經濟上的 例：economic growth

electrical 與電相關的	electric 電動的裝置
例：an electrical engineer	例：an electric car
fun 有樂趣的	funny 好笑的
例：a fun time	例：a funny joke
gold 金的	golden 金色的
例：a gold ring	例：golden sunshine
historical 歷史的，過去的	historic 具歷史重要性的

This is the advance program for the 2020 Conference of the Advanced Technologies.

Why do I feel lonely even when I am not alone?

（lonesome 類似於 lonely）

The economic forecast for next year is not good, so economical cars become quite popular.

He suggested tomorrow's historic event be held at a historical site.

3.4.2　分詞形容詞

　　分詞形容詞（participle adjectives）是形容詞中重要的子類，有很多時候，我們常搞不清應該用現在分詞還是該用過去分詞，下表及例句是關於「感覺」的分詞形容詞：

現在分詞 Present Participle	過去分詞 Past Participle	
annoying	annoyed	煩擾的
boring	bored	厭煩的
confusing	confused	困惑的
exciting	excited	興奮的
interesting	interested	感興趣的
tiring	tired	疲倦的

annoy	An annoying person makes me feel annoyed.
bore	We were really bored because it was a boring flight.

confuse	He was confused by the confusing street signs in the city.
excite	The story was exciting, and the children were excited.
interest	English is interesting. I am interested in English.
tire	This work was tiring, so we all felt tired.

　　現在分詞表示「感覺的原因」，如 a frightening movie，電影是害怕的原因。過去分詞則是「本身的感覺」，如 The dog is frightened，表示狗很害怕，是狗自己的感覺。或者說，過去分詞是效果，例如上述的第四句，故事是令孩童興奮的原因，用 exciting；孩童興奮是效果，用 excited。

　　我們最常犯的錯誤是在該用過去分詞形容詞時，錯用了現在分詞，例如想要表達某人感到厭煩，正確句子是 He is bored，但卻寫成了 He is boring（他是一個無趣的人）。另外，interested in～表示對某事感興趣；interesting person 是有趣的人。

　　注意：現在分詞形容詞可用在人、動物、或事物，但過去分詞僅能用於人或動物，不能用於無生命、無感覺的事物，不能說 The film was bored，因為 film 是沒有感覺的。

　　除了「感覺」之外，分詞形容詞當然還有其他的用法，以下僅舉兩個例子，稍微說明置於名詞之前的分詞的語法：

1. 現在分詞具主動的意義，如 barking dogs, a crying baby, a laughing monkey, the running water。過去分詞具被動的意義，如 a broken heart, a cracked window, the sliced apple。

2. 現在分詞表示正在進行之中（說話的同時），如 The falling snow is beautiful. 過去分詞表示過去已經完成的，如 The fallen snow is 10 centimeters deep.

　　分詞形容詞一般是由動詞字尾變形而來：現在分詞是動詞加 ing，過去分詞是加 ed。但是，有少數分詞是由名詞變形而成的，其中又以過去分詞居多，如 renowned, skilled, talented。

3.4.3 名詞用作形容詞

名詞除了可以當作主詞、受詞、補語、同位語等之外，還具有形容詞的修飾性質，如便利商店 convenience store 中的 convenience，注意：它是名詞，不是形容詞。這樣的片語是複合名詞（compound noun）的一種，置於前面的名詞（convenience）被當作形容詞，置於後面的名詞（store）才是真名詞，所以：

race boat	→ 比賽的船
boat race	→ 船的比賽

中文也有類似情形，如蜂蜜 / 蜜蜂；豬肉 / 肉豬；水井 / 井水。

名詞當形容詞的複合名詞如 credit card, book store, history teacher, rock band, show business, ticket office, traffic light, wedding ring 等；這種詞也常以連字號（hyphen）連接，如 book-case, ice-cream, pain-killer；或者，兩個字連成一體，如 bedroom, driveway, earphone, football, keynote, ladybug, milestone, railroad, sunglass, toothbrush。

如果要表達多數時，則改變第二個字（真名詞）的複數形即可，如 apple pies, palm trees, sports cars 等。

另外，在名詞的前面用形容詞來修飾，或用名詞來修飾，意思常有差別，如：

名詞＋名詞		形容詞＋名詞	
fashion industry	時裝行業	fashionable industry	時下流行的行業
heart disease	心臟病	hearty welcome	熱情的歡迎
history class	歷史課	historical event	歷史的事件

3.4.4 複合形容詞

複合形容詞（compound adjective）是指由兩個（或以上）字用連字號連接的一個形容詞，這種形容詞被視為是一個字，通常置於名詞之前（如 an eye-catching headline）。複合形容詞的組成如下（其中最常見的是 名詞＋形容詞）：

名詞＋形容詞	→ a world-famous **scholar**, a sugar-free **drink**
名詞＋分詞	→ a record-breaking **heat**, a sun-dried **fruit**
名詞＋名詞	→ a bullet-proof **vest**, part-time **staff**
形容詞＋分詞	→ an easy-going **attitude**, a long-legged **beauty**
形容詞＋名詞	→ a full-time **job**, a blue-collar **worker**
副詞＋分詞	→ never-ending **complaints**, well-paid **jobs**
數字＋名詞	→ a 5-star **hotel**, a 6-story **building**
數字＋時間	→ an 8-hour **shift**, a 10-minute **break**

連字號的有無會造成不同的意思，如：

I saw a man-eating tiger.

I saw a man eating tiger.

man-eating 是複合形容詞，表示「吃人的老虎」，但如果沒有連字號，第二句就聽起來像是「人在吃老虎」！又如：

small city mayor	→ 意思模糊：矮小的市長？小城的市長？
small-city mayor	→ 意思明確：小城的市長

大部分的複合形容詞只能放在名詞之前，如果是在修飾的名詞之後（在 be 動詞之後），就不再用連字號，如：

She is an 8-year-old girl.	→名詞之前要用連字號，year 用單數
The girl is 8 years old.	→名詞之後不用連字號，years 用多數
It is a 5-foot wall.	→名詞之前要用連字號，foot 用單數
The wall is 5 feet high.	→名詞之後不用連字號，feet 用多數

3.4.5 代名詞用作形容詞

有些代名詞常被置於名詞之前，作為名詞的修飾，這類代名詞的功能與形容詞相似，因此，它們亦可歸類於形容詞（或稱為 determiners），如：

The dog growled and bared its teeth.

Those babies in the nursery have been crying for hours.

I don't want any more water because I'm not thirsty anymore.

第一句的 The 是冠詞，its 是所有代名詞；第二句的 those 是指示代名詞；第三句的 any more 是數量詞（句尾的 anymore 則是副詞）；它們都在修飾名詞，這類置於名詞之前的代名詞包括：

冠詞	a, an, the
指示代名詞	this, that, these, those
所有代名詞	my, your, his, her, our, their, its
疑問代名詞	what, which, whose
不定代名詞（數量詞）	a few, one, each, many, much, some, ten

除了冠詞之外，其他的都已在前面章節陳述，下一節將只討論冠詞。

3.4.5.1 冠詞

冠詞（Article）是一種名詞的標誌，看到冠詞，就表示其後會有名詞。冠詞分為定冠詞（the）與不定冠詞（a, an）。定冠詞指特定的事物；不定冠詞則指一般的事物。中文常不須冠詞，例如：我是 Jolin 迷，不需要說：我是 Jolin 的一個迷，聽起來很怪。但在英文中，就必須加不定冠詞，如：

I am a big fan of Jolin.

再舉幾句：

Terry has a strong interest in history.
Robert looks up the history of coffee cups.
Calvin is reading a history book.

第一句的 history 指一般的歷史（general），不需冠詞；第二句的定冠詞 the 是指特定的咖啡杯歷史（specific）；第三句的不定冠詞 a 則是指非特定的一本歷史書（indefinite）。

單數名詞前可加不定冠詞 a 或 an，這取決 a 或 an 後面單字的第一個音（注意：不是字母），如果是子音，加 a：

a book

a unicorn, a union, a university

a historic moment

a once-in-a-lifetime chance

如果是母音，加 an：

an apple

an umbrella, an uncle

an honorable fellow, an only child

an FBI agent, an MBA degree

由於冠詞屬於功能字，美式口語一般都發輕音 a /ə/, an /ən/，但在強調時，有時則發強音 a /e/, an /æn/。

定冠詞 the 的唸法決定於它之後的單字，如果是子音開頭，the 要發 /ðə/，如 the book, the school, the unicorn；如果是母音，要唸 /ði/，如 the apple, the hour, the owl。另外，有時如果要特別強調某件事物，會將 the 唸成 /ði/（即使是在子音之前），如：That was「the」worst romance I've ever read.

也有部分的文法書中把冠詞視為一個詞類（part of speech），獨立於形容詞之外。

3.4.6 形容詞排列順序

如果在名詞或代名詞之前，有超過 1 個的形容詞來修飾，習慣上，有個大家默認的排列順序，例如：

I bought 8 nice big old blue Italian leather chairs.

這只是個極端的例子，不可能同時有這麼多形容詞，2,3 個就夠多了。一般形容詞排列的大體順序如下：

形容詞類型	例子
冠詞、代名詞、所有格…	a/an/the, my, your, these, Bob's
數字	eight, second, first five
意見看法品質	nice, expensive, beautiful, new, honest

實質描述	大小	big, small, tall, short, heavy
	年紀	old, young, new
	形狀	square, round, triangular
	顏色	blue, white, yellow
	來源	Italian, aboriginal, African
	質料	leather, silk, steel
	目的	sports, cleaning

　　其他例子如 a wonderful old Chinese jade ring；the two big white houses；some disgusting pink sofas 等。這些例子中的每個形容詞都是不同類型的，可相互累積的，以 two blue cars 為例，blue 是形容名詞 cars 的，而 two 是形容 blue cars 的，這種情況的形容詞不要以逗號（comma）相隔。

　　如果是同一類型的形容詞，每個形容詞都可獨立地形容名詞，the big and tall tree，big 是形容 tree 的，tall 也是形容 tree 的，都可獨立，而不像 two blue cars 那樣累積。這種情況的形容詞之間要用 and 或用逗號相隔，如 a warm and gentle father; a blue, white, and red shirt。

　　當然，上表不是全然的固定規則，畢竟語言是活的，但還是有參考價值。如果完全不照順序，有時可能會感覺不太順。

3.5　副詞

　　adverb 的拉丁語源是「ad 與 verb」，隱喻「加在動詞之上」，符合它的功能：「修飾動詞」。大多數的副詞是由形容詞改變字尾而生成。除了修飾動詞的主要功能之外，它也可以修飾形容詞，或其他副詞，甚至整個句子。以副詞 amazingly 為例：

Teresa sang Tian Mi Mi amazingly.	→ 修飾動詞 sang
Dilraba is amazingly beautiful.	→ 修飾形容詞
Hebe performed amazingly well.	→ 修飾副詞 well
Amazingly, Bingbing wore a dragon robe.	→ 修飾整個句子

副詞在文句中表達和句子其他部分的關係，包括：地方 Where, 時間

When, 方法 How, 原因 Why 等訊息。

3.5.1 副詞的位置

副詞可說是 8 大詞類中最具彈性的詞類了，它幾乎可以擺在句子中的任何地方，如：

> I sometimes read a book before bed.
> I read a book before bed sometimes.
> Sometimes I read a book before bed.

頻率副詞 sometimes 可在句首、句中、或句尾，這增加了我們的困擾。第三句的 Sometimes 置於句首，作為強調，也可在它之後加一個逗號，如果是講話，要 stress 這個副詞。

雖然副詞可放在許多位置，但不能置於動詞與受詞之間：

> I read sometimes a book before bed.　　　→ 錯誤

副詞的位置太具彈性，不太能歸納出規則，有個原則是：副詞應盡量靠近它所修飾的字詞，不應離開太遠。

3.5.2 副詞類型

副詞的類型有很多，包括：

manner	情狀	- How
place	地方	- Where
time	時間	- When
frequency	頻率	- How often
degree	程度	- How much
connecting	連接	

情狀、地方、時間副詞

如果上述的前三種副詞（情狀、地方、時間）同時出現在一個句子中，通常次序是 mpt（manner, place, time），例如：

A-mei sang a song beautifully on this stage yesterday.

情狀 beautifully 擺在最前，地方 on this stage 次之，時間 yesterday 最後：情狀→地方→時間。

中文的順序大大不同，我們會說：A-mei 昨天在這裡唱得好美，順序是：時間→地方→情狀。

情狀副詞如 angrily, beautifully, fast, generously, happily, loudly, politely, repeatedly, well（大多數情狀副詞是形容詞字尾＋ly）；地方副詞如 here, in, inside, nearby, on, over, somewhere, upstairs；時間副詞如 now, today, the other day, last week 等。

頻率副詞

許多頻率副詞所代表的發生的可能性各有不同，依一般認知的機率，大略排列如下：

always usually frequently often	100%
sometimes occasionally seldom rarely	50%
never	0%

除了 sometimes 和 occasionally 之外，頻率副詞通常在動作動詞之前，但在 be 動詞之後，如：

He rarely goes to extremes.

They hardly ever go to the movies.

War is seldom the answer.

There is usually a long wait on the weekends at that restaurant.

程度副詞

程度副詞用以表達某種強度（動詞、形容詞、副詞），如 absolutely, awfully, barely, completely, extremely, hardly, rather, slightly, somewhat, totally, very。通常，程度副詞的位置是在形容詞或副詞之前，如 absolutely beautiful, rather slow。enough 可當副詞、也可當形容詞，當副詞時，擺在形容詞之後，如 old enough, strong enough, tall enough；當形容詞時，擺在名詞之前，如 enough food, enough money, enough time。

連接副詞

連接副詞（Conjunctive Adverb）也可算是連接詞的一種，如 consequently, however, nevertheless, therefore……，詳見【3.6】節的連接詞中的【3.6.4】。

3.5.3 副詞與形容詞

中文的副詞通常是將形容詞加上「地」，例如：快樂地、高興地。很多英文的副詞也都是從形容詞變更而來，最普通的方式是將形容詞字尾用某些方式改成 ly：

Adjective	Adverb
bad	badly
interesting	interestingly
luck	luckily
lazy	lazily
terrible	terribly

也有不少是不規則的，例如，good 是形容詞，它的副詞是 well。還有一些形容詞與副詞是一樣的，如 daily, early, far, hard, long, only, straight, weekly 等。舉例：

It's a monthly magazine.	→ 形容詞
I receive it monthly.	→ 副詞

He is a very fast runner.	→ 形容詞
He can run very fast.	→ 副詞

She is late.	→ 形容詞
She got up late this morning.	→ 副詞

另外，有些字的字尾加上 ly 之後與原字的意義完全不同。舉例來說，hard 是努力，但是，hardly 的意思是幾乎不：

Are you working hard or hardly working?

short 是短；shortly 是馬上：

It is a short talk.	→ 短
The book will appear shortly.	→ 不久

其他例子如：late（晚的）和 lately（近來）；near（近的）和 nearly（幾乎）等。

有些字雖然字尾是 ly，但它們是形容詞，不是副詞，如 costly, friendly, lively, lonely, lovely, silly, worldly 等，這些字無法改成副詞，如果它們與動詞連用，需用其他方式表達：

She smiled in a lovely manner.	→ NOT She smiled lovely.

另有一些動詞的字尾是 ly，如 apply, rely, supply 等。還有一些名詞的字尾是 ly，如 ally, bully, melancholy 等。

good 與 well 都是極常用到的單字，如：

She sings well.	→ well 是副詞，修飾 sings
She is good at singing.	→ good 是形容詞，是補語

但是，well 也可以當形容詞，如果有人問 How are you（doing）？回答：

I'm good.（or I'm fine）	→表示一般狀況（心情、生活……）
I'm well.	→表示身體不錯（可能前一陣子不適）

3.5.4 比較級與最高級

　　形容詞與副詞的比較級與最高級將於此節中合併說明。比較級用於兩件事情的比較；最高級用於三件或更多的比較。

　　首先是形容詞，它的比較級與最高級要比副詞的複雜很多，可分類為單音節、雙音節、多音節三種不同的狀況：

 1. 單音節

  形容詞在字尾加 er 與 est 就成為比較級與最高級了，如 cheap, cheaper, cheapest；large, larger, largest。有少數例外需加 more/most，如 fun, more fun, most fun；loved, more loved, most loved。

 2. 双音節

  双音節字則較複雜，可能性包括：

  a. ＋ more/most

   字尾是 ful, ive, less, ous, ing, ed 等

   如 active, hopeless, famous, boring, worried

   （例：more useful, most useful）

  b. ＋ more/most 或 字尾改為 er/est 皆可

   如 common, friendly, gentle, lovely, narrow, simple

   （例：more friendly 或 friendlier 皆可）

  c. 改成 ier/iest

   字尾是 y。如 angry, busy, early, easy, lucky, pretty

   （例：early, earlier, earliest）

 3. 多音節

  三音節及以上的單字則需加 more/most

  如 more expensive, most expensive

　　另外，如果是描述比較級中的劣等，則 less/least 是唯一的用法，例如 dry, less dry, least dry；hungry, less hungry, least hungry；interesting, less interesting, least interesting。

　　相對於形容詞，副詞的比較級與最高級就非常簡單了，大多數是用 more 與 most 表示，如 sweetly, more sweetly, most sweetly。也有在字尾加 er 與 est 的情形，如 fast, faster, fastest；soon, sooner, soonest。

還有一些不規則的形容詞與副詞的比較級與最高級如下：

	詞類	比較級	最高級	註
bad	形	worse	worst	
badly	副	worse	worst	
far	形、副	farther	farthest	指距離
	形、副	further	furthest	指程度（或距離）
good	形	better	best	
late	形、副	later	latest	指時間
	形	latter	last	指次序
little	形、副	less	least	
many	形	more	most	
much	形、副	more	most	
old	形	older	oldest	可指人獸物等
	形	elder	eldest	僅指家人
well	副	better	best	

以 little 為例，它可當形容詞，也可當副詞，它的比較級 less 與最高級 least 也是如此，如：

I have less money than I need.　　→ less 是比較級形容詞

She walks less than she should.　　→ less 是比較級副詞

注意：不可重複使用比較級或最高級，如 more prettier, most tallest, least busiest 是錯的，應改為 prettier, tallest, 和 least busy。

最高級意味著「到現在為止，最…」，因此，它常跟著現在完成式，如：

I just want to let you know that I think you're the most beautiful woman that I've ever seen. You're the best I've ever had.

有些形容詞或副詞是不可用比較級或最高級的，如 unique 的意思是僅此一家，既然獨一無二，比較級就無意義了。其他如 absolute, complete, dead, entire, eternal, final, perfect, round, universal 等。近來這規則變得較寬鬆，有些人也接受 less complete, more perfect 等，但正式寫作時最好不要。

有句常用的慣用語：put one's best foot forward（全力以赴），如以嚴格的文法來看，best 表示至少三個，但我們只有兩隻腳。兩個之中最好的是 better，如 my better half。

※ 練習題－形容詞與副詞 （請參考【附錄 2】的習題解答）

( ) 1. Yao is _____ to do that.
   (a) tall enough   (b) enough tall

( ) 2. Kobe saved _____ to buy a ranch.
   (a) enough money   (b) money enough

( ) 3. Michael played basketball so _____ .
   (a) well   (b) good

( ) 4. Sylvester's soup smells _____ .
   (a) well   (b) good

( ) 5. Brad hasn't seen her _____ .
   (a) late   (b) lately

( ) 6. Leonardo cooks really _____ .
   (a) amazing   (b) amazingly

( ) 7. Denzel's food tastes _____ .
   (a) amazing   (b) amazingly

( ) 8. Russell finished work very _____ yesterday.
   (a) late   (b) lately

( ) 9. This is a _____ course.
   (a) six-month   (b) six-months   (c) six months

( ) 10. It's dark, I can _____ see anything.
   (a) hard   (b) hardly

( ) 11. This is a _____ report.
   (a) month   (b) monthly

( ) 12. I was _____ by the image.
   (a) fascinating   (b) fascinated

( ) 13. I have worked _____ on this project.

(a) hard   (b) hardly

(   ) 14. Yesterday's meeting was _____ .

     (a) tiring   (b) tired

(   ) 15. She spoke _____ to the child.

     (a) lovingly   (b) lovely

(   ) 16. She sings _____ than her sister.

     (a) sweeter   (b) more sweetly

(   ) 17. _____ , he comes from England.

     (a) Interesting   (b) Interestingly

(   ) 18. Jane is _____ by her stories.

     (a) boring   (b) bored

(   ) 19. Tom's stories are _____ .

     (a) boring   (b) bored

(   ) 20. Our progress seemed _____ .

     (a) slow   (b) slowly

(   ) 21. Al cut his speech _____ .

     (a) short   (b) shortly

(   ) 22. I will call you back _____ .

     (a) short   (b) shortly

(   ) 23. Michael is a _____ good singer.

     (a) wonderful   (b) wonderfully

(   ) 24. They were _____ by the news.

     (a) surprising   (b) surprised

(   ) 25. Anthony looked _____ at the man wearing the trench coat.

     (a) suspiciously   (b) suspicious

(   ) 26. The new was _____ .

     (a) surprising   (b) surprised

(   ) 27. Morgan bought a _____ piece of new watch.

     (a) costly   (b) costy

(   ) 28. My dog runs unusually _____ when she's chasing cats.

     (a) quick   (b) quickly

(   ) 29. Keanu's car goes _____ than Al's.

(a) fast　(b) faster

（　）30. Tom is the _____ among three of us.

(a) wealthier　(b) wealthiest

（　）31. _____ all the people enjoyed it very much.

(a) Almost　(b) Most

（　）32. _____ every person agreed.

(a) Almost　(b) Most

（　）33. She didn't feel _____ when she lied to her teacher.

(a) good　(b) well

（　）34. He has the flu and does not look _____ .

(a) good　(b) well

（　）35. Lionel is the _____ of the two brothers at skiing.

(a) best　(b) better

（　）36. He did _____ on the test.

(a) bad　(b) badly

（　）37. There is _____ European hotel on that street.

(a) a　　(b) an

（　）38. The clown was riding _____ one-wheel bike.

(a) a　　(b) an

（　）39. There is _____ university in my hometown.

(a) a　　(b) an

（　）40. He has _____ ugly dog.

(a) a　　(b) an

（　）41. He is _____ English teacher.

(a) a　　(b) an

（　）42. It is _____ honor meeting you.

(a) a　　(b) an

（　）43. That is an _____ wall.

(a) eight-foot　(b) eight-feet

（　）44. Paul is an _____ actor.

(a) blue-eyed　(b) blue-eye

（　）45. She is a _____ girl.

(a) six-year-old　　(b) six-years-old

（　　）46. Sean is 60 _____ old.

(a) year　　(b) years

（　　）47. George wore _____ to the dinner party.

(a) suit　　(b) a suit

（　　）48. We wish you _____ !

(a) Happy New Year　　(b) a Happy New Year

（　　）49. Why do I feel _____ even when I'm around many people?

(a) lonely　　(b) alone

（　　）50. _____ online registration is required.

(a) advance　　(b) advanced

（　　）51. I decided to learn French, just for _____ .

(a) fun　　(b) funny

（　　）52. He's acting _____ today.

(a) fun　　(b) funny

（　　）53. He finished his homework in 20 minutes. He was very _____ .

(a) quickly　　(b) quick

3.6　連接詞

　　被尊稱為「中國語言學之父」的趙元任曾說：「漢語連詞的地位如此的不確定，以至於龍果夫不承認它是一個單獨的詞類。」龍果夫是前蘇聯知名的漢學家。前面已說過：英文重形合，中文重意合。英文的連接詞非常的重要，它是英文句子中的膠水、漿糊，用來連接單字、片語、或子句，定義了句子中的從屬關係。中文連接詞很有彈性，沒有具體的規則，句子的從屬關係常由語意來決定，並非只靠連接詞。

　　一般來說，中文句子短，英文句子長。英文文章通常要長句與短句穿插應用才是好文章，而長句子主要就是靠連接詞來串接不同的子句，這是中英文的一個很大的不同。英文語言考試中常會測試對長句子的了解程度。

　　遇到長句子時，要能夠先將它拆解成多個短小的子句與片語，才容易

清楚來龍去脈，這是我們不熟悉以及欠缺的，好在英文連接詞的邏輯與規則很明確，值得我們花些時間去學。連接詞會出現在句首、句中，但不會在句尾。連接詞分 3 種：

> 對等連接詞（coordinating conjunction）
> 相關連接詞（correlative conjunction）
> 從屬連接詞（subordinating conjunction）

3.6.1 對等連接詞

對等連接詞就如字面上的意義，是用來連接兩個「重要性對等」的單字、片語、或子句。最常用的有 7 個：

F	A	N	B	O	Y	S
for	and	nor	but	or	yet	so

這 7 個字的第一個字母排起來是：FANBOYS（小男粉），可幫助記憶。其中，以 and, but, or 的使用頻率最高。舉例：

> The game will be held rain or shine.
> To see a world in a grain of sand and a heaven in a wild flower...
>
> —— William Blake
>
> I am good, but not an angel. I do sin, but I am not the devil.
>
> —— Marilyn Monroe

第一句是以對等連接詞 or 來連接兩個對等的單字：rain 或 shine；第二句是以 and 來連接兩個對等的片語：a world in a grain of sand 和 a heaven in a wild flower；第三句則是以 but 連接兩個對等的獨立子句如：I do sin 和 I am not the devil。

3.6.2 相關連接詞

相關連接詞類同於對等連接詞，只不過，相關連接詞成雙成對出現（如

either/or），相互對應。與對等連接詞一樣，它用於連接兩個對等的單字、片語、或子句。相關連接詞包括：both/and, either/or, neither/nor, not only/but also, not/but, whether/or, hardly/when, scarcely/when, rather/than, no sooner/than。例如：

> The game is good for both children and adults.　→ 連接單字
> You can go either by bus or by taxi.　→ 連接片語
> The more you can dream, the more you can do.　→ 連接子句

相關連接詞所連結的是「兩個成對的平行元素」，如第一句的 children 和 adults，第二句的 by bus 和 by taxi。

3.6.3　從屬連接詞

從屬連接詞句型的關鍵點在於將兩個「重要性不相等」的子句連結成一個句子。重要性高的子句是「主要子句」，重要性低的子句叫「從屬子句」。主要子句可獨立存在（所以又稱為獨立子句），從屬子句則不行，只是添加額外資訊到主要子句中。從屬連接詞很多，包括 after, although, as, because, before, if, once, since, than, unless, until, when, where, while，也有不只 1 個字的，如 as if, as soon as, even though, no matter how, so that。例句：

> Even if the sky is falling down, you'll be my only.

主要子句 you'll be my only 是表達的重點，可單獨成句；而從屬子句 Even if the sky is falling down 是次要資訊，雖不能單獨成句，但可添料加味，讓主要子句更加完美。又如：

> Whenever I'm discouraged, she knows just what to do.
> ——Lobo (lyrics from "How Can I Tell Her")

主要子句是 she knows just what to do；從屬子句是 Whenever I'm discouraged。

從屬連接詞將在第四章 4.2.2 節的副詞子句中做更詳細的介紹。

3.6.4 連接副詞

有一種副詞叫連接副詞（conjunctive adverbs），如 accordingly, finally, however, meanwhile, moreover, nevertheless, otherwise, subsequently, then, therefore, thus，常見的錯誤寫法如：

> He wanted to be just friends, however, she wanted much more.

這樣寫不正確，不能用連接副詞兩邊打逗號來分開兩個獨立子句，正確的寫法如下：

> He wanted to be just friends; however, she wanted much more.
> He wanted to be just friends. However, she wanted much more.

兩種寫法是一樣的，要小心標點符號的用法。另外，however 可以放在不同的位置，如下：

> He wanted to be just friends. She, however, wanted much more.
> He wanted to be just friends. She wanted much more, however.

※ 練習題 – 連接詞　（請參考【附錄 2】的習題解答）

(　) 1. I will be in bed ＿＿＿＿ the time you get back.

　　　(a) by　(b) before　(c) when

(　) 2. I like sugar in my tea, ＿＿＿＿ I don't like milk in it.

　　　(a) and　(b) but　(c) or

(　) 3. The sun was warm, ＿＿＿＿ the wind was a bit too cool.

　　　(a) and　(b) nor　(c) yet

(　) 4. ＿＿＿＿ Katy was watching TV, his wife was sleeping on the couch.

　　　(a) While　(b) And　(c) So

(　) 5. I'll call you ＿＿＿＿ I have the info.

　　　(a) what　(b) as soon as　(c) where

(　) 6. I will be relieved ＿＿＿＿ it is finished.

　　　(a) before　(b) by　(c) when

（　　） 7. I'll text you _____ I've arrived in Bangkok.

　　　　(a) after　(b) so　(c) then

（　　） 8. They climbed Mount Everest _____ it was very windy.

　　　　(a) or　(b) although　(c) so

（　　） 9. They do not smoke, _____ do they play cards.

　　　　(a) yet　(b) or　(c) nor

（　　） 10. You have to finish it _____ you can leave.

　　　　(a) before　(b) until　(c) when

（　　） 11. We were very tired _____ happy after our flight to Sydney.

　　　　(a) so　(b) but　(c) or

（　　） 12. I paid Pat, _____ garden design work is top-notch.

　　　　(a) Because　(b) who　(c) whose

（　　） 13. Neither the shirt _____ the jacket fit.

　　　　(a) nor　(b) or　(c) and

（　　） 14. Scarcely had I gone to bed _____ the doorbell rang.

　　　　(a) before　(b) when　(c) than

（　　） 15. No sooner had I closed my eyes _____ I fell asleep

　　　　(a) before　(b) when　(c) than

3.7　介系詞

　　介系詞（preposition）的字源可視作為：「pre + position」，意思是在什麼之前。實質上，介系詞必在受詞之前，換言之，介系詞不能單獨存在，介系詞之後必有受詞，而受詞必定是名詞（包括代名詞、動名詞、名詞片語、名詞子句），例句如下：

I haven't seen you for ages.	→ 介系詞＋名詞
I'll go with you.	→ 介系詞＋代名詞
My mom has difficulty in sending SMS.	→ 介系詞＋動名詞
He is stiff from yesterday's long practice.	→ 介系詞＋名詞片語
You must pay attention to what I say.	→ 介系詞＋名詞子句

介系詞的文法功能在於顯示「兩個名詞之間的相互關係」，這種相互關係大多數是指時間與位置，其他的則如屬性、方法、因果等。例如下面兩個句子中的介系詞 in, to, of，其中，in, to 表示位置（或時間）的相互關係，of 表示屬性：

> The car in which the superstar arrived to the party is an Aventador.
>
> The pop star is in the middle of her worldwide solo concert tour.

　　介系詞雖然都是些小字小詞，但大多沒有一定的規則，許多人將介系詞視為八大詞類中最不易掌握與運用的前茅之一。常見的介系詞錯誤用法大致分為三類：

1. 用錯了介系詞

Jennifer was married with Brad.	→ with 應更正為 to
I'll contact you with email.	→ with 應更正為 by
I found a solution of your problem.	→ of 應更正為 to
This is the tallest building of the world.	→ of 應更正為 in
The surgeon was accused for negligence.	→ for 應更正為 of
The sun rises from the east and sets to the west.	→ from, to 更正為 in

　　第一句的 is married to 表示婚姻狀態，如果是 She is married with 3 children. 則表示她結婚了而且有 3 個小孩。最後一句或也可寫成 The sun rises in the east and moves from east to west.

2. 該用而未用介系詞

He asked （　　） a coffee.	→ 填入 for
Do you believe （　　） God?	→ 填入 in
I listened （　　） the radio last night.	→ 填入 to
Whiners are usually not easy to deal （　　）.	→ 填入 with
Did you hear （　　） the renovation project?	→ 填入 about
The manufacturer promises quality you can depend （　　）	→ 填入 on

3. 不該用而多用了介系詞

下面例子中的介系詞依序是 to, at, for, into, about, with，它們都是多餘的，都要刪除：

Where are you going to?	→ 刪除 to
Where is your school at?	→ 刪除 at
I appreciate for your help.	→ 刪除 for
She is entering into the kitchen.	→ 刪除 into
They are discussing about the news of the day.	→ 刪除 about
I tried to contact with him at his office, but he wasn't in.	→ 刪除 with

discuss 相當於 talk about，所以 discuss 後面直接加受詞即可，其他類似的動詞如 mention, consider，也都是直接加受詞。contact 也是直接加受詞（人）。

如前所述，介系詞表達名詞相互間的關係，位置及時間應是最常用的相互關係了，以下兩節將討論位置及時間介系詞。

3.7.1　介系詞 – 位置

表示位置關係的介系詞，如 at, above, across, below, beside, between, by, from, in, in front of, into, on, onto, near, through, toward, under 等。其中，有些介系詞的意義很清楚，如 above（在上面）、behind（在後面）、by（在旁邊）等，很容易了解與運用。但是，有些則容易混淆，如 arrive in 表示到達一個城市、國家，arrive at 則是到達一個定點（小的地方，buildings），舉例：

> He arrived at the Louvre Museum an hour ago.
> He arrived in Paris yesterday.

at, in, on 可說是日常生活中最常用也容易混淆的三個位置介系詞了，下表有幾個規則可幫助我們了解它們的用法，是幫助記憶的一種「概念性的歸納」：

位置介系詞	意涵	例子
at	定點	at a party, at the bus stop, at home at the door, at 28 Fifth Avenu
on	線、面	on the second floor, on the wall, on her forehead, on the beach, on Main street
in	空間	in a room, in the kitchen, in the park in LA, in Libya, in Asia, in the world

如果概略地以大小來說，at 最小，on 較大，in 最大。以住址為例：

Steph lives at 56 Park Avenue.　　　　　→ at：特定地址

Kevin's house is on Grand Boulevard.　　→ on：街道

LeBron lives in Riverside County.　　　　→ in：市縣省國

Kawhi lives at 18 Main Street, in an apartment, on the eighth floor.

還有一些 at, on, in 的片語則較抽象，譬如：

　　　in a book, in a movie, in a newspaper

　　　on TV, on the radio, on the internet

如果要形容一個人在某個交通工具裡，常用到介系詞 on 與 in。幾乎只有 car, taxi 用 in，其他都用 on。這主要是習慣用法，或者可以說，大型的或公共的交通工具用 on，小型的或私人的交通工具用 in，如：

　　　on a boat, on a bus, on a train, on a plane, on a ship

　　　in a car, in a taxi

如果是說坐什麼交通工具去某處，則用介系詞 by，如 by car, by train, by plane, by boat 等。

3.7.2 介系詞 – 時間

表示時間關係的介系詞，如 after, before, by, during, for, since, to, until, within 等。如同位置介系詞，有些時間介系詞的意義很清楚，如 after（之

後）、before（之前）、since（從～起）等，很容易了解與運用。但是，有些則容易混淆，如常用的 at, in, on，下表也是幫助記憶的一種「概念性的歸納」：

時間介系詞	意涵	例子
at	特定時間點（如一天中的某個時間）、假期	at 7:30 p.m., at noon, at lunchtime at midnight, at Thanksgiving
on	特定的日子（如星期幾）、日期（如幾月幾號）	on Tuesday, on Saturday night, on the weekend, on January 2, 2020
in	特定的時期（較長）：數天、星期、月份、季、年、世紀	in a few days, in a week in March, in winter, in 2018, in the 1980s, in the 21st century

如果概略地以時間的長短來說，at 最短，on 較長，in 最長。和幾乎所有的英文規則一樣，都會有很多例外、很多灰色的地帶，以早上、中午、晚上為例：in the morning, in the afternoon, in the evening，但是，卻用 at night。所以，最重要的 還是：習慣用法。講到特定節日，可以說 on Christmas Day, on New Year's Day，也可以用 at Christmas, at New Year。另外，on the weekend 是美式，英國人則用 at the weekend。

如果日期之前已有時間形容詞，如 every, last, next, this 等，則不需再加 on, at, in，如：

> Let's meet next Tuesday.
> They got married last December.
> We sing Auld Lang Syne every New Year's Eve.

3.7.3 幾個容易混淆的介系詞用法

among vs. between

among：兩個以上
between：兩個

例句：The bees are buzzing among the flowers.

They tried to break up the fight between Justin and Drake.

beside vs. besides

beside：在什麼的旁邊

besides：除……之外

例句：Would you come and sit beside me?

He wants to learn other languages besides English.

by vs. until

by 表示：在某時間點之前

until 表示：直到某時間點

例句：You can have the bike until tonight, but you must return it by 12:00.

except vs. besides

except：除……之外，都不

besides：除……之外，也都

例句：All of us will go except Vladimir. → Vladimir 不去

All of us will go besides Vladimir. → Vladimir 也去

in vs. into

in：狀態，是靜態的

into：動作，隱含動態

例句：The silverware is in the cupboard.

Chloe drove her car into the garage.

to vs. at

例句：She shouted to me. → 她叫我（因為距離遠，聲音大些）

She shouted at me. → 她因為生氣而對我大聲叫

attend vs. attend to

attend：參加、出席

attend to：照料、處理

例句：He regularly attends yoga classes. → 參加

He'll attend to the problem tomorrow. → 處理

in time vs. on time

in time：即時

on time：準時

例句：They managed to get to the airport in time.

Why is it that the buses never run on time?

lack vs. lack of

lack 當動詞時，直接加受詞

lack 當名詞時，需用 lack of

例句：This soup lacks salt. → 動詞

The lack of salt made the food tasteless. → 名詞

3.7.4 介系詞，連接詞，副詞

有的介系詞也同時是從屬連接詞，如 before, after, since, until，如何判斷是介系詞還是從屬連接詞呢？要記得詞類的區別端視它們在句子中所擔任的功能：介系詞表達一個名詞與另一個名詞間的相互關係，其後必接名詞（包括動名詞）；從屬連接詞則帶領著從屬子句，連結獨立子句，如：

He stood before the wall.	→ before 是介系詞
Let's eat before we go.	→ before 從屬連接詞
I have learned a lot since coming here.	→ since 介系詞
I have learned a lot since I came here.	→ since 是從屬連接詞

有些介系詞也可以是副詞，如 above, on, out, up 等，如：

His house is half-way down the hill.	→ down 是介系詞

The computer broke down.	→ down 是副詞
The work is in progress.	→ in 是介系詞
Please chip in with your comments.	→ in 是副詞

當 down, in 是副詞時，其後就不必跟著受詞。副詞是內容字，讀的時候要加重；當它們是介系詞（功能字）時，要輕讀。

3.7.5 介系詞 to ＋ Ving

單字 to 可以用作介系詞，也可以用作不定詞的標誌，兩者在文法上有極大的區別：

> 介系詞的後面＋名詞（動名詞）
> 不定詞的後面＋原形動詞

不定詞 to ＋原形動詞是最常見的用法，我們非常習慣：

We decided not to go out.

Do you swear to tell the truth?

我們非常不習慣 to ＋動名詞，這時候的關鍵點是：to 是介系詞。通常有下面幾種情形：

1. 某些以 to 結尾的 phrasal verbs
   如：admit to, come down to, confess to, object to, resort to

   I'm really looking forward to seeing what life brings to me.
   ——Rihanna

2. 某些 形容詞＋ to 的組合
   如：be accustomed to, be addicted to, be committed to, be dedicated to, be devoted to, be opposed to, be used to, get used to
   這些片語中的 accustomed, addicted 等是形容詞（過去分詞）

We love life, not because we are used to living but because we are used to loving. ——Friedrich Nietzsche

3. 某些 名詞＋to 的組合

如：alternative to, addiction to, dedication to, commitment to, devotion to, reaction to 等

His addiction to surfing the Internet is a problem.

有個很好的測試法可以如何決定 to 之後該用原形動詞或是動名詞：先在 to 之後加上一個名詞（如 something），如果句子合乎文法邏輯，就用動名詞；如果不合邏輯，就用動詞原形。如：

I am used to（something）.	→ 合。加動名詞
He might object to（something）.	→ 合。加動名詞
I wanted to（something）.	→ 不合。加原形動詞
I used to（something）.	→ 不合。加原形動詞

提醒：to + gerund 的前提是 to 是介系詞。另外，當 to 是介系詞時，其後也都可以加名詞（代名詞等）

I'm hopelessly devoted to you.

——Olivia Newton John
(lyrics from "Hopelessly Devoted to You")

※ 練習題 – 介系詞　（請參考【附錄 2】的習題解答）

註： No prep. 指不需介系詞

（　　）1. I like watching fight scenes ＿＿＿＿ Jacky Chen movies.

(a) in　(b) on　(c) at

(　) 2. Batman is one of my favorite cartoons _____ TV.

(a) in　(b) on　(c) at

(　) 3. I had a cup of tea _____ Elva's house.

(a) at　(b) in　(c) by

(　) 4. I had a cup of tea _____ Elva.

(a) at　(b) with　(c) by

(　) 5. I'm seeing my children _____ Christmas.

(a) on　(b) at　(c) in

(　) 6. I killed two birds _____ one stone.

(a) by　(b) in　(c) with

(　) 7. Parents would do just about anything _____ their children.

(a) at　(b) for　(c) to

(　) 8. Luckily, we arrived just _____ time to catch the train.

(a)on　(b) at　(c) in

(　) 9. She's been a good friend _____ me.

(a)with　(b) of　(c) to

(　) 10. The class had ended _____ the time I arrived.

(a) by　(b) in　(c) at

(　) 11. Do you need help _____ your homework?

(a) about　(b) to　(c) with

(　) 12. They all arrived _____ the same time.

(a) by　(b) in　(c) at

(　) 13. They met _____ a wedding.

(a) at　(b) in　(c) on

(　) 14. The teacher read a story _____ the class.

(a) at　(b) to　(c) for

(　) 15. Are you interested _____ mobile games?

(a) in　(b) for　(c) with

(　) 16. We have to turn off cell phones when we get _____ the plane.

(a) in　(b) on　(c) No prep.

(　) 17. Please read the details _____ our website.

(a) in   (b) on   (c) at

(   ) 18. We're going _____ home soon.

(a)to   (b) for   (c) No prep.

(   ) 19. He walked _____ the kitchen and opened the oven.

(a) to   (b) into   (c) No prep.

(   ) 20. She entered _____ my office without knocking.

(a) to   (b) into   (c) No. prep.

(   ) 21. The kitchen is _____ the first floor.

(a) at   (b) in   (c) on

(   ) 22. They've lived _____ this address for many years.

(a) at   (b) in   (c) on

(   ) 23. The supermarket is _____ the corner of Nanjing Street.

(a) to   (b) in   (c) on

(   ) 24. Let's meet _____ the corner of Miami Street and Beach Road.

(a) at   (b) in   (c) on

(   ) 25. We arrived _____ our destination.

(a) at   (b) in   (c) on

(   ) 26. He met her _____ visiting Beijing.

(a) in   (b) while   (c) since

(   ) 27. I'm going shopping _____ lunchtime.

(a) at   (b) in   (c) on

(   ) 28. I have complete confidence _____ Robert.

(a) at   (b) in   (c) on

(   ) 29. What's the solution _____ the problem?

(a) about   (b) to   (c) with

(   ) 30. He stuck a magnet _____ the refrigerator.

(a) at   (b) in   (c) on

(   ) 31. Have you heard _____ this book?

(a) from   (b) of   (c) No prep.

(   ) 32. I'll contact _____ him right away.

(a) with   (b) to   (c) No prep.

(   ) 33. It is up for people to make _____ their own minds.

(a) for　(b) of　(c) up

(　　) 34. He is different _____ the rest.

　　　　(a) from　(b) than　(c) among

(　　) 35. Can you write _____ your left hand?

　　　　(a) by　(b) for　(c) with

(　　) 36. What's the reason _____ your decision?

　　　　(a) for　(b) of　(c) with

(　　) 37. The rumor was spread _____ the public.

　　　　(a) among　(b) between　(c) around

(　　) 38. He worked on his math homework from 8 _____ midnight.

　　　　(a) during　(b) to　(c) since

(　　) 39. Are you worried _____ the exam?

　　　　(a) about　(b) for　(c) of

(　　) 40. 「All of us will go besides Joe.」 means Joe:

　　　　(a) will not go　(b) will go　(c) has not decided

(　　) 41. He got an 88 _____ the final exam.

　　　　(a) at　(b) on　(c) in

(　　) 42. She got a B _____ physics last semester.

　　　　(a) at　(b) on　(c) in

(　　) 43. This option is preferable _____ any other.

　　　　(a) than　(b) to　(c) by

(　　) 44. I am taller than _____ .

　　　　(a) they　(b) he　(c) him

(　　) 45. She is married _____ an Egyptian.

　　　　(a)from　(b) with　(c) to

(　　) 46. He gave a speech _____ the dangers of texting and driving.

　　　　(a) on　(b) to　(c) at

(　　) 47. I really admire his dedication _____ animal rights.

　　　　(a) about　(b) for　(c) to

(　　) 48.　She has a talent _____ learning languages.

　　　　(a) for　(b) about　(c) with

(　　) 49.　They have got lots of previous experience _____ management.

(a) in　(b) for　(c) of

（　）50.　Most people have little awareness _____ world events.

(a) at　(b) of　(c) in

3.8　感嘆詞

　　感嘆詞是一些較小的字詞，通常表達一種感情或驚嘆，不與句子中的其他元素有文法上的關連，可以說是完全獨立的。如 Aha! Boo! Blah! Good grief! Hey! Heavens! Hurray! Oh! Oops! Ouch! Ugh! Wow! Yay!

　　　　例句：Shh! Keep your voice down, please.
　　　　　　　Hurray! I won the lottery.
　　　　　　　Wow, you're on a winning streak.

CHAPTER 4

句子結構

　　句子是語言表述的基本單位。語文通常是由單字到片語，由片語到句子，再由句子到文章。簡單地說，英文句子是由一個或數個子句（clause）組成，子句由片語（phrase）與單字組成。

　　句子的核心架構是主詞與動詞，其他的詞類（如形容詞與副詞）都是架構之外的修飾，不是必要的核心。

　　中英文句子架構的邏輯不同，譬如：妳很漂亮。吃飯了沒？前一句沒動詞；後一句沒主詞。都不符英文句子的條件。

　　英文文章常有很長的句子，了解句意的先決條件在於分析句子的架構、各部分的關連與規則，將長句分解成多個子句與片語，分辨其間的相互關係，這是讀寫的基本功，卻也是我們較欠缺的練習。因此，有時會覺得為什麼單字全都認得，卻無法讀懂，這是主要的原因。

4.1　基本分類

　　英文句子是由一個或數個子句連結而成。子句分為兩種：

　　　　獨立子句 independent clause（或 main or complete clause）
　　　　從屬子句 dependent clause（或 subordinate clause）

　　獨立子句（主要子句）具備完整意義，是一個句子最基本的建構單元，可以單獨成句；從屬子句雖然也有主詞與動詞，但意義不完整，不能獨立存在（只具備形容詞、副詞、名詞的功能），必須依附於主要子句。例如：

When tears are in your eyes, I'll dry them all.

—— Simon & Garfunkel

(lyrics from "Bridge Over Troubled Water")

When tears are in your eyes 是從屬子句，不具完整意義；I'll dry them all 是主要子句，可獨立存在。

子句與片語都是有意義的字詞組合，兩者的不同在於子句必須具備主詞與動詞，而片語則否。

句子有 4 類句型：

簡單句（simple sentence）
複合句（compound sentence）
複雜句（complex sentence）
複合複雜句（compound complex sentence）

讀文章時，先將句子拆解為前三類型，才容易了解句子的意思。而寫文章時，要記得英文非常注重表達方式的變化，包括（1）上下文盡量不重複相同的字詞，用其他意義相近的同義字，（2）文章不過度重複相同的句型，盡量靈活穿插簡單句、複合句、複雜句，才是好文章。

4.1.1 簡單句

簡單句中只有一個獨立子句。

簡單句是指它的結構性很基本，但不表示句子很短或很容易，理論上，一個簡單句中可以有幾十個片語及單字。簡單句也可以少到只有一個字：

Go!
Look!
Run!
Stop!

這幾個命令句 imperative sentences，看似只有動詞一個字，其實，都只是將主詞 You 省略了而已（除命令句之外，句子都不能缺少主詞）。這

幾個動詞都是不及物動詞；如果是及物動詞，就不成句，如 I want 不是一個句子，因為 want 必須有受詞。

簡單句主要的元素可大致分為主詞 Subject（S）、動詞 Verb（V）、受詞 Object（O）、補語 Complement（C）。

簡單句的基本句型一般可簡略地分為五類：

SV	主詞＋動詞
SVO	主詞＋動詞＋受詞
SVC	主詞＋動詞＋補語
SVOO	主詞＋動詞＋間接受詞＋直接受詞
SVOC	主詞＋動詞＋受詞＋受詞補語

Michael laughed.	→ SV。laugh 是不及物動詞
Magic kissed her.	→ SVO。kiss 是及物動詞
Larry was a coach	→ SVC。a coach 是主詞補語
Kareem gave him a ball.	→ SVOO。him 是間接受詞，a ball 是直接受詞
Isiah made him angry.	→ SVOC。him 是受詞，angry 是受詞補語

4.1.2　複合句

複合句包含兩個（或更多）獨立子句，中間用對等連接詞連結在一起，「對等」代表是兩個平行且同等重要的獨立子句。

如前所述，對等連接詞有 7 個：for, and, nor, but, or, yet, so（FANBOYS）。記住它，就能在一些冗長的句子中，清楚分辨複合句。如：

You may say I'm a dreamer, but I am not the only one.

—— John Lennon (lyrics from "Imagine")

句中的 You may say I'm a dreamer 和 I am not the only one 是兩個同等

重要的獨立子句，中間以對等連接詞 but 相連，要注意在前面的獨立子句之後要加逗點，句型是：

獨立子句＋逗號＋對等連接詞＋獨立子句

依照正式英語的文法規則，逗號是必須的，然而，非正式英語的趨勢是簡單化：如果兩個子句都很短而且強相關時（尤其是主詞又相同），逗號可省略，如：

You have to do it now or you'll be punished.

4.1.3 複雜句

複雜句由一個獨立子句和至少一個從屬子句組成，獨立子句和從屬子句「重要性不相等」，獨立子句是主要的，可單獨成句；從屬子句是次要的，必須依附於獨立子句。複雜句是增添英文寫作深度與多樣性的重要一環。獨立子句與從屬子句之間用從屬連接詞（如 after, although, as, as if, because, before, if, once, since, so that, than, when, where, whether, while）相連。如：

If you can dream it, you can do it.　　　　——Walt Disney

If 是從屬連接詞，前面的 If you can dream it 是從屬子句，置於後的 you can do it 是獨立子句，兩子句之間須加逗號。複雜句也可將從屬子句擺在後面，如：

How many times must the cannon balls fly before they're forever banned?　——Bob Dylan (lyrics from "Blowin' In The Wind")

從屬子句 before they're forever banned 擺在後面，這樣的句型，就不需要逗號了。複雜句有兩種句型：

1. 從屬子句＋逗號＋獨立子句
2. 獨立子句＋從屬子句（兩句中間沒逗號）

另一種記憶的方法是：當連接詞在句首時，要用逗號分隔後面的子句；當連接詞在句子中間時，不要用逗號。

因為從屬子句的功能基本上與形容詞、副詞、名詞類同，所以從屬子句分為 3 種：形容詞子句、副詞子句、名詞子句：

The person who made the mess needs to clean it.	→ 形容詞子句
He didn't call her because he is shy.	→ 副詞子句
What the billionaire did shocked the whole world.	→ 名詞子句

複合句與複雜句的區別如下：

1. 複合句是平行對等子句的組合，沒有誰修飾誰的問題；
   複雜句中的子句的重要性不相等
   從屬子句依附於主要的獨立子句
2. 複合句的對等連接詞不能擺在句子的開頭；
   複雜句的從屬連接詞可以擺在句子的開頭或中間

4.1.4 複合複雜句

複合複雜句是複合句與複雜句的合體，包含至少一個複合句和一個複雜句，或者說，至少兩個獨立子句和至少一個從屬子句，如：

He likes to sleep in, but he can get up early if he has work to do.

先找出：but 是對等連接詞，if 是從屬連接詞。這樣，就可以很容易地分析出 He likes to sleep in 以及 he can get up early 是兩個獨立子句，而 if he has work to do 是從屬子句。

討論完英文的 4 類句型後，簡單說明拆解句子的步驟：

1. 先找出有幾個主詞與動詞的配對	→ 決定有幾個子句？
2. 分辨連接詞	→ 決定對等？從屬？
3. 分辨子句	→ 決定獨立？從屬？

確定了句子中有幾個獨立子句與從屬子句之後，由相互間的從屬關係就可讀出句子的意思了，如：

We are all in the gutter, but some of us are looking at the stars.

——Oscar Wilde

If I stay here, won't you listen to my heart?

——Rod Stewart (lyrics from "I Don't Want To Talk About It")

　　第一句中主詞與動詞組合有：We + are 以及 us + are looking 兩組，表示有兩個子句，由對等連接詞 but 連接，因此，是複合句，兩個子句的重要性相等。第二句中主詞與動詞組合有：I + stay 以及 you + listen，也表示有兩個子句，而 If 是從屬連接詞，因此，If I stay here 是次要資訊，輔助後面的主要子句。

　　分析句子會先對懂英文有很大幫助，練習久了，不但較容易讀懂，寫作的功力也會提升，寫出多樣化的句型（簡單句、複合句、複雜句），增加文章色彩、豐富寫作風格。

4.2　從屬子句

　　從屬子句雖然具備主詞與動詞，但不是獨立的句子，從文法功能的角度來看，它就如同一個單一的形容詞、或副詞、名詞，按照這樣的性質，從屬子句有 3 大類：

　　　形容詞子句（adjective [or relative] clause）
　　　副詞子句（adverb clause）
　　　名詞子句（noun clause）

4.2.1　形容詞子句

　　大部分的形容詞子句（又稱為關係子句）由關係代名詞引領。關係子句一定緊跟於它所修飾的名詞之後，用來增添這個名詞的相關訊息，作用與單一的形容詞類同。關係子句分為兩種：

限定關係子句 Restrictive (Defining) Relative Clause

非限定關係子句 Non-restrictive (Non-defining) Relative Clause

4.2.1.1　限定／非限定關係子句

　　限定關係子句提供必要的訊息；非限定關係子句僅提供非必要的參考。關係子句通常由關係代名詞引導，包含 who, which, that, whom, whose（詳如【3.3.1】代名詞的分類）。例句：

　　　　The man who is sitting next to the door is very smart.

　　限定關係子句 who is sitting next to the door 緊跟著它所修飾的主詞 The man，是必要的訊息，如果沒有它，就不知道主詞 who 指的是誰。如果句子改成：

　　　　Albert, who is sitting next to the door, is very smart.

　　這句話重點在說 Albert is very smart，交談的雙方都知道 Albert 是誰。, who is sitting next to the door,（前後都有逗號）是非限定關係子句，可有可無，只是增添訊息，作為非必要的參考（口語中，講到非必要訊息時，通常會稍作停頓並且降低音調），即使刪除，也不會影響句子的重點。

　　注意：非限定關係子句的前後都要加逗號，限定關係子句則不加逗號。

　　再以例子說明如下：

　　　　His sister who lives in Nairobi visited him.

　　　　His sister, who lives in Nairobi, visited him.

　　在正式文法中，雖然這兩個子句的差別只在於一個有逗號，一個沒有，但意思不同。第一句的 who lives in Nairobi 是限定關係子句，隱含他有不止一個 sister，來訪的是那個從 Nairobi 來的 sister；第二句的 , who lives in Nairobi, 是非限定關係子句，隱含的意義是他只有一個 sister。

　　選擇用限定或是非限定句法取決於你想表達什麼。

　　關係代名詞 which 有個較特別的用途，它可以用來修飾它之前的整個子句：

　　　　Leonardo finally got his award, which is fantastic.

這裡的 which is fantastic 不是指 award，而是指終於得獎了這件事，修飾整個子句 Leonardo finally got his award。注意：which 之前須加逗號（,）。

形容詞子句有時可由關係副詞（where, when, why）引領，如下兩句的 where 和 when：

> The house where Mozart was born is now a museum.
>
> I remember the day when we first met.

4.2.1.2　關係代名詞的省略與取代

常有人問：關係代名詞可以省略嗎？答案是：某些情況下可以省略，尤其是在口語中，幾乎經常被省略。原則是：

1. 在限定關係子句中
   作為主詞 → 不可以省略
   作為受詞 → 可以省略
2. 在非限定關係子句中
   → 不可以省略

> 例句：The customer who called me was unhappy.
>
> 　　　The customer（whom）I called was unhappy.

第一句中的 who 是主詞，不可以省略。第二句中的 whom 是 called 的受詞，可以省略。

另一種說法是：經過省略後，關係子句的句首不可以沒有主詞；如果關係子句有自己的主詞（如第二句的 I），就可以省略關係代名詞。再舉兩個例句：

> The fanny pack (which) my mom bought for me was stolen.
>
> These are the wireless earphones (that) young people love so much.

這兩句中 which 與 that 是受詞，關係子句都有自己的主詞（my mom 和 young people），所以 which 和 that 都可以省掉。

如何判定關係代名詞是主詞還是受詞呢？有一個簡單的判別方法是：

1. 如果它後面緊跟著動詞	→ 是主詞
2. 如果它後面緊跟著的不是動詞	→ 是受詞

另外一個常問的問題是：關係代名詞（who, which, whom）可以被 that 取代嗎？原則是：

1. 在限定關係子句中	→ 可以被 that 取代
2. 在非限定關係子句中	→ 不可以被 that 取代

who 和 which 可以用於限定或非限定關係子句中，但 that 只能用於限定關係子句中。

但是，正式的美式英文在 that, which, who 的用法上較為分明：

    1. 限定關係子句中描述事物時，用 that

    2. 非限定關係子句中描述事物時，用 which

    3. 描述人時，用 who (口語中則常用 that)

這幾個原則恰好讓我們能清楚分辨限定與非限定關係子句，而且，它們很簡短，我們可以快速記住 that, which, who 在正式美式英文關係子句中的用法，這樣，自己寫文章時會比較放心。英式英文則略有不同。

如果關係代名詞前面是介系詞，那只能用 which 或 whom，不能被 that 取代，如：

    The party at which he spoke was noisy.

    "From whom did you get this?" she asked.

4.2.1.3　形容詞子句的精簡

形容詞子句常被精簡（reduced）為形容詞片語，讓整個句子更緊密、更流暢。這樣的精簡要有兩個先決條件：

1. 關係代名詞是形容詞子句的主詞
2. 只有 3 個關係代名詞可以被精簡：which, that, who

    Hockey is a sport that requires skill, strength, and focus.

The NBA playoffs, which are held in different U.S. and Canada cities, are often sold-out events.

這兩句的形容詞子句分別是 that requires ～以及 which are held ～，關係代名詞 that 和 which 都是子句中的主詞，因此，這兩個子句都可以精簡為片語，步驟：

1. 將關係代名詞 which, that, who 拿掉
2. 將 be 動詞（is, are,…）拿掉
3. 主動語態的動詞 → 改為現在分詞
   被動語態的動詞 → 保留過去分詞
4. 子句中如果有逗號 → 保留逗號

Hockey is a sport requiring skill, strength, and focus.
The NBA playoffs, held in different U.S. and Canada cities, are often sold-out events.

有些不能精簡的例子如：

The FIFA World Cup Trophy, which France won in 1998 and 2018, is sought after by almost every country.
This is the guy whose sister is a supermodel.

第一句的形容詞子句 which France won in 1998 and 2018 中的關係代名詞 which 不是主詞，不能被精簡；第二句的 whose 不在精簡之列。

4.2.2 副詞子句

副詞子句是從屬子句的一種，它的文法功能與單一的副詞類同。副詞子句的種類很多，像是時間、地方、原因、條件、對照等，它須由一個從屬連接詞引領，將副詞子句與獨立子句連結，從屬連接詞很多，如下表：

時間	地點	原因	條件	對照
after, before,	where, wherever	as, because,	if, in case,	although, though,

until,		since,	provided	while
when		so that	that	

從屬連接詞可以幫忙找出副詞子句，如：

(You) only hate the road when you're missing home.

(You) only know you love her when you let her go.

──Passenger (lyrics from "Let Her Go")

第一句的主詞＋動詞有兩組：You + hate 以及 you + are missing，表示有兩個子句，副詞子句 when you're missing home 由從屬連接詞 when 帶領，修飾主要子句 You only hate the road。

當一個句子中的有多個子句時，要小心彼此的順序，如：

I rarely eat bacon, although I like it, because it's unhealthy.

Although I like bacon, I rarely eat it because it's unhealthy.

上述兩句話都各有 3 組主詞＋動詞：I + eat; I + like; it + is，表示有 3 個子句（一個主要子句以及兩個副詞子句）。第一句話雖然文法沒問題，但子句的順序不對，because it's unhealthy 容易被誤解是在修飾 I like it！改為第二句，意思就很清楚了。

4.2.2.1　副詞子句的精簡

副詞子句的種類很多，不是所有的類型都可以被精簡，通常僅有時間（time）、原因（cause）、對照（contrast）等三種副詞子句可被精簡成副詞片語。精簡的先決條件是：

副詞子句的主詞＝主要子句的主詞

以下三節簡述時間、原因、對照等三種副詞子句的精簡。

1. 時間副詞子句的精簡

After Meghan and Harry had lunch, they went back to the palace.

以上面的句子來說，副詞子句的主詞 Meghan and Harry 與獨立子句

的主詞 they 相同，句子可以精簡成：

> After having lunch, Meghan and Harry went back to the palace.

副詞子句 After Meghan and Harry had lunch 精簡成了副詞片語 After having lunch。精簡步驟為（以上句為例）：

　　a. 將副詞子句中的主詞（Meghan and Harry）刪除

　　　視情況調整主要子句中的主詞（they → Meghan and Harry）

　　b. 如果副詞子句中有助動詞，刪除

　　c. 將副詞子句中的動詞改為動名詞（had → having）

2. 原因副詞子句的精簡：

> Because she didn't understand the question, she asked him for help.
>
> 精簡為 →
>
> Not understanding the question, she asked him for help.

這精簡步驟與上述的時間副詞類似，再加上（a）從屬連接詞 because 被刪除，（b）否定字 Not 放在分詞之前。又如：

> I try to avoid going up high buildings because I'm afraid of height.
>
> 精簡為 →
>
> Being afraid of height, I try to avoid going up high buildings.

3. 對照副詞子句的精簡：

　　原句：Although the room is big, it won't hold all that furniture.

　　精簡：Although big, the room won't hold all that furniture.

　　　保留形容詞（big）

對照副詞子句的精簡步驟（以上句為例）：

　　a. 保留從屬連接詞（Although）

　　b. 刪除主詞與 be 動詞（the room is）

　　c. 保留形容詞（big）或名詞，或將動詞改為動名詞

原句：Though he was an excellent student, he failed to pass the test.

精簡：Though an excellent student, he failed to pass the test.

　　保留名詞（student）

原句：While William works in the city, he lives in the country.

精簡：While working in the city, William lives in the country.

　　更改動詞（works）

　　時間、原因、對照副詞子句的精簡通常用在文章上，不在會話中。要注意精簡後的副詞片語雖然沒有主詞，但隱含著和主要子句的主詞是同一個。

4.2.3　名詞子句

　　名詞子句在文法的作用上可以看成子句型式的名詞，它和句子的其他部分是經由特定的字詞來連結，這些字包括：

連接詞	（if, that, whether…）
疑問詞	（Wh question words）
關係代名詞	（who, which, that…）

　　名詞子句在句子中可擔任的角色包括：主詞、受詞（在動詞之後）、受詞（在介系詞之後）、補語等。

　　當主詞的例子如下句中的名詞子句 All you have to do：

All you have to do is call, and I'll be there.

——Carol King (lyrics from "You've Got A Friend")

當受詞的例子如：

My mama always said life was like a box of chocolates.

——Forrest Gump

Wrinkles should merely indicate where the smiles have been.

——Mark Twain

第一句中的子句 life was like a box of chocolates 是動詞 said 的受詞；第二句中的子句 where the smiles have been 是 indicate 的受詞。當介系詞的受詞的例子如下句中的子句 what you do today，它是 on 的受詞：

> The future depends on what you do today.——Mahatma Gandhi

當補語的例子如下句中的 nobody can take it away from you：

> The beautiful thing about learning is nobody can take it away from you.
> ——B.B. King

4.2.3.1 名詞子句中 that 的省略

名詞子句的連接詞 that 在什麼情況下可以省略？基本原則是：名詞子句用作主詞時，不可省略 that；用作受詞時，可以省略 that。如：

> That you asked me so many questions shows me (that) you are really trying to learn.

句首的名詞子句 That you asked me so many questions 在主詞的位置，所以 That 不能省略；而句尾的名詞子句 that you are really trying to learn 是動詞 shows 的直接受詞，可以省略。

以下參考英語學家 Michael Swan (2016). *Practical English Usage*（4th ed.）. Oxford University Press，進一步說明相關可能：

1. 間接引述句

引述性動詞如 admit, agree, believe, claim, feel, know, say, suggest, think，可省略 that：

I thought (that) he likes baseball, but he said (that) he loves tennis.

另有一些動詞，則通常不省略 that，如 reply, shout 等：

He replied that he did not do it.

2. 在形容詞之後，通常可省略

I was surprised (that) he won the prize.

It's important (that) the press be independent.

3. 在名詞之後，通常不省略

There is a rumor that he hit the jackpot.

Do you regret the fact that you married me?

即使是在上述可省略 that 的情況時，最重要的還是要先考慮省略 that 是否會造成意義模糊，甚至誤會，如：

She believed Richard was a liar.

The doctor feels Nicole's leg will soon be better.

這兩句話乍聽之下，會先聽到 She believed Richard 以及 The doctor feels Nicole's leg，容易造成誤會，聽完全句後才會了解。但如果保留連接詞 that，讀者就清楚知道後面跟著的是一個子句（而不是單字 Richard 或片語 Nicole's leg），不會造成任何誤會：

She believed that Richard was a liar.

The doctor feels that Nicole's leg will soon be better.

許多時候，是否省略 that 是一個「選擇性」的問題，而不是「必要性」的問題。雖然，省略不必要的字可使文句簡潔，但有造成意義不清或文法錯誤的風險，而保留 that 則比較不會有危險。如果有任何疑慮時，建議還是保留 that。

此外，非正式英文中兩個字的連接詞如 now that, provided that, so that, such that 等，可省略 that。

這裡可以看到英文的一個有趣的（煩人的？）現象：一方面正規文法的規則與要求繁多，另一方面，日常英語的整體趨勢卻又是想方設法地簡化省略非必要的字詞。

4.2.3.2 名詞子句的精簡

名詞子句的精簡可大抵可分為兩類：1. 精簡為動名詞片語，2. 精簡為不定詞片語（請參考【3.1.6.5】不定詞與動名詞的抉擇：哪些動詞接動名詞？哪些動詞接不定詞？），簡略地說明於下：

1. 精簡為動名詞片語：

將名詞子句中的連接詞與主詞刪除，動詞改為動名詞，如：

原句：I remember that I visited you once.

精簡：I remember visiting you once.

2. 精簡為動不定詞片語：

將名詞子句中連接詞與主詞刪除，動詞改為不定詞，如：

原句：She asked me if I could help her.

精簡：She asked me to help her.

※ 練習題 – 句子種類　（請參考【附錄 2】的習題解答）

（　　）1. At the age of 39, Emmanuel Macron became the youngest President in the history of France.

    (a) simple　(b) compound　(c) complex

（　　）2. Taylor Swift is an American singer-songwriter, but Emma Thompson is a British actress and screenwriter.

    (a) Simple　(b) compound　(c) complex

（　　）3. As Prince Harry watched a volleyball match at the 2017 Toronto Invictus Games, a little girl sneakily swiped his popcorn.

    (a) Simple　(b) compound　(c) complex

（　　）4. A famous movie star was wearing a brown linen suit, a white shirt, a blue tie, dark sunglasses, and black loafers.

    (a) simple　(b) compound　(c) complex

（　　）5. Dustin wishes he could be younger, for everyone else in the program is half his age.

    (a) simple　(b) compound　(c) complex

（　　）6. If I get married someday, I hope to buy a house in the suburbs and plant a garden.

    (a) simple　(b) compound　(c) complex

（　　）7. Neither wind nor rain can stop the postal service from delivering the mail.

    (a) simple　(b) compound　(c) complex

(　) 8. Can I go home with you, so we can do our homework together?

      (a) simple　(b) compound　(c) complex

(　) 9. Leave while you can.

      (a) simple　(b) compound　(c) complex

(　) 10. The passengers and crew went through Customs and left.

      (a) simple　(b) compound　(c) complex

(　) 11. Matt drove to the park, and then he walked to the beach.

      (a) simple　(b) compound　(c) complex

(　) 12. The brown fox, which is next to the tree, jumped over the lazy dog quickly.

      (a) simple　(b) compound　(c) complex

(　) 13. With much consideration, he decided to study abroad.

      (a) simple　(b) compound　(c) complex

(　) 14. I am counting my calories, yet I really want dessert.

      (a) simple　(b) compound　(c) complex

(　) 15. Robert retired when he turned 65.

      (a) simple　(b) compound　(c) complex

辨別是否可省略 who, which, that, whose：

(　) 1. George Lucas, whose movies are popular, is a great filmmaker.

      (a) Yes　(b) No

(　) 2. That's the actor who was in The Godfather.

      (a) Yes　(b) No

(　) 3. She is the girl who we saw in the gym.

      (a) Yes　(b) No

(　) 4. That's the girl who you like.

      (a) Yes　(b) No

(　) 5. That's the boy who likes you.

      (a) Yes　(b) No

(　) 6. The customer who called me was unhappy.

(a) Yes (b) No

(　) 7. Have you seen the painting that they sold for 10 million dollars?

(a) Yes (b) No

(　) 8. This is the bag which I found in the sales.

(a) Yes (b) No

(　) 9. Where's the portable charger which was on the table?

(a) Yes (b) No

(　) 10. This jacket, which I found in the sales, was made in Italy.

(a) Yes (b) No

(　) 11. I have a good friend that I've known since elementary school.

(a) Yes (b) No

(　) 12. I've told him secrets which no one else knows.

(a) Yes (b) No

根據語言專家的研究，世界上有 6000 多種語言，每一種的文法都完整成熟，沒有所謂的正在進化中的文法。每種文法都有獨自的特性，最基本的差別之一是字詞排列的順序與規則。

語序的大架構是以主要元素（主詞 S、動詞 V、受詞 O）的順序來分類的，世界上前三名的語序為依次為：

我妳愛	SOV	→	韓文、日文、西班牙文
我愛妳	SVO	→	中文、英文、法文
愛我妳	VSO	→	阿拉伯文、愛爾蘭文

前兩名各大於 40%，第三名大於 10%。所幸，中文與英文同屬第二大語序 SVO（主詞＋動詞＋受詞），是我們學英文的一個幫助，但即使兩者的語序大結構屬於同一類，還是有許多字詞順序以及邏輯規則有很大的差別，這是本章討論的主題。

字詞順序大多數是相沿成習的，並非都是硬性規定，所以自然會有許多例外，但對學習者來說，先有個基本的認識，是會有幫助的。

5.1 基本順序

一個完整句子主要表達的含意不外乎：誰 Who、做了什麼 What、什麼地方 Where、什麼時間 When、什麼情狀 How、以及什麼原因 Why 等。簡單陳述句的常見順序如下：

Who + What + Where + When

Sherlock solved a tough case at home yesterday.

Watson bought a bowler hat in London last month.

Subject	What （Verb + Object）	Where	When
Sherlock	solved a tough case	at home	yesterday
Watson	bought a bowler hat	in London	last month

中文的語序則不同，通常會是 Who + When + Where + What（如：Watson 上個月在倫敦買了一個圓頂帽子）。

如果從詞類的角度來看，英文句子最主要的順序是：主詞→動詞→受詞。修飾性的單字、片語、子句則穿插其間或置於句首、句尾。

副詞通常不擺在動詞與直接受詞之間，如下例的副詞 wide 與副詞片語 very much：

He opened wide the door. → 錯

He opened the door wide. → 對

I like very much ice cream. → 錯

I like ice cream very much. → 對

5.2　直接受詞與間接受詞

有些及物動詞常跟著兩個受詞：直接受詞 direct object（DO）和間接受詞 indirect object（IO）。這類動詞如 buy, give, leave, pass, offer, sell, send, write 等。美式英語的順序多將間接受詞（通常指人）置於前，直接受詞（通常指事、物）置於後，如下：

A salesperson sold me a new TV.

I bought my mom a new TV.

第一句中店員賣的電視是直接受詞，me 是間接受詞。第二句中的直接受詞也是電視，my mom 是間接受詞。另種說法：

> A salesperson sold a new TV to me.
>
> I bought a new TV for my mom.

這兩句直接受詞在前，間接受詞在後，這樣的句型需要用介系詞（to, for 是最常用的兩個），介系詞之後的是間接受詞。

有少部分的動詞（如 admit, describe, explain, introduce, propose, return）只適用 DO + IO 的句型，如：

> The poet explained the poem to me.
>
> Could you change a $20 bill for me?

不能說成：

> The poet explained me the poem.
>
> Could you change me a $20 bill?

第二句會讓人誤會要把你換成 20 元了！

另外，當直接受詞是代名詞（如 it, them）時，也只能用 DO + IO 的句型，如：

I bought my mom it	→ 錯
I bought it for my mom.	→ 對

5.3　倒裝句法

英文是 SVO 型語言（主詞在前，動詞在後），一般只有「疑問句」會將主詞與動詞倒置，這是大家習慣的句型。但有些特殊的「陳述句」也是將主詞與動詞順序顛倒：（助）動詞在前，主詞在後，這種句型叫做倒裝句（inversion）。例如：

> With great power comes great responsibility.
>
> ——Spider-Man

句子的主詞其實是句尾的 great responsibility，倒裝之後比原來平淡的陳述（Great responsibility comes with great power.）要鏗鏘有力得多。這種刻意修辭性的倒裝句日常很少見，中文也有類似的倒裝句，多見於文學作品、詩詞中。

平時常會看到的倒裝句都受限於一些特殊句型，比較下面兩句：

> Brad Pitt starred in this film, and he also directed it.
>
> Not only did Brad Pitt star in this film, but he also directed it.

第一句是陳述句，第二句是倒裝句，意思也相近，但倒裝句顯得多彩。以下舉一些倒裝句的句型規則：

1. 否定副詞的倒裝

句首是帶有否定意味的副詞時，要用倒裝句型，如：

> Under no circumstances should you trust a lean cook.
>
> Seldom had they met such an intriguing person.

以第一句為例，句首的 Under no circumstances 為否定意味的副詞片語，助動詞 should 倒裝於主詞 you 之前。這類否定字詞包括 at no time, hardly, little, never, rarely, scarcely。

2. 句型 No sooner ～ than; Hardly（Scarcely）～ when

> 例句：No sooner had he reached the station than the train came.
>
> Hardly had he reached the station when the train came.

這兩個倒裝句都表示：我一到車站，火車就來了。要點：

a. no sooner 是比較級，與 than 配合。hardly 與 when 連用

b. 兩件事在過去發生，依據文法，先發生的事用過去完成式，後發生的事用過去式（雖然兩件事幾乎同時發生）

c. 然而，因為句中的 time words 讓事件發生的順序極為清楚，在非正式用法上，也可用過去式取代過去完成式，如 No sooner did he reach the station than the train came.

d. 也可以寫成 As soon as I reached the station, the train came.

3. 條件句的倒裝（省略 if）

    a. Conditional 2 的句型：

    Were it not for their assistance, our life would be difficult.

    = If it weren't for their assistance, our life would be difficult.

    b. Conditional 3 的句型：

    Had I known it was your birthday, I would've bought you a present. = If I had known it was your birthday, I would've bought you a present.

這種倒裝句型很正式，一般文句及口語中少見。

4. 地方副詞置於句首

地方副詞或片語的倒裝句常用在口語中，如：

    Here comes the bus, at last.

    There goes my money – my wife is shopping.

5. 驚嘆句

    例句：Isn't it a wonderful day today?

這個句子並不是真的疑問句，而是一種表示驚嘆的語法。

6. wishes/blessings

    例句：May the Force be with you!

也可以寫成如 I hope the Force will be with you. 但不像倒裝句那麼有力！

7. 其他（so, neither, nor）

    例句：I like the film and so does she.

           He doesn't like the boss. Neither do I.

           "I don't like that." "Nor do I."

5.4 附帶問句

　　附帶問句（tag questions）是一種特殊順序、特殊結構的句法，它多用在口語或非正式寫作中。英國人比較愛用這種句子。

　　附帶問句是在陳述句的句尾附加一個小的疑問短句（tag）。肯定陳述句要搭配否定的疑問短句；否定陳述句則搭配肯定的疑問短句。附帶問句的目的有二：

1. 提出疑問

　　需要對方確認提出的疑問。如果是談話，疑問短句句尾的音調要提高（rising intonation），如：

> You are coming to the party, aren't you?
>
> He fell in love with road cycling, didn't he?
>
> She's been teaching for a while, hasn't she?
>
> He's never at school, is he?
>
> You won't go without me, will you?

　　雖然句型中的陳述句與附加問句是相反的肯定與否定，但無論如何，回答仍與一般問句相同，以上面第一句為例，如果你要去，就回答 Yes, I am。如果不去，就回答 No, I am not.

2. 發表意見

　　用這種句型來發表意見。這時候雖然句中有個問號，但實際上僅是修辭的作用，不是問句，並不真的需要對方給答案，而是希望對方同意。如果是談話，疑問短句句尾的音調要降低（falling intonation），如：

> Teaching is rewarding, isn't it?
>
> It wasn't a nice day yesterday, was it?

5.5 先小後大

　　英文句子中如果包含大小不同的成分，如時間、地點等，它們的順序

要由小而大。中文正好相反，是由大而小。

時間的大小順序是：

The conference started at 9:00 AM on Thursday last week.

9:00 AM 最小，再來是 Thursday，最後是 last week。

地點的大小順序是：

He lives at No. 4, Lane 68, Section 2, Shuang-Shih Road, Taichung.（台中市雙十路 2 段 68 巷 4 號）

She lives at Apt. 1045, 9395 SW 77 Avenue, Miami, FL 33156.

注意：公寓號碼也可寫在街道之後（這反而更普遍），如：

9395 SW 77 Avenue, Apt. 1045（or #1045）

美式日期的寫法則稍有例外，例如 2020 年 10 月 18 日，英式是 18 October, 2020（18/10/2020），按照日、月、年的先小後大的順序。美式則是月份在前：October 18, 2020（10/18/2020）。世界上大多數國家的日期格式與英式相同，美國通常不按國際標準，其他如：重量、長度、體積、溫度、音標符號、紙張尺寸等，也都是如此。（註：如果在電腦檔案加註日期，反而是 20201018 比較方便日後作檢索）

5.6 分裂不定詞

不定詞（to ＋動詞原式）的字詞順序，曾引起很大的爭議，有著名的詞典編纂學家曾說：No other grammatical issue has so divided the nation. 這裡指的就是分裂不定詞（split infinitive）。

著名的影集 Star Trek 有句很有名的台詞：

To boldly go where no man has gone before.

其實，To boldly go 是舊時文法規則所不接受的，很多英文語言專家認為不定詞是一個整體（如 to go），不能分開，不能在中間加副詞 boldly，應該寫成 to go boldly。

這個舊規則已經過時，在現代英語中，分裂不定詞已經相當普遍，但是，正式文章中，使用 split infinitive 還是要謹慎，尤其不要在 to 與原形動詞之間加上很長的修飾片語，如：

I like to on a nice day walk in the woods.

這句話是不被接受的，可以改成：

On a nice day, I like to walk in the woods.

5.7　介系詞位於句尾

舊式文法有個關於字詞順序的規則：介系詞不能置於一個句子的尾巴（stranded prepositions）。preposition 這個字源於拉丁文，意思是「置於……之前」，而拉丁文的文法規定介系詞必須置於名詞之前，如果在句尾就不合這個規定了。這個舊規則已經過時了，現代英語早已不受此束縛，如下兩句句尾的介系詞 to, with，通順自然：

Who(m) were you talking to?

This is the sort of nonsense which I will not put up with.

如果依照舊式文法，則須改成：

To whom were you talking?

This is the sort of nonsense up with which I will not put.

第一句雖然文法沒問題，但日常生活中不會這樣說；第二句則是英國前首相邱吉爾因為不同意某些人過份強調介系詞不能置於句尾，而刻意造了這個怪句子來反諷舊文法規則。

5.8　錯置與虛懸的修飾語

任何修飾語（單字、片語、子句）都要注意擺放的位置，如果順序不對，句子的意義就模糊不明，甚至完全錯誤。

錯置修飾語（misplaced modifiers）是指修飾語擺錯了位置，距離它所修飾的字詞太遠，如：

> Eddy wore a bicycle helmet on his head that was too large.

這句話原意是說安全帽很大，但修飾語 that was too large 離 helmet 太遠，會被誤會為在形容 head，改成下面的句子就不會有誤會了：

> Eddy wore a bicycle helmet that was too large on his head.

再舉一例：

> The doctor told him that he was overweight this morning.

聽起來可能會誤會為他今早過重，顯然，原意應該是醫生在早上告訴他……，可改成：

> This morning, the doctor told him he was overweight.

有一位美國前總統曾說：

> I remember meeting a mother of a child who was abducted by the
> North Koreans right here in the Oval Office.

這句話讓人嚇了一大跳，因為 right here in the Oval Office 應該是要形容 meeting 的，但卻錯放在 the North Koreans 之後，聽起來像是在白宮橢圓形辦公室執行的綁架！原意是：

> I remember meeting, right here in the Oval Office, a mother of a
> child who was abducted by North Koreans.

5.8.2 虛懸修飾詞

虛懸修飾詞（dangling modifiers）和錯置修飾語實質上可以歸為一類，只不過，「虛懸」表示在它所修飾的字詞並不存在於句子中。寫作時最常

發生的虛懸修飾語是分詞片語，如：

　　　　Walking down the beach, the sunset was so beautiful.

　　乍看之下，好像通順（如果用中文思維，是沒問題的），但在英文的嚴謹結構下，是完全錯誤的。因為，分詞片語 Walking down the beach 原本是要形容主詞的，但主詞落日（sunset）是不可能自己走路的！顯然，Walking down the beach 所修飾的主詞並不在句子之中，需要額外加上主詞，可以改成：

　　　　Walking down the beach, she thought the sunset was so beautiful.

Walking down the beach 修飾 she（主詞），很合理。另外有一種不同的寫法：

　　　　While I was walking down the beach, the sunset was so beautiful.

　　這則是一個複雜句，有兩個子句，兩個不同的主詞。

CHAPTER 5 字詞順序

★5.9 中文視角 – 字詞順序

　　中文與英文在字詞順序方面存在不小的差異，我們要特別注意的地方包括：

　　1. 中英文語序大架構 SVO 相同，但字詞順序則相異。
　　2. 英文的時間與空間的敘述順序是從小到大；中文相反。
　　3. 美式的單位通常與國際用法不同，如：重量、長度、溫度等。

CHAPTER 6

寫作時常見的文法錯誤

　　保持主詞與動詞一致性（subject-verb agreement）是英文寫作的核心關鍵，中文沒有這樣的概念，因此容易出錯。重點是：一定先要確定主詞，再決定動詞。以下是一些應注意的地方：

1. 主詞是動名詞、不定詞、名詞子句時
　　→ 動詞要用單數

Downloading videos **takes too much time.**	→動名詞片語
To get good grades **is my goal.**	→不定詞片語
Whichever restaurant you pick **is fine with me.**	→名詞子句

　　主詞如果是複合名詞，要注意分辨那個是主詞，例如 Swimming lessons are quite popular in the summer. 中的 lessons 是主詞，所以動詞用 are。而動名詞 Swimming 在複合名詞中修飾 lessons，如同形容詞，不是主詞。

2. 複合主詞的多個元素用 and 連結時
　　→ 動詞要用複數

Olivia and I are going to visit Rome.

A good head and a good heart are always a formidable combination.　　　　　　　　　　　　——Nelson Mandela

當兩個名詞是描述同一個人或事時，則用單數，如下句中的 poet 和 novelist 指的是同一人（注意 novelist 前沒冠詞）：

The poet and novelist is dead.

3. 複合主詞的兩個元素用 either/or, not only/but also 等連結
   → 最靠近動詞的那個元素決定動詞的形式
   這意味著句子強調的重點是後者

Either he or I am right.	→ I 最靠近動詞
Neither Marie nor her sisters like doing dishes.	→ sisters 最靠近
Not only Al but also his friends are well over 190.	→ friends 最靠近

相關連接詞（either/or 等）所連結的是兩個成對的平行元素。
當一個元素是單數，另一個是多數時，最好將多數的元素置於
最後，避免混淆，如第二句的 sisters, 以及第三句的 friends。

4. 主詞包含不定代名詞
   a. 不定代名詞 anybody, anyone, each, every, everyone,
      much, neither, one, someone, somebody, something 等
      → 動詞要用單數
      Every one of my friends has a smartphone.
      Every boy and every girl in this class has applied TOEFL.
      Something is wrong with you today.

      注意：something 表示「某件事」，用單數動詞；some things
      　　　表示「一些事」，是複數，如：
      Some things are better left unsaid.

   b. 不定代名詞 few, many, others, several 等
      → 動詞要用複數
      Several of us are going to the movies.

c. 不定代名詞 all, any, most, none, some 等
　　→ 可單可複，視其後的主詞的性質而定

Some of the wine has been drunk.	→ 主詞：不可數
Most of his ideas are silly.	→ 主詞：可數複數

5. 主詞包含量詞
　a. 量詞 a number of, a few 等
　　→ 量詞之後要跟複數名詞，動詞用複數
　　A number of students were late for class.

　　注意：a number of 表示「一些」，是複數；the number of 則
　　　　　是指某種東西的「數量」，用單數動詞，如：
　　　　　The number of people lined up for the face masks was a
　　　　　hundred.

　b. 量詞 an amount of, a great/good deal of, a little 等
　　→ 量詞之後要跟不可數名詞，動詞用單數
　　There is a great deal of truth in what she said.
　　A small amount of salt, around a tablespoon or so, is enough.

　c. 量詞 a lot of, lots of, plenty of, 45 % of, 1/3 of 等
　　→ 視其後所跟的主詞的性質決定單數或複數動詞

A lot of flour is needed for that recipe.	→ 主詞：不可數，單數
Three-fourths of the cake has been eaten.	→ 主詞：可數單數
One-third of the drivers were texting.	→ 主詞：可數複數

6. 主詞表示一個特定的數量
　→ 動詞要用單數

Nine hundred kilometers is too far.	→ 主詞：900 公里
A million dollars is a lot of money.	→ 主詞：一百萬元

7. 集體名詞：audience, class, crowd, family, team …

→ 美式用單數，英式較用複數

15% of the population lives below the poverty line.	→美式

15% of the population live below the poverty line.　→英式偏多數

8. 主詞與動詞之間的附加片語

附加片語（常以介系詞開頭）如 along with, as well as, in addition to, together with 等

→ 動詞要跟著在句子前面的主詞

The earthquake, along with its aftershocks, has caused panic among the city's residents.

Marie as well as her brothers does not like doing dishes.

附加片語在文法上的作用是修飾主詞，並非用來形成複合主詞，所以，動詞要跟著在句子前面的主詞。

附加片語常被錯誤地視為和連接詞 and 同義。and 連結兩個同等重要的元素；附加片語的重心則是它前面的主詞，如第二句的重心是 Marie，不是 her brothers。

（註：在 not only/but also, not/but 的句型中，則強調的是後者，如 Ellen is not only intelligent but also funny. 重點在 funny）

9. 形容詞字句（關係子句）

→ 關係代名詞的先行詞決定動詞

Kevin gave me the letter, which was in a white envelope.

The boys who were lazy didn't win.

上兩句的關係代名詞是 which 和 who，代表的先行詞分別是 letter 和 boys，因此動詞分別用單數 was，與複數 were。

10. 主詞在動詞之後的句子

→ 先確定那個是主詞，再決定動詞的一致性

a. there is, there are

→ there 不是主詞，主詞在 be 動詞之後

There is an opossum in the yard.

There were a girl and a boy in the garden.

There is some milk in the fridge.

這 3 句的主詞分別為 an opossum（單數）、a girl and a boy（複數）、milk（不可數），因此，三句的 be 動詞分別是 is, were, is。

b. 其他主詞在動詞之後的情形

In the middle of chaos lies opportunity. ——Bruce Lee

Here come Laurel and Hardy.

Off in the corner sat Ed, Edd, and Eddy.

這 3 句的主詞分別為 opportunity、Laurel and Hardy、Ed, Edd, and Eddy，因此，三句的動詞分別是 lies, come, sat。

11. 不要被主詞與動詞之間的詞語誤導

The repetition of the drumbeats helps to stir motions.

Corruption of political operations causes the entire nation to suffer.

The library, with its collection of books, benefits the community.

第一句主詞是 repetition，動詞用單數的 helps，不要被後面的 drumbeats 誤導；同樣的，第二句的主詞是 Corruption，不是 operations；第三句的主詞則是 library，不是 books。

6.2 少用贅字贅詞

好的文章往往用詞配句都非常簡明直接，但因為英文不是我們的母語，我們常會希望盡力表達清楚，有時反而畫蛇添足，造成贅字贅詞，甚

至出錯，例如：

Although I really hate grammar, but it is extremely useful.

　　→刪除 Although，或刪除 but

中文說「雖然……但是」，但英文只選擇其一

Because I am a vegetarian, so I don't eat any meat.

　　→刪除 Because，或刪除 so

中文說「因為……所以」，但英文只選擇其一

一些贅字贅詞如下表：

贅述		精簡
50th-year anniversary	→	50th anniversary
advance forward	→	advance
at 8:30 PM tonight	→	at 8:30 PM
because of the fact that	→	because
blue in color	→	blue
completely finished	→	finished
contact with him	→	contact him
discuss about the problem	→	discuss the problem
end result	→	result
enter into	→	enter
final conclusion	→	conclusion
free gift	→	gift
fundamental basis	→	basis
future goal	→	goal
join together	→	join
longer in length	→	longer
new innovation	→	innovation
past history	→	history
repeat again	→	repeat
return back	→	return
small in size	→	small

summarize briefly	→	summarize
time period	→	time（or period）
true fact	→	fact
he is a man who is	→	he is
in a place where	→	where
at the present time	→	now
due to the fact that	→	because
I'll go with you together.	→	I'll go with you.
It is a fact that most of us like to be praised.	→	Most of us like to be praised.
I wish you have a happy New Year.	→	I wish you a happy New Year.
There are many people who play Sudoku online.	→	Many people play Sudoku online.
Welcome you to Taiwan.	→	Welcome to Taiwan.

中文也常有贅字，例如，有人會說「他做了一個關門的動作」，實在很累贅，門到底關上了沒？還是只做了一個動作？

6.3 句子的平行結構

平行結構能吸引讀者特別注意到文句中相互對稱的字詞（就如中文詩詞用對仗來表現修辭的對稱之美），如：

... government of the people, by the people, for the people, shall not perish from the earth. —— Abraham Lincoln

Ask not what your country can do for you; ask what you can do for your country. —— John F. Kennedy

上述第一句是片語的對稱，第二句是子句的對稱，優美地呈現平行的形式。即使是日常英文寫作，也應注意詞性、結構等的對稱性。

She loves to draw, dance, and playing mobile games.

　　draw 與 dance 是動詞，但 playing 是動名詞，詞性不平行，若將動名詞也改為動詞 play，會更順：

She loves to draw, dance, and play mobile games.

　　另舉一個例子：

Renee is beautiful, attractive, and has intelligence.

　　beautiful 與 intelligent 是形容詞，但 has 是動詞，詞性不平行，若都是形容詞，會更好：

Renee is beautiful, attractive, and intelligent.

　　當兩件事物在做比較或對照時，平行結構可以讓讀者更清楚地加以辨識，如下面句子中的不定詞 to postpone 與 to vote（在 speaking 時，比較或對照的字詞要唸得重）：

The board decided to postpone the motion rather than to vote on it.

　　句子中有相關連接詞子時，如 either/or, neither/nor, both/and, not only/but also, not/but, whether/or 等，要注意平行性：

We expected to be not only late but also exhausted.	→好
We expected not only to be late but also to be exhausted.	→次之
We expected not only to be late but also exhausted.	→不平行

　　如果描述一系列的項目，冠詞如 a, an 或代名詞如 his, her, their 等可以僅用在第一個項目，或者用在每一個項目：

We liked his courage, stamina, and style.	→平行
We liked his courage, his stamina, and his style.	→平行
We liked his courage, his stamina, and style.	→不平行

| He owns a car, motorcycle, bicycle, and skateboard. | →平行 |
| He owns a car, a motorcycle, a bicycle, and a skateboard. | →平行 |

> He owns a car, motorcycle, bicycle, and a skateboard.　　　→不平行

> I bought a laptop and antivirus program.　　　→不平行
> I bought a laptop and an antivirus program.　　　→平行

　　另外，也要注意句子中動詞語態的平行，如下述第一句是平行的兩個主動語態動詞；而第二句則不平行，因為兩個動詞中，一個是主動，一個是被動，不順：

> He prepared the speech last night and delivered it this morning.
> He prepared the speech last night, and it was delivered this morning.

　　在比較句中，也要注意對稱性，也就是，兩件事情是否可以相互比較，如：

> The forests of US are more extensive than UK.　　　→錯誤
> The forests of US are more extensive than those of UK　　　→正確

forests 要與 forests 相比較；forests 不能與 UK 比較。

6.4　短句的結合技巧

　　中文多短句，中文語意大多透過小短句來表達，這也反映在我們的英文寫作中。雖然，短句是英文寫作的一個不可或缺的方式，它具有強調的作用，常用來引發讀者的注目，但是，英文寫作很注重多樣化，句子有長有短，穿插簡單句、複合句、複雜句，太多的短句會降低文章的品質。對我們來說，如何結合短句成長句是練習寫作的重要課題。結合短句時要先決定那一個比較重要，至於那個短句比較重要，則大多取決於寫作者自己想表達什麼。結合的技巧分為兩大類：

1. 重要性相等的短句

a. 以相關連接詞（FANBOYS）來結合

短句甲：Web surfing is a wonderful escape.

短句乙：It interferes with my writing.

結　合：Web surfing is a wonderful escape, but it interferes with my writing.

b. 以連接副詞（consequently, however, therefore 等）來結合

短句甲：You must do your homework.

短句乙：You might get a bad grade.

結　合：You must do your homework; otherwise, you might get a bad grade.

c. 用分號來結合

短句甲：In youth we learn.

短句乙：In age we understand.

結　合：In youth we learn; in age we understand.

2. 重要性不等的短句

原則是將重要短句置於主要子句中；將次要資訊放在附屬架構的子句或片語中。

a. 將次要短句置於從屬子句中

短句甲：The alarm goes off.

短句乙：I hit the snooze button.

結　合：As soon as the alarm goes off, I hit the snooze button.

b. 將次要短句置於關係子句中

短句甲：My father goes swimming every day.

短句乙：My father is 86.

結　合：My father, who is 86, goes swimming every day.

c. 將次要短句改為同位語

短句甲：Karate is a type of martial arts.

短句乙：It teaches the art of self-defense.

結　合：Karate, a type of martial arts, teaches the art of self-defense.

d. 將次要短句改為分詞片語

短句甲：Ethan shouted with happiness.

短句乙：He celebrated the chance to interview at Amazon.

結　合：Shouting with happiness, Ethan celebrated his chance to interview at Amazon.

6.5 逗號的錯誤用法

據調查，逗號可說是美國人寫作時最大的問題之一，最常見的錯誤是 run-on sentences（連續句）：連接兩個或更多的獨立子句時，未使用正確的標點符號以及連接詞。連續句有兩類：

1. comma splice（逗號連接）
   兩個或多個子句僅以逗號連接，如：
   Usain ran a 100m dash, he loved it.
2. fused sentences（融合句）
   兩個或多個子句直接連寫在一起，如：
   Usain ran a 100m dash he loved it.

上述兩種狀況都包含兩個子句：Usain ran a 100m dash. 和 He loved it. 但連結的方式都錯了。依上節【6.4】所述，修訂的方法很多，僅舉兩例：

Usain ran a 100m dash, and he loved it. 　　　→ 複合句

Usain ran a 100m dash because he loved it. 　　→ 複雜句

在特殊情況下，短句有時可以只用逗號連接，包括（1）在非正式書寫、句子很短、不會被誤解時；（2）另外，文學作品、歌詞等，為了韻律，也可能只用逗號，如：

It was the best of times, it was the worst of times, it was ...

——Charles Dickens (from "A Tale of Two Cities")

6.6　不完整句

　　不完整句（sentence fragments）也是寫作時常見的錯誤之一。不完整句是一組字詞，但不成為一個完整的句子，因為它至少缺少了完整句的三項要素之一：

1. 主詞：句子的主角（人、事、物）
2. 動詞：主角在做什麼，或者，是什麼狀態
3. 一個完整的想法

不完整句通常以下列幾種形式出現：

1. 缺少主詞或動詞（or both）

Ran from his room, slamming the door behind him.　　→ 缺少主詞

A science fiction book on the table in his living room.　→ 缺少動詞

2. 雖有主詞與動詞，但只是從屬子句

The party was canceled. Because he had a car accident.

When you have time. Come and see me.

上面的 Because he had a car accident 與 When you have time 只是從屬子句，不是一個完整想法，不成句，可以改成：

The party was canceled because he had a car accident.

When you have time, come and see me.

3. 分詞片語常會被誤用為完整句

Mickey comforted Minnie. Terrified after watching a scary movie.

分詞片語 Terrified after watching…不成句，可改為：

Mickey comforted Minnie, terrified after watching a scary movie.

4. 其他：同位語、清單……

Boris displayed symptoms of COVID-19. Coronavirus disease 2019.

They love 1960s rock bands. Such as Beatles, Bee Gees, and Eagles.

第一句的 Coronavirus disease 2019.（同位語），第二句的 Such as Beatles, Bee Gees, and Eagles（清單）都不是完整的句子，可將句子中間的句號改為逗號：

Boris displayed symptoms of COVID-19, Coronavirus disease 2019.

They love 1960s rock bands, such as Beatles, Bee Gees, and Eagles.

要注意不完整句與文字的長短沒有直接的關係，很長的敘述仍可能不是一個完整句，而只是個片語或從屬子句；而很短的文字卻可能是一個完整句，如：He jumped. 或 She wept.。

在口語與非正式英文中，不完整句出現地極為頻繁，例如問：Why did you do that? 答：Because I had to. 另外，有些作家、廣告等會刻意地使用不完整句來增加修辭效果，這些都不在正式寫作的範圍內。

6.7 主動語態 vs. 被動語態

主動語態（active voice）句子中的主詞是動作的執行者，它的表達較為直接、明確、有力。被動語態（passive voice）顯得較薄弱，主要是因為它的主詞是動作的接受者，而不是執行者。大多數英語專家及教師都建議寫作時盡量用主動語態，不要濫用被動式，然而，也有不少情境則相當適合用被動語態，增加文章的多樣性。通常，使用被動式的情況包括：

1. 要強調的重點是動作的接受者

Mona Lisa was painted by Leonardo da Vinci.

Jurassic Park was directed by Steven Spielberg.

The Great Wall was built as a military defensive line to resist invasions.

2. 不知道是誰做的，或誰做的並不重要

My friend's car has been stolen.

My room is being painted.

A mall will be built nearby.

3. 動作的執行者明確，不須說明

She was born in 2001.	→ 媽媽生的
The mail has been delivered.	→ 郵差送的
The thief was arrested last week.	→ 警察抓的

4. 責任模糊化，避免遭質疑

Mom, my wireless earbuds were broken.	→ 小孩怕被罵
The decision has been made to increase taxes.	→ 政府怕被罵

有時候，用被動式是好意，例如你的書不見了，說 My book was taken. 這種方式比較隱晦，保護了拿書的人。口語中很少用被動式。

被動語態在科技文章中經常被使用，尤其是學術性論文，因為重點是執行過程與實驗結果，而不是誰是執行者，被動式正好可以突出這個角色，如：

10ml of distilled water was poured into a 100ml beaker.

主動語態與被動語態有時在字面上的差異很小，但意義上卻可能截然不同，如：

First come, first serve.	→ 錯誤
First come, first served.（FCFS）	→ 正確

FCFS 是常見的商家用語，表示先到的先「被」服務，第一句將 served 誤寫成 serve，會讓人以為先到的先服務別人。

中文的被動語態通常是用副詞「被」來輔助動詞，如：唐納被我痛罵了一頓。

及物動詞才可能有被動語態，不及物動詞沒有受詞，所以不會有被動語態，如 The accident was happened. 是錯誤的，應改為 The accident happened. 其他如 die, laugh, occur, reach, sit, sleep 等。

如果不及物動詞與介系詞連用時，介系詞之後得跟受詞，這樣就可以形成被動語態了，如下面例子中 laughed at 與 run over：

She laughed at me.	→ I was laughed at (by her).
A truck ran over a cat.	→ A cat was run over (by a truck).

正式文章中，使用動詞時，除了考量主動與被動的句型之外，也應盡量使用簡潔有力的動詞。通常，包含 be 動詞的片語較為缺乏活力，因為 be 動詞屬於非動作動詞，表達一種狀態，不直接執行動作。比較下面兩句：

Hiding assets is in violation of the tax laws.

Hiding assets violates the tax laws.

第二句的動詞 violates 比 is in violation of 簡潔有力。下表左邊列出幾個包含動詞的片語，比較冗長無力，可考慮以右邊的簡潔有力的單一動詞取代，如：

包含動詞的片語	單一動詞簡潔有力
conduct an investigation of	investigate
give assistance to	assist
have a discussion on	discuss
make payment to	pay
perform an analysis of	analyze

6.8 直接引述 vs. 間接引述

在寫作中，有時會引用其他人的話語或文字，來增添文章觀點的權威性或客觀性等，引用的方式分為直接引述（direct speech）或間接引述（indirect speech）。直接引述要用引號「…」（quotation marks），將原始話語放在引號裡，如果是完整句子，第一個字要大寫；間接引述基本上是把直接引述時所用的引號中的話語改為「名詞子句」。直接引述與間接引述的轉換如：

直接：He said, "I am hungry now."

間接：He said that he was hungry then.

直接："I did it last week," he confessed to her.

間接：He confessed to her that he had done it the week before.

直接：She said, "I've been waiting here for an hour."

間接：She said that she had been waiting there for an hour.

直接：The students said, "We will take an English class."

間接：The students said they would take an English class.

以上面句子為例，直接引述轉換成間接引述的步驟如下：

1. 拿掉逗號與引號
2. 調整引句主詞：如第一句的代名詞由 I 改為 he
3. 轉換動詞時態：如第一句的 am 改為 was，以與 said 相對應
4. 轉換時間副詞：如第一句中的 now 改為 then
5. 轉換地方副詞：如第三句中的 here 改為 there

下表列出時態序列（sequence of tenses）的轉換規則：

需轉換的時態序列

Direct quotation	需轉換	Indirect quotation
現在	→	過去
現在進行式	→	過去進行式
現在完成式	→	過去完成式
現在完成進行式	→	過去完成進行式
過去	→	過去完成式
can, may, will	→	could, might, would

也有些不需轉換的情況，如下表及例句：

不需轉換的時態序列

Direct quotation	不需轉換	Indirect quotation
過去完成式	=	過去完成式
unreal conditionals	=	unreal conditionals
should, could, might	=	should, could, might

直接：He said, "I had moved to the US before I learned English."
間接：He said he had moved to the US before he learned English.

直接：He said, "If I had more money, I would travel a lot."
間接：He said if he had more money, he would travel a lot.

直接：She told her students, "You should finish it today."
間接：She told her students that they should finish it that day.

時間副詞與地方副詞轉換的例子如下：

Direct quotation	需轉換	Indirect quotation
today	→	that day
tomorrow	→	the next（following） day
yesterday	→	the day before
last week	→	the previous week
next time	→	the next（following） time
here	→	there

如果引述的是個 Wh 疑問句（what, who, why, how……），須將疑問句改為陳述句（將問號改為句號），如：

直接：The teacher asked me, "How many days will you study?"
間接：The teacher asked me how many days I would study.

直接：He asked me, "Where did you visit?"
間接：He asked me where I had visited.

如果引述的是個 Yes/No 疑問句，間接句中要用 whether（or not），或者 if（註：if 不能與 or not 連用），如：

> 直接：Tom asked Jerry, "Do you like cartoon?"
> 間接：Tom asked Jerry whether he liked cartoon（or not）.
> 　　或 Tom asked Jerry if he liked cartoon.

一般而言，直接引述讓讀者的感受較強烈，但要確認引述內容的真確性。

6.9　嵌入式問句

嵌入式問句（embedded questions），是將一個問句嵌入一個主問句（母句）之中，如：

> What time did she leave?
> Could you tell me what time she left?

第一句是直接問句，第二句則將第一句嵌入了一個母句中。兩相比較，嵌入式問句用詞較委婉，比直接問句更禮貌、圓順。我們常犯的錯誤是未更改嵌入問句的字詞順序，而直接錯寫成 Could you tell me what time did she leave?

改變嵌入問句字詞順序的步驟如下（以上句為例）：

1. 將嵌入問句改為主詞＋動詞的順序（陳述句）
2. 將助動詞拿掉（如上例中的 did）
3. 將動詞改為適當的時式（如上例中的 leave → left）
4. 將改好的嵌入式問句放入母句中

除了放入主問句，嵌入問句也可以被放進陳述句中，這時，句尾要改為句點，如：

I'm not sure what time she left.

　　如果嵌入句是 Yes/No 問句，則置於母句中時需加入 whether（or not）或 if，例如：將嵌入式問句 Did she leave? 放入不同母句中：

I wonder if she left.	→ 陳述句
Could you tell me whether she left（or not）?	→ 疑問句

　　分裂句（Cleft Sentences）是將一個訊息分裂（cleft 的意思：一分為二）為兩部分，一部分為想要強調的重點（新資訊），一部分為次要訊息（舊資訊）。分裂句在 writing 與 speaking 都常見，在口語時，新資訊的音調要加重，舊資訊則平弱。分裂句有很多種句型，本節僅將簡單地介紹其中的幾種基本用法（it, wh, all）：

1. It cleft

　　It cleft 的句子通常是將一個簡單句分裂為兩個子句，變成了複雜句，其中，主要子句包含要強調的新資訊，附屬子句（關係子句）則是次要舊資訊。例如 Garfield ate my pizza yesterday 是個簡單句，但如果你要強調句中的某些字詞，則：

It was Garfield that ate my pizza yesterday.	→ 強調 Garfield
It was my pizza that Garfield ate yesterday.	→ 強調 my pizza
It was yesterday that Garfield ate my pizza.	→ 強調 yesterday

　　上面三句都是含有兩個子句的複雜句，基本句型是：

　　　　It is/was ＋強調的重點＋ that 子句

　　前面的主要子句中，動詞 is/was 之後的是強調的重點，其後的子句則是次要訊息。第一句強調的重點是 Garfield，子句 that ate my pizza 是

次要訊息（that 也可用 who）。

2. Wh cleft

Wh 包含 what, where, why, how 等，僅以 what 為例：

What they like is pearl milk tea.	→強調 pearl milk tea
What I want to know is how he got there.	→強調 how he got there
What I did was call the police.	→強調 call the police

What cleft 的基本句型是：

What 開頭的名詞子句＋ be 動詞＋強調的重點

3. All cleft

All I want for Christmas is you.	→強調 you
All I have to do is dream.	→強調 dream

All cleft 句型與 What cleft 類似。All 表示是唯一的選擇。

★ 6.11　中文視角－寫作

中英文寫作上概念的差異包括：

1. 英文必須保持主詞與動詞的一致性；中文沒有這種顧慮。
2. 英文：不過度使用相同的字詞；中文：較不要求。
3. 英文：不過度重複單一的句型；中文：較不要求。

※ 練習題－綜合題　（請參考【附錄 2】的解答）

(　) 1. (a) He wore jeans.　　(b) He wore a jean.

(　) 2. (a) My dad explained me the poem.

　　　　 (b) My dad explained the poem to me

(　) 3. (a) He got a high pay job.

(b) He got a high-paying job.

(　) 4. (a) This is a six-month course.

(b) This is a six-months course.

(　) 5. (a) Women commit less crimes than men.

(b) Women commit fewer crimes than men.

(　) 6. (a) How many advice do you have?

(b) How much advice do you have?

(　) 7. (a) It was so long ago.

(b) It was so long time ago.

(　) 8. (a) I have an advice for you.

(b) I have a piece of advice for you.

(　) 9. (a) She stopped him making a mistake.

(b) She stopped him from making a mistake.

(　) 10. (a) The boss let them leave work early.

(b) The boss let them to leave work early.

(　) 11. (a) She worked a lot in last week.

(b) She worked a lot last week.

(　) 12. (a) I usually get to home from work at 6:30.

(b) I usually get home from work at 6:30.

(　) 13. (a) I'm sorry. What was your name again?

(b) I'm sorry. What is your name again?

(　) 14. (a) I forget my hat at home.

(b) I left my hat in the house.

(　) 15. (a) He lent to me some money.

(b) He lent some money to me.

(　) 16. (a) I'm looking for Al. Has he gone to Iran?

(b) I'm looking for Al. Has he been to Iran?

(　) 17. (a) I have gone to Argentina.

(b) I have been to Argentina.

(　) 18. (a) If I will go, I will tell you.

(b) If I go, I will tell you.

(　) 19. (a) If I went, I would tell you.

(b) If I would go, I would tell you.

( ) 20. (a) She didn't save money enough.

(b) She didn't save enough money.

( ) 21. (a) I like coffee, he likes tea.

(b) I like coffee; he likes tea.

( ) 22. (a) We need to redo our garden completely.

(b) We need to completely redo our garden.

( ) 23. (a) Ask Tom to quickly come here.

(b) Ask Tom to come here quickly.

( ) 24. (a) It's rained = It is rained

(b) It's rained = It has rained

( ) 25. (a) Where are we?　　(b) Where are we at?

( ) 26. (a) He is our common friend.　　(b) He is our mutual friend.

( ) 27. (a) They go to church on Sunday.

(b) They go to church on Sundays.

( ) 28. (a) Let's meet next Wednesday.

(b) Let's meet on next Wednesday.

( ) 29. (a) Moon Festival falls on Friday this year.

(b) Moon Festival falls on a Friday this year.

( ) 30. (a) She said, "I am happy." = She said she is happy.

(b) She said, "I am happy." = She said she was happy.

( ) 31. (a) Cecilia and I are going to visit Paris.

(b) Cecilia and I am going to visit Paris.

( ) 32. (a) Here comes Bonnie and Clyde.

(b) Here come Bonnie and Clyde.

( ) 33. (a) Today morning I woke up late.

(b) This morning I woke up late.

( ) 34. (a) There is no room in the hall.

(b) There is no place in the hall.

( ) 35. (a) People are seated on a first come, first serve basis.

(b) People are seated on a first come, first served basis.

( ) 36. (a) She walks the dog every day, except Thursday.

(b) She walks the dog every day, except Thursdays.

( ) 37. (a) Has the film started yet?　　(b) Has the film been starting yet?

( ) 38. (a) What have you done? You're all wet.

(b) What have you been doing? You're all wet.

( ) 39. (a) How long have you been knowing her?

(b) How long have you known her?

( ) 40. (a) Neither you nor I am good at driving.

(b) Neither you nor I are good at driving.

( ) 41. (a) He has two son-in-laws.　　(b) He has two sons-in-laws.

( ) 42. (a) Get up early is good for one's health.

(b) Getting up early is good for one's health.

( ) 43. (a) You, he and I will do it together.

(b) I, you and he will do it together.

( ) 44. (a) They are sales at a furniture store.

(b) They are salespeople at a furniture store.

( ) 45. (a) They had no sooner arrived then they were arguing.

(b) They had no sooner arrived than they were arguing

( ) 46. (a) Take this medicine after meals.

(b) Eat this medicine after meals

( ) 47. (a) Do not make noise when you drink soup.

(b) Do not make noise when you eat soup.

( ) 48. (a) How's going?　　(b) How's it going?

( ) 49. (a) More people today die of cancer.

(b) More people today die of the cancer.

( ) 50. (a) Tell me why did you do that?

(b) Tell me why you did that.

( ) 51. (a) You like chocolate, isn't it?

(b) You like chocolate, don't you?

( ) 52. (a) Alex forgot his 20th wedding anniversary.

(b) Alex forgot his 20th-year wedding anniversary.

( ) 53. (a) I wish you merry Christmas and Happy New Year!

(b) I wish you a merry Christmas and a Happy New Year!

(   ) 54. (a) He has good knowledge of English grammar.

            (b) He has a good knowledge of English grammar.

(   ) 55. (a) He is so manly.   (b) He is so man.

(   ) 56. (a) Here are 10 tips to increase weight.

            (b) Here are 10 tips to gain weight.

(   ) 57. (a) I like apple.   (b) I like apples.

(   ) 58. (a) Justin is a mature man.

            (b) Justin is a matured man.

(   ) 59. (a) It happened a few hours before.

            (b) It happened a few hours ago

(   ) 60. (a) There is someone knock at the door.

            (b) There is someone knocking at the door.

在 speaking 時，我們可以視狀況選用停頓、加強、轉變等各種不同語調的表達方式，但在 writing 裡，我們就只能靠標點符號（punctuation）來協助，因此，它對於語意表達的重要性不言而喻，用錯了標點符號，不僅是瑕疵，往往會造成語意不清，甚或完全錯誤。

中文的標點符號，是 1919 年由胡適等人在前人的基礎上，參考西方國家的用法，訂出 12 種符號，提請教育部頒行的。有關標點符號最有名的故事就是「下雨天留客天天留我不留」了，有人用標點符號將這句話拆解，居然可以有 7 種方式，不過基本上，有兩種完全不同的解釋：

下雨天，留客天，天留，我不留。

下雨天，留客天，天留我不？留。

原本主人想攆客，不好意思開口，留了張紙條給客人，沒想到客人的文法技高一籌，用標點符號拆解，硬是留了下來。不管故事的真假，它說明了標點符號的重要性。英文也有類似的狀況，一個在網上有名的例子：

Let's eat Grandma.

這句話問題大了，如果加一個（,），就可救一條人命：

Let's eat, Grandma.

再舉個例子，有位英語文法教授在黑板上寫了一句話：

A woman without her man is nothing.

他要求學生加上標點符號，所有的男學生都改為：

A woman, without her man, is nothing.

所有的女學生都改為：

A woman: without her, man is nothing.

以下僅就幾個我們常遇到的英文標點符號簡略說明：

7.1　句號

一個英文句子只可以用 3 種標點符號來終結：

句號（.）
問號（?）
驚嘆號（!）

句號（period）是上述 3 種最常用的終結。根據一些語言性的實驗，華人在中文寫作時，對於句號（。）的用法不是掌握得很好，往往寫了一大段的文字，用了許多的逗號（，），最後才用一個句號結束。相反的，我們在寫英文時，因為喜歡用簡單句，整篇文章大多數都是用英文句號（.）。可以這麼說，寫中文時很逗，一路逗到底；寫英文時則很句（懂），一路句到底！

7.2　逗號

逗號（comma）表達句中訊息之間的停頓，增加節奏與清晰。有統計顯示句號與逗號是英文最常用的兩種標點符號，出現的頻率差不多（句號稍多）。而逗號是標點符號中最容易出錯的符號，其中最常見的錯誤是該加而未加逗號（missing a comma）。逗號的功能很多，主要有：

1. 分隔一系列對等的事或物

例句：She bought peaches, pears, lemons, and mangos.

在 and 之 前 的 最 後 一 個 逗 點 叫 做 serial comma 或 Oxford comma，美式英文普遍使用它，英式則偏向省略。省略逗點有時較易造成混淆，如：

I love my brothers, Ben, and Matt.
I love my brothers, Ben and Matt.

第一句表示你愛你的兄弟、和 Ben、和 Matt；第二句則可能被誤會成你愛你的兄弟，而你的兄弟是 Ben 和 Matt。

2. 分隔對等的獨立子句（用對等連接詞 FANBOYS）

例句：Give a girl the right shoes, and she can conquer the world.

——Marilyn Monroe

3. 分隔從屬子句與主要子句

例句：When you hit rock bottom, the only way is up.

4. 分隔非限定關係子句

例句：His grandfather, who is 80, still goes jogging.

5. 分隔同位語

例句：Michal Jackson, the King of Pop, died at age 50.

6. 分隔前導式片語 (Introductory Phrase)

顧名思義，它是在句首的片語，為整個句子先佈好舞台：

Thinking of the possible consequences, he decided not to sue her.
To stay in shape for competition, athletes must exercise every day.

兩句分別由分詞片語及介系詞片語開頭，常見的錯誤是片語之後少加了逗號。有時也可以是一個單字（通常是副詞）：

Finally, it's Friday.
Yes, I've made mistakes. Life doesn't come with instructions.

7. 分隔中斷詞（**Interrupter**）

中斷詞是在句子中加入一些字詞（表達情感、強調等），因而造成句子中斷，它的前後要加逗號（如果是口語，則要停頓）來凸顯它提供的資訊，如：

What you just ate, if you must know, was jellied moose nose.

Terry, as you know, is planning to go abroad next year.

8. 信頭稱謂語（**salutation**）

常用的信頭稱謂語如 Dear Luke,; Hello, Han,; Hi, Darth, 等，這樣的用法，Dear 是形容詞，Hello 與 Hi 是驚嘆詞。但一般常省略了 Hello 及 Hi 之後的逗號，而寫成 Hello Han, 或是 Hi Darth,，雖然較不符文法，可是似乎已經被大家接受，非常普遍，甚至超過了原來的寫法。

在非正式英文中，如果句首是簡短的片語或子句，趨勢是可省去逗號，但前提是意思很清楚，不會造成混淆，如：

When Yoda appeared(,) we started applauding.

Before eating, Leia always washes her hands with soap and water.

第一句因為子句簡短、句意清晰，可以省略逗號。第二句如果省略逗號，可能造成誤解，不該省略逗號。

逗號雖小，但有時對句子的意義影響巨大，例如：

Because I wanted to help, Rey, I pulled my car to the roadside.

Because I wanted to help Rey, I pulled my car to the roadside.

第一句表示你對 Rey 說：我因為想幫忙，所以在路邊停下車來。第二句則是：我因為想幫助 Rey，所以……。

7.3 分號

分號（semicolon ;）可以將兩個獨立子句連接，但這兩個獨立子句必須是對等子句而且密切關聯，如：

Dessert is the best meal of the day; it's definitely my favorite!

Europe doesn't have a true desert; it's the only continent without one.

使用分號時，第二句的第一個字不大寫。另外，兩個對等子句的連結可以用（1）分號＋連接副詞（2）逗號＋對等連接詞。下例的 otherwise 是副詞，or 是對等連接詞：

Hurry up; otherwise, you will be late for the train.

Hurry up, or you will be late for the train.

7.4　引號

引號（quotation mark " "）可用來標示引用的詞句。例如：

Shakespeare once said, "I cried when I had no shoes, but I stopped crying when I saw a man without legs."

引述句放在句首的例子如：

"Pass me the ball," Kobe shouted at his teammate.

句首的引述句要用逗號結尾（不是句號），並且將逗號置於引號內。引述句也可放在句子兩端，如：

"I would love to," she explained, "but I really ought to go home."

上句中 to 之後的逗號與 home 後的句號，都要放在引號裡，這是美式的用法。如果在引句中又有引句（a quote within a quote），美式用單引號。如：

"Did he say 'I love you' yet?" her mother asked.

英式與美式很不一樣，英式引句用單引號，引句中的引句則用双引號，而逗號與句號則放在引號之外（但如果原文中有標點符號，則放在引句裡）。

7.5 撇號

撇號（apostrophe '）的功能包括：
　　1. 所有格
　　　　a. 單數名詞，如 Zack's, cat's, someone else's, 2020's
　　　　b. 複數名詞，如 ladies', children's, women's, mice's
　　　　c. 複合名詞，如 mother-in-law's, post offices'
　　　　d. 不定代名詞，如 another's, someone's, no one's

　　2. 省略符號
　　　　a. 如 he's = he is/has, he'd = he had/would
　　　　　 what's = what is/has
　　　　　 who's = who is/has
　　　　b. '90s = 90s = 90 年代

　　在每年的 12 月，常見到有些廣告將聖誕節錯誤地簡寫為 X'mas，正確為 Xmas。

7.6 連字號

連字號（hyphen - ）的主要功能包括：
　　1. 斷字
　　　 文章常有每一行的右邊行尾邊界參差不齊，如要版面整齊，就得用連字號斷字，將一個字分為兩部分，分別置於行尾與下一行的行首。斷字通常只在音節之間分割。而單音節的字一般不斷字，如 stretched, strength, throbbed, through。遇到複合字時，如果本身就有連字號，則在連字號斷字，如 ex-ᵈᵉ wife, high-ᵈᵉ tech, mother-ᵈᵉ in-law, mother-in-ᵈᵉ law。

　　2. 複合字
　　　 由兩個（或以上）的字所組成，單字之間用連字號連接，如

名詞 father-in-law, long-term, mountain-climbing，以及形容詞 eighteen-year-old, up-to-date, well-known 等。

3. 前綴

有時在前綴之後加上連字號，alt-right, ex-husband, ill-tempered, mid-July, Neo-Nazism, post-truth, semi-naked 等等。

4. 數字（21-99）；分數

twenty-one … ninety-nine；nineteen forty-five（1945）
one-third; three-fifths, one-hundredth; two-thousands

★ 7.7 中文視角 – 標點符號

中文與英文在標點符號方面存在不小的差異，如：
1. 我們寫英文時常一路用句號，寫中文則常一路用逗號。
2. 英文標點最容易出錯的是逗號；中文較不易把握的是句號。

Part 3

字彙篇

英國著名的語言學家 David Wilkins 曾說：" ～ without grammar very little can be conveyed; without vocabulary nothing can be conveyed." 也就是說：沒有文法，寫不出什麼來；沒有字彙，什麼也寫不出來。

根據 1989 年出版的《牛津字典》（Oxford English Dictionary, OED）的統計，英文有 171476 個在用單字，老舊不用的有 47156 個單字，是世界上大體公認的單字最多的語言之一。

另外，英文在歷史演進上，曾與許多語言交流，據統計，單字約有 25% 源自於 Old and Middle English，約 28% 源自法文，另有約 28% 源自拉丁文，約 5% 源自希臘文，這樣不同字源的背景，更增加龐大字彙庫的複雜度。

除了龐大的字彙量之外，極多單字又有不同的意思，以及不同的詞類，以 run 來說，在 Oxford 字典中，名詞與動詞都各有 10 多個意思。而單字 like 可以用作 6 種詞類：動詞、名詞、形容詞、副詞、連接詞、介系詞。

CHAPTER 8　單字的形成方式

　　擴充英語字彙需要大量的記憶與練習，除了多看、多聽、多讀、多寫（最好能有外語環境）之外，有效的方法包括：

　　　　1. 多查各種字典，包括中英與英英字典
　　　　2. 多查同義字，練習用近義的字詞表達類似的意思
　　　　3. 以興趣（如書報、運動、影劇）出發，漸漸延伸擴展
　　　　4. 多了解外語母國的歷史文化、風俗習慣等
　　　　5. 放開母語，以外語思考（至少在上課或自修的時候）

　　上述的都是很好的增加單字的方法，都需要長時間持之以恒地去做，唯有如此，才能真正豐富你的字彙庫。

　　如果想在較短的時間內有效與有系統地擴充一些字彙，最好的方法之一是先對英文單字的生成與演化有個概念。英文在歷史上演進的過程中，單字的生成（word formation 構詞，即：從舊字造出新的字詞）方式很多，包括衍生、複合、轉換等等，其中，了解單字的衍生是公認的能在短時間內快速擴充字彙的方法之一。不過，建議初學者要先下功夫累積一定的字彙基礎後，再來探索單字的生成與演化，才容易吸收養分。

8.1　單字的衍生

　　衍生（derivation）的主要方式是新字由原字加上前綴（prefix）、後綴（suffix）而產生。許多單字可以從它的前綴、後綴、與字根（root），幫助你知道（猜到）它大概的意思，如果能對單字的語源（etymology）有些了解，更有效果。

在語言學中，單字中最小的、有意義的、不能再分的元素，叫做做詞素（morpheme，單字的組成元素）。以 discoverable 為例，它由前綴 dis、字根 cover、後綴 able 三個詞素組成，dis 代表「排除」，cover 是「遮蓋」，able 是「可」並且將詞性改為形容詞，所以，discoverable 表示形容詞「可發現的」。

前綴、後綴、字根常用連字號 (-) 註記，更可彰顯其意思，前綴 dis- 表示可在其後加字根，後綴 -able 表示可在前面加字根，字根 -cover- 表示前可加前綴、後可加後綴。

我們有個通俗的說法「有邊讀邊，無邊讀中間」，雖然與「前綴、後綴、字根」的意義相差很大，但僅就「利用單字的組成元素來幫助認識這個單字」這角度來說，也有相似之處。

8.1.1 前綴

前綴不能單獨存在，它最大的功能是改變原字的意思，但通常不改變原字的文法詞性，如：

前綴		源自	例子	意思
anti-	相反	希臘	antiseptic	a. 消毒劑
chrono-	時間	拉丁	chronology	n. 年表
de-	分離	拉丁	denuke	v. 無核化
dis-	不	拉丁	disagree	v. 不同意
extra-	額外	拉丁	extraordinary	a. 特別的
inter-	相互	拉丁	interact	v. 互動
intra-	內部	拉丁	intramural	a. 同一校內的
hyper-	高	希臘	hypertension	n. 高血壓
infra-	下	拉丁	infrastructure	n. 基礎建設
macro-	大	希臘	macromolecules	n. 大分子
micro-	小	希臘	microscope	n. 顯微鏡
para-	旁	希臘	paramedic	n. 醫務輔助人員
omni-	全	拉丁	omnipotent	a. 全能的
re-	再次	拉丁	remix	n. v. 混音
super-	超	拉丁	superimpose	v. 加上去

sym-	共同	希臘	symphony	n. 交響樂
syn-	共同	希臘	synchronize	v. 同步
trans-	跨	拉丁	transgender	n. a. 跨性別（者）

以 re- 為例，用作前綴可以當 again 的意思，常見的單字如 reassure, rebuild, recreate, redo, regain, reproduce, revisit, rewind，可見前綴應用的廣泛。要注意：如果單字中有連字號，意思與合為一體的字可能不一樣，如 reform 是「改革」，但 re-form 則是「重新製作」。

有些前綴加在原字之前可以否定原來的意思，這樣的前綴如 un-, il-, im-, in-, ir-, dis- 等，例子：happy → unhappy, legal → illegal, possible → impossible, active → inactive, regular → irregular, like → dislike 等。原則上，im- 加在 b,p,m 等閉唇音之前，如 imbalance, impure, immoral；il- 加在 l 開頭的字之前，如 illogic；ir- 加在 r 開頭的字之前，如 irrelevant。

前綴通常不會改變原字的文法詞性，譬如，tidy 是形容詞，加上前綴 un- 成為 untidy，仍然是形容詞。但少數的前綴會改變文法詞性，如 embody 的前綴 em-，將 body 從名詞變為動詞；enlarge 的前綴 en-，將形容詞 large 變為了動詞。

有些英文單字用拉丁前綴，有些則用希臘前綴，增加了字彙的複雜度。以數字 1 到 10 來說，舉例如下表：

數字	前綴	語源	例子	中文
1	uni-	拉丁	unicorn	獨角獸公司
	mono-	希臘	monopoly	獨佔專賣
2	bi-, duo-	拉丁	biceps	二頭肌
	di-	希臘	dilemma	兩難
3	tri-	拉丁	tripod	三腳架
	tri-	希臘	triathlon	三鐵運動
4	quadri-, quart-	拉丁	quarter	四分之一
	tetra-	希臘	tetrahedron	四面體
5	quint-	拉丁	quintet	五重奏（唱）
	penta-	希臘	pentagon	五角大樓
6	sex-	拉丁	sextuple	六倍
	hex-	希臘	hexadecimal	十六進位

7	sept-	拉丁	September	9 月
	hept-	希臘	heptathlon	七項運動
8	oct-	拉丁	October	10 月
	oct-	希臘	octopus	八爪章魚
9	novel-	拉丁	November	11 月
	ennead-	希臘	enneagon	九角形
10	dec-, de-	拉丁	decimal	十進位
	dec-	希臘	decathlon	十項運動

　　September, October, November, December 的拉丁前綴代表 7, 8, 9, 10，那為什麼會是 9, 10, 11, 12 月呢？簡單的說，在古代的羅馬日曆，它們的確是 7, 8, 9, 10 月，後來經過兩次修訂重排，由最早的 Roman Calendar 改為 Julian Calendar，再改為沿用至今的曆法 Gregorian Calendar，過程中產生了些更動，又為了紀念 Julius 與 Augustus 這兩位凱撒，將 7 月定為 July，將 8 月定為 August，因此，後面的 4 個月份被順延兩個月，September, October, November, December 就這樣被變成了 9, 10, 11, 12 月。

8.1.2 後綴

　　後綴不能單獨存在，它最大的功能是改變詞性，如：

單字	後綴	功能
hospital-ize	-ize	名詞→動詞
friend-ly	-ly	名詞→形容詞
establish-ment	-ment	動詞→名詞
attract-ive	-ive	動詞→形容詞
real-ity	-ity	形容詞→名詞
ampl-ify	-ify	形容詞→動詞
slow-ly	-ly	形容詞→副詞

　　常見的動詞後綴如 -ize, -ify, -en；常見的名詞後綴如 -ment, -ity, -ation, -ism, -ness；常見的形容詞後綴如 -al, -able, -ant, -ative, -ish, -less, -ous；而最常見的副詞後綴是 -ly。

有時候，suffix 也會改變原字的意思，如 teach-er 由 teach（動詞）改變成老師；social-ist 由 social（形容詞）改變成社會主義者；king-dom 由國王改變成王國。

文法上單字的詞形變化如：單複數、時態、比較級等，絕大時候是以 suffix 表示，如：加 s 表示複數、加 ed 表示過去式、加 ing 表示進行式、加 est 表示最高級等等。

英文除了前綴、後綴，還有很罕見的中綴 infix，例如 passerby 的多數形是 passersby，因為單字 passer 的多數是 passers。

中文也有前綴與後綴，是以單字的形式表現的，前綴如：非賣品、非正式、非婚生的「非」；後綴如：科學、文學、形而上學的「學」。

8.1.3 字根

字根是不能再加以細分的單字的基本形式（base form）。字根可能出現在一個單字的不同位置上，它可以是一個獨立存在的有意義的字，也可能需要與其他字結合，才有意義（前綴與後綴則必須依附著字根才能存在）。大多數的字根是源自 Latin 和 Greek，如：

字根	意思	源自	例子
cycle	圓形、環繞	希臘	bicycle, tricycle Cyclops, recycle
graph	寫、畫	希臘	autograph, photograph phonograph, telegraph
lect	選擇	拉丁	collect, elect neglect, select
scope	看	希臘	microscope, periscope stethoscope, telescope
scrib, script	寫	拉丁	describe, inscribe manuscript, transcript

字根 cycle 源自希臘的 kuklos 'circle'，代表圓形，前綴 bi- 代表兩個，tri- 表三個，bicycle 是二輪車，tricycle 是三輪車。

如上所述，衍生是單字生成最多的方式，還有不少其他的方式，簡述如下：

複合

複合（compounding）是由兩個（或多個）單字組合成新字，通常是經過長期的演化。有的複合字是在兩個字中間加連字號，這類的字如果常被使用，會拋開連字號，進化成一個字，近年來的例子如 electronic mail → e-mail → email；on line → on-line → online。這兩個字被用地太頻繁，因此演化時程很短，屬於特殊狀況。

複合字有許多詞類的可能，包括：

複合字	
名詞	airplane, baseball, brainstorm, doublespeak, cowboy, great-grandfather, honeymoon, mother-in-law, president-elect, raincoat, superman, toothache, weekday
形容詞	airsick, good-looking, heartbreaking, mass-produced, self-taught, sugar-free, well-known, water-proof
動詞	double-click, baby-sit, oven-bake, chain-smoke
副詞	good-naturedly, nevertheless, sometimes, thereafter

大部分這類字從字面上即可看出它的意思，譬如 computer-aided 是電腦輔助。但是，也有不少例外，如 greenhouse 是培養植物的溫室，分開寫 green house，才是綠色的房子。

中文有極多的複合詞，如新車、地震、收視率等，其中以兩個字的複合詞最多。和英文一樣，有的詞可以由組成的單字讀出它的意思，有的則否，例如「鬧新房」中的「新房」並不一定指「新建的房屋」。

轉換

不經任何形態變化，直接由原字轉換（conversion）成該字的其他詞類，如：

詞類轉換		
chair　　n. 主席	名詞→動詞	v. 主持
email　　n. 電郵		v. 電郵
Google (google)		v. 網上搜尋
text　　n. 本文		v. 傳訊息
cook　　v. 做菜	動詞→名詞	n. 廚師
dry　　a. 乾的	形容詞→動詞	v. 弄乾
down　adv. 向下	副詞→動詞	v. 吞下
model　　n. 模範	名詞→形容詞	a. 模範的

　　這種詞類轉換演化在近年最明顯例子包括 email 原先是名詞，現在也可當動詞；Google 是公司名，現在也可用作動詞的搜尋（小寫 google）。

修剪

　　修剪（clipping ）與縮寫（abbreviation）的意思類似，例如：

縮寫	詞類轉換	原字
app	剪掉字尾	application
bra		brassiere
disco		discotheque
fax		facsimile
gym		gymnasium
copter	剪掉字首	helicopter
gator		alligator
wig		periwig
flu	前後裁減	influenza
fridge		refrigerator
pub	片語裁減	public house

　　很多字詞經過充分演化，已融入生活中，人們已不再介意起源了，如：o'clock 是由 of the clock 縮減演變的；jack-o'-lantern 則是 Jack of the Lantern 的縮減。

Initialism

Initialism 指的是將一個片語的幾個單字的第一個字母連接起來，形成新字，須一個字母一個字母地讀，，如：

不能連在一起讀	意思
AI	Artificial Intelligence
CIA	Central Intelligence Agency
OMG	Oh My God
MPH	Miles Per Hour
NYC	New York City
PPE	Personal Protective Equipment
TBA	To Be Announced
VIP	Very Important Person

Acronym

Acronym 和 Initialism 定義相同（也有人將兩者均歸為 acronym），只不過，它是要連起來讀的，如：

連起來當字讀	意思
AIDS	Acquired Immune Deficiency Syndrome
DAEMON	Disk And Execution MONitor
LOL	Laughing Out Loud
NASA	National Aeronautics & Space Administration
POTUS	President Of The United States
SCUBA	Self Contained Underwater Breathing Apparatus

LOL 可連著唸也可分開唸，都有群眾。使用 acronym 要小心，有人在友人逝世時發了短訊給友人的親戚，為了跟上時代，結尾時寫上 LOL（也可以是 Lots Of Love），造成誤會。

Acronym 在英語中用的非常廣泛，各行各業都在用，因此，要注意一個 acronym 可能代表的意思極多，在不同的領域有不同的解釋，例如，大家都知道 AI 是 Artificial Intelligence，但它也可能有其他的意思，如 American Idol（TV show）, Amnesty International, Appreciation Index,

Artificial Insemination……。

Blending

Blending 是將兩個字各取一部分，合成另一個具有新的意思的字，通常稱為 portmanteau word（合成字），又稱為 frankenword（Frankenstein 與 word 的合成）或者是 centaur word。日常生活中常見到這類單字，尤其是和現代科技有關的，如：

連起來當字讀	意思	意思
bionics	biology + electronics	仿生學
blog	web + log	部落客
camcorder	camera + recorden	攝影機
cyborg	cybennetic + organism	半機械人
email	electronic + mail	電郵
freeware	free + software	免費軟體
Internet	international + network	網際網路
Linux	Linus + Unix	
malware	malicious + software	惡意軟件
netizen	network + citizen	網民
pixel	pix + element	像素
Skype	sky + peer-to-peer	
vlog	video + blog	影片部落格
Wi-Fi	wireless + fidelity	無線熱點

其他日常生活的例子：

Portmanteau	Two words	中譯
affluenza	affluence + influenza	富貴病
Bollywood	Bombay + Hollywood	寶萊塢
Brexit	British + exit	英國脫歐
bromance	brother + romance	兄弟情
brunch	breakfast + lunch	早午餐
burkini	burqa + bikini	布基尼
cellfish	cellphone + selfish	手機＋自私

cheeseburger	cheese + hamburger	乳酪漢堡
cosplay	costume + play	角色扮演
cronut	croissant + donut	可頌甜甜圈
dramedy	drama + comedy	劇情喜劇
dumbfound	dumb + confound	目瞪口呆
edutainment	education + entertainment	寓教於樂
emoticon	emotion + icon	表情符號
Eurasia	Europe + Asia	歐亞
facekini	face + bikini	臉基尼
froyo	frozen + yogurt	霜凍優格
glamping	glamor + camping	豪華露營
hangry	hungry + angry	又餓又氣
jeggings	jeans + leggings	牛仔緊身褲
motel	motor + hotel	汽車旅館
motorcycle	motor + bicycle	摩托車
Oxbridge	Oxford + Cambridge	牛津劍橋
phubbing	phone + snubbing	低頭滑手機
sci-fi	science + fiction	科幻小說
sitcom	situation + comedy	情境喜劇
smog	smoke + fog	煙霧
spork	spoon + fork	叉匙
telethon	television + marathon	電視馬拉松
workaholic	work + alcoholic	工作狂

　　微軟公司 Microsoft 是兩個字 microprocessor 和 software 的組合；Intel 是和 integrated 和 electronics 的組合。

　　sitcom 是指系列電視劇，基本上每集故事不同，但都在同一場景，如公寓或餐廳；telethon 是長時間的電視節目，大多數是為了慈善募資。

Borrowing

　　有非常多的英文單字是從其他語言轉借而來，包括約 28% 源自法文，約 28% 源自拉丁文，約 5% 源自希臘文，還有許多其他語言。舉些通俗的

例子：

源自	例子
法文	a la carte, ballet, café, cuisine, resume
拉丁文	agenda, alias, cancer, circus, e.g., July, August
希臘文	Amazon, echo, marathon, narcissus
德文	Autobahn, hamburger, kindergarten, waltz
中文	cha, dim sum, ketchup, Kung fu, tofu
日文	karaoke, karate, origami, sushi, tsunami
梵文	Avatar, Buddha, guru, karma, nirvana

西元 1066 年，法國諾曼地公爵（Duke of Normandy）征服英國，加冕為英王威廉一世（William the Conqueror），法語因而成為英國政府及上層階級的語言約三百年之久，至今仍是英文的最大外來語源之一。

拉丁（羅馬）與希臘對英文的影響自然不在話下，非但英文，西方文明也處處有他們的影子，其中，希臘與羅馬神話就扮演很大的角色，以我們每天都會接觸到的月份與星期的名稱來說，幾乎都源自希臘與羅馬神話。希臘神話與羅馬神話基本上是一一對應，故事類同，一般認為希臘神話在先，羅馬神話在後。這些神明非常的人性化，七情六慾樣樣有，通常，希臘神比羅馬神更人性化，甚至更荒唐淫蕩。神話中有極多各類的神，祂們的名字在兩種語言中當然不一樣，因此，也對應著兩種不同的英文名稱。

有些月分和星期的名稱源自臘羅馬神話，如：

月分或星期	源自羅馬神	神	對應的希臘神
January	Janus	門神	
March	Mars	戰神	Ares
May	Maia	女神	Maia
June	Juno	天后	Hera
Saturday	Saturn	農神	Cronus

月份 February, April 雖不是源自神的名字，但都出自 Roman Calendar；至於 7-12 月，則已在【8.1.1】節說明過了。Tuesday, Wednesday, Thursday, Friday 源自北歐神話，但也都可以追溯到拉丁的傳承，如 Thursday 是依北歐的雷神 Thor 命名，而 Thor 又可以對應到羅馬的主神 Jupiter（掌管打雷

閃電）。星期天Sunday來自sun，Monday來自moon，也都有拉丁字的源頭。

　　九大行星的名字源自羅馬神話中的幾位特別重要的神（天王星是唯一以希臘神命名的行星），下表列出地球外的八大行星：

星座	星座名	源自羅馬神	特色	對應的希臘神
金星	Venus	愛神	最亮	Aphrodite
木星	Jupiter	主神	最大	Zeus
水星	Mercury	信差神	離太陽最近	Hermes
火星	Mars	戰神	最紅	Ares
土星	Saturn	農神	有土星環	Cronus
天王星	Uranus	天神	唯一希臘神	Uranus
海王星	Neptune	海神	最藍,	Poseidon
冥王星	Pluto	冥王	最黑最遠	Hades

其他

　　有些字源自地名、人名、神話、聖經、品牌名等等，如：

單字	中譯	源自
bikini	比基尼	地名
cantaloupe	哈密瓜	
china	瓷器	
jeans	牛仔褲	
marathon	馬拉松	
tuxedo	晚禮服	
boycott	抵制	人名
guillotine	斷頭臺	
jacuzzi	按摩浴缸	
lynch	私刑	
sandwich	三明治	
saxophone	薩克斯風	
sideburns	絡腮鬍	

Amazon	亞馬遜	神話
cereal	麥片	
chaos	混亂	
echo	回音	
music	音樂	
odyssey	漫長旅程	
abacus	算盤	聖經
apocalypse	末日	
babble	說話模糊	
scapegoat	替罪羊	
sodomy	雞姦	
google v.	網上搜尋	品牌名
xerox v.	影印	

★8.3 中文視角－單字生成

中文與英文在單字生成方面的差異很大，我們應注意：

1. 對英文單字的生成方式以及語源的認識對擴充字彙有幫助。
2. 多了解前後綴及字根是短時間內快速增加字彙的方法。
3. 英文受西方各語言的影響很大，特別是法文拉丁希臘。
4. 一個 acronym 可能有多種不同的意思，要謹慎。

　　每種語言都有自己獨特的表達方式，本章所謂「特殊的」字詞指的是我們可能比較不習慣的一些英文字詞，尤其是在中文思維裡不熟悉的表達方式。

9.1　字詞搭配

　　很多字詞的搭配（collocation）是習慣成自然，常常沒有為什麼，這正是困難的地方。美國人說 up north, down south, back east, out west。我們習慣說東南西北，沒人會說西東北南。

　　許多語文專家認為，具備靈活運用搭配詞彙的能力是任何語言要說寫流利及準確的主要關鍵之一。

　　形容雨大時，中文的思維會翻成 big rain，美國人說 heavy rain；吃藥是 take medicine，我們可能會說 eat medicine；洗衣服是 do the laundry，不是 wash the laundry；常聽到 cost down，應該是 reduce costs。這些都是受到了母語直譯的影響。

　　同樣地，美國人學中文時當然也會受他們母語的影響，譬如將戴眼鏡講成「穿眼鏡」，是 wear glasses 的直譯；將喝湯講成「吃湯」，顯然來自 eat soup。我們聽得懂，但味道不一樣！

　　下表是日常一些單字、片語、短句的中式思維與英文語法的對照。美國人可能也聽得懂中式思維，但不會那樣說：

	中式思維	英文說法
預先付款	advanced payment	advance payment
好消息	a good news	good news

保母	baby sister	baby sitter
大霧	big fog	thick/heavy/dense fog
大風	big wind	strong/high wind
雞腿肉	black meat	dark meat
吹長笛	blow the flute	play the flute
身體健康	body is healthy	is in good health
露營很好玩	camping is funny	camping is fun
便宜	cheap price	low price
關燈	close the light	turn off the light
恭喜	congratulation	congratulations
便利商店	convenient store	convenience store
降低成本	cost down	reduce costs
喝湯	drink soup	eat soup
吃藥	eat medicine	take medicine
到外面吃飯	eat outside	eat out
覺得生病	feel uncomfortable	not feel well
亞洲四小龍	Four Asian Dragons	Four Asian Tigers
加薪	get more salary	get a raise
拜訪你	give you a visit	pay you a visit
給你	give you	here you go
全球暖化	global heating	global warming
考了 85 分	got 85 points	got an 85
他有男子氣概	he's so man	he's so manly
總部	headquarter	headquarters
想家	home sick	homesick
怎麼拼…	How to spell …?	How do you spell …?
貴賓	honor guest	honored guest
你好嗎	How's going?	How's it going?
我怕冷天氣	I'm afraid of cold weather	I don't like cold weather
我很興奮	I am high	I am excited
我剪頭髮了	I cut my hair	I got my hair cut
我有個疑問	I have a problem	I have a question

我很喜歡妳	I very like you	I like you very much
我很丟臉	I lost my face	I lost face
我要化妝	I'll make up	I'll put on make-up
我載你去	I'll ride you there	I'll take you there
我煩了	I'm boring	I'm bored
我對…感興趣	I'm interesting in	I'm interested in
增重	increase weight	gain weight
很痛	It's so hurt	It hurts (so much)
參加考試	join an exam	take an exam
參加派對	join a party	go to a party
洛杉磯湖人隊	LA Laker	LA Lakers
現場轉播	life broadcast	live broadcast
淡季	light season	low season
聽我講	listen me	listen to me
住在飯店	live in a hotel	stay at/in a hotel
沒關係	no mind	no worries
古老歷史	old history	ancient history
開支票	open a check	write a check
開燈	open the light	turn on the light
開戰	open war	wage war
異地會議	outside meeting	off-site meeting
超車道	passing line	passing lane
和朋友出去玩	play with friends	hang out with friends
貼文	po	post
平行會議	parallel sections	parallel sessions
嫉妒的	red eyed	green eyed
紅糖	red sugar	brown sugar
紅茶	red tea	black tea
減重	reduce weight	lose weight
榜樣	road model	role model
搽香水	rub perfume	wear perfume
售貨員	sales	salesperson

她很時尚	she is so fashion	she is so fashionable
酸雨	sour rain	acid rain
小吃	snack	street food
濃妝	thick makeup	heavy makeup
濃茶	thick tea	strong tea
喉嚨痛	throat ache	sore throat
白麵包	toast	bread
兩百元	two hundreds dollars	two hundred dollars
等我	wait me	wait for me
溫室效應	warm house effect	greenhouse effect
看報紙	watch newspapers	read newspapers
穿太少	wear too less	wear too little
發生了什麼事	What's happen?	What happened?
白髮	white hair	gray hair
寫日記	write a diary	keep a diary

非但搭配詞，有些常用的單字也容易受到中文思維的混淆，譬如：

1. borrow/lend

在中文裡，借錢給別人或向別人借錢，都可以用「借」，這可能混淆我們對 borrow 和 lend 的了解，borrow（from）是向別人借錢，lend（to）是借錢給別人，不能混為一談。

A bank is a place that will lend you money if you can prove that you don't need it.　　　　　　　　　　　　—— Bob Hope

English seems to have borrowed words from many languages.

2. hear/listen；talk/speak

hear 與 listen 的中文都是「聽」，英文的 hear 是自然的感官聽覺；listen 是有意識的行為，專注的聽（後面有受詞時要用 listen to）。talk 與 speak 都是「講」，talk 是非正式氛圍，著重在與他人對話；speak 較正式，著重發表的個人。

I saw....people talking without speaking, hearing without listening.

—— Simon & Garfunkel
(lyrics from "The Sound of Silence")

I am listening but I can't hear anything.

3. see/look/watch

三個字的中文都是「看」，而英文的 see 是自然感官視覺；look
表示專注地看（有受詞時與 at 連用：look at）；watch 是專注
看一段時間。

I'm looking but I don't see it.

They watched the house all night but nobody entered or left.

另外，看電影可翻成 see a movie，這表示去電影院看電影，如
在家中電視上看電影，則用 watch a movie。

4. rise/raise

中文都是「升」，rise 是自然升起，是不及物動詞，沒有受詞；
raise 是受外力而升，是及物動詞，必有受詞。

As the sun rose in the sky, the temperature climbed.

We're having a lottery to raise money for homeless families.

9.2　一字多義

下表列出一些中小學程度的單字，但是，每個單字都可能有我們沒注
意到的解釋（如 doctor 是醫生，但當動詞時，意思是「竄改」）。表中的「第
一義」是大家都熟悉的解釋，「另一義」則是我們可能比較不熟悉的意思
或詞類，但絕大多數都曾出現於近年英美主流媒體，也就是說，它們都是
活的。

表中的很多單字還有許多其他的解釋，為了簡潔，只各選一個解釋列
於「第一義」與「另一義」。即使僅列出一個解釋，在這個解釋之下，也
可能有好幾種詞類，以單字 row 來說，在當作「爭吵」/raʊ/ 時，可作名
詞，也可作動詞，這裡也僅列出一個詞類。（n. 名詞，v. 動詞，a. 形容詞，
adv. 副詞）。

	第一義	另一義
aside	(adv.) 旁邊	(n.) 題外話
bananas	(n.) 香蕉	(a.) 瘋狂的
bank	(n.) 銀行	(n.) 堤岸
bar	(n.) 酒吧	(v.) 禁止
bark	(n.) 狗叫	(n.) 樹皮
barrel	(n.) 桶子	(v.) 高速前進
base	(n.) 基地	(a.) 卑下的
beard	(n.) 鬍鬚	(v.) 對抗
beggar	(n.) 乞丐	(v.) 使不足
best	(a.) 最好的	(v.) 勝過
brave	(a.) 勇敢	(v.) 勇於面對
brand	(n.) 商標	(v.) 加污名於
cake	(n.) 蛋糕	(v.) 結塊
can	(n.) 罐頭	(v.) 解雇
cap	(n.) 無邊帽	(v.) 勝過
car	(n.) 汽車	(n.) 電梯車廂
catholic	(a.) 天主教的（大寫）	(a.) 廣泛普遍的
champion	(n.) 冠軍	(v.) 擁護支持
cheek	(n.) 臉頰	(n.) 傲慢無禮
club	(n.) 俱樂部	(n.) 高爾夫球桿
coin	(n.) 硬幣	(v.) 創造新詞
coke	(n.) 可口可樂（大寫）	(n.) 焦炭
concern	(n.) 關心	(n.) 公司
corn	(n.) 玉米	(n.) 陳腐老套
court	(n.) 法庭	(v.) 求愛
distress	(n.) 苦惱	(n.) 遇險
doctor	(n.) 醫生	(v.) 竄改
down	(adv.) 向下	(v.) 吞下
drum	(v.) 打鼓	(v.) 灌輸
duck	(n.) 鴨子	(v.) 躲避
duke	(n.) 公爵	(v.) 打鬥

felt	(v.) 感覺	(n.) 毛氈
field	(n.) 原野	(v.) 成功答覆
flare	(n.) 火光	(v.) 張開
float	(v.) 浮	(n.) 花車
foil	(n.) 錫箔	(n.) 陪襯者
foot	(n.) 腳	(v.) 支付
game	(n.) 遊戲	(n.) 野味獵物
gift	(n.) 禮物	(v.) 天賦
give	(v.) 給	(n.) 彈性
given	(v.) 給	(n.) 假定事實
go	(v.) 去	(n.) 嘗試
heavy	(a.) 重的	(n.) 彪悍壯漢
husband	(n.) 丈夫	(v.) 節省地使用
industry	(n.) 工業	(n.) 勤奮
list	(n.) 名單	(v.) 傾斜
live	(v.) 活著	(a.) 現場直播
lock	(n.) 鎖	(n.) 髮
main	(a.) 主要的	(n.) 水管
make	(v.) 製造	(n.) 品牌
meet	(v.) 遇見	(n.) 運動比賽
meter	(n.) 公尺	(n.) 韻律
milk	(n.) 牛奶	(a.) 榨取
mint	(n.) 薄荷	(n.) 造幣廠
minutes	(n.) 分鐘	(n.) 會議記錄
moonlight	(n.) 月光	(v.) 兼職
moonshine	(n.) 月光	(n.) 私酒
needle	(n.) 針	(v.) 刺激
nose	(n.) 鼻子	(v.) 探問
nuke	(n.) 核武器	(v.) 用微波爐加熱
optics	(n.) 光學	(n.) 公眾觀感
paint	(n.) 油漆	(n.) 籃球三秒禁區
part	(n.) 部分	(v.) 分離

pen	(n.) 筆	(n.) 禽畜之圍欄
pepper	(n.) 辣椒	(v.) 布滿
pound	(n.) 磅	(v.) 猛襲
pride	(n.) 驕傲	(n.) 一群（獅子）
pupil	(n.) 學生	(n.) 瞳孔
purse	(n.) 女提包	(v.) 嘟（嘴）
racket	(n.) 球拍	(n.) 喧鬧聲
rail	(n.) 鐵軌	(v.) 抱怨
railroad	(n.) 鐵路	(v.) 強迫
rap	(n.) 饒舌樂	(v.) 責難
rent	(n.) 房租	(n.) 破洞
roast	(v.) 烘烤	(n.) 拷問
rib	(n.) 肋骨	(v.) 嘲弄
rock	(n.) 石塊	(n.) 靠山
row	(n.) 列	(v.) 爭吵
scale	(n.) 比例	(v.) 攀登
school	(n.) 學校	(n.) 一群（魚）
scoop	(n.) 杓	(n.) 內幕消息
score	(n.) 分數	(v.) （電影）配樂
second	(n.) 秒	(v.) 贊同
see	(v.) 看見	(n.) 主教轄區
shoulder	(n.) 肩膀	(v.) 承擔
side	(n.) 旁邊	(v.) 支持
skirt	(n.) 裙子	(v.) 繞開
shrink	(v.) 縮小	(n.) 精神醫師
soul	(n.) 靈魂	(n.) 人
spell	(v.) 拼字	(n.) 魔咒
spring	(n.) 春天	(v.) 彈躍
sport	(n.) 運動	(v.) 炫耀
staff	(n.) 職員	(n.) 枴杖
stamp	(n.) 郵票	(v.) 踩踏
stock	(n.) 股票	(a.) 老套的

stomach	(n.) 胃	(v.) 承受
stool	(n.) 凳子	(n.) 大便
study	(v.) 學習	(n.) 書房
stump	(n.) 殘幹	(n.) 巡迴演說
swear	(v.) 發誓	(v.) 粗口
take	(v.) 拿取	(n.) 反應
takeaway	(n.) 外帶	(n.) 重點
tank	(n.) 坦克	(v.) 股票慘跌
tap	(v.) 輕拍	(v.) 裝竊聽器
tax	(n.) 稅	(v.) 使負重擔
tender	(n.) 溫柔	(v.) 提出
top	(n.) 頂端	(n.) 陀螺
trip	(n.) 旅行	(v.) 絆到
vector	(n.) 向量	(n.) 傳染媒介
wasted	(a.) 浪費的	(a.) 大醉的
well	(n.) 井	(v.) 湧出
weather	(n.) 天氣	(v.) 度過（難關）

9.3 複數形態

英文對於單字的單數或複數是很敏感的！有些名詞的複數形態具有特定的意義，一些常用的例子如下表：

名詞單數	意思	名詞複數	意思
custom	習俗	customs	海關
future	未來	futures	期貨
gut	腸子	guts	膽量
honor	榮譽	honors	成績優等
letter	信	letters	學問
mean	平均數	means	手段
premise	前提	premises	建物及土地

regard	考慮	regards	問候
security	安全	securities	證券

上表沒有列出每個名詞單字的所有意思，重點擺複數時的意義。有些常用的字詞必須用複數形態，如：

Bottoms up!	乾杯！
Cheers!	喝吧！
Congratulations!	恭喜！

有些平日生活中常見的單字（特定的人事物）以 s 結尾，這種字通常是因為它隱含複數的意義而衍生的，如：

Dallas Cowboys	達拉斯牛仔美式足球隊
Los Angeles Lakers	洛杉磯湖人籃球隊
Niagara Falls	尼加拉瓜瀑布
NY Yankees	紐約洋基棒球隊
Starbucks	星巴克
Windows	Microsoft 作業系統
Rio 2016 Olympic Games	2016 奧林匹克運動會
2020 Oscar Awards Ceremony	2020 奧斯卡頒獎典禮

球隊的名稱要用複數，如果是指某一位球員時才用單數。微軟的作業系統是 Windows，不是 Window。

有些源自英國的姓氏以 s 結尾，如 Bill Gates, Charles Dickens, Julia Roberts, Keanu Reeves, Peter Sellers, Robin Williams, Tom Hanks, Tiger Woods。

由於中文單字沒有單複數的概念，因此容易忘了單數形的可數名詞之前須加冠詞的規則，祝人聖誕與新年快樂時，如果寫成：We wish you Merry Christmas and Happy New Year! 是不對的，少了兩個不定冠詞 a，應該是：We wish you a Merry Christmas and a Happy New Year!

還有些單字在字尾加 s 時，除了意義不同之外，連詞類也有可能變了，

但與單複數無關，一些常用單字的例子如下表：

名詞單數	詞類	意思	字尾 + s	詞類	意思
beside	prep.	在旁邊	besides	prep.	此外
good	adj.	好的	goods	n.	商品
headquarter	v.	設總部	headquarters	n.	總部
proceed	v.	繼續做	proceeds	n.	收益
remain	v.	餘留	remains	n.	遺跡
summon	v.	傳喚	summons	n.	傳票

9.4　破音字

「朝辭白帝彩雲間，千里江陵一日還」，李白的名句中的「還」讀作「環」，它也可讀作「孩」，這是個破音字 heteronym：同形、異音、異義。破音字在英文中也很多，如：

> I wound a bandage around my wound.　　→我將膠帶纏繞在傷口上

句中第一個 wound /waʊnd/ 是動詞（wind 的過去式），後面的 wound /wund/ 是名詞，是破音字。下表是一些常用的例子（左邊是我們較熟的意思；有些字有多個意思，僅列其一為代表）：

破音字			
attribute	n. /ˈætrəˌbjut/ 特性	v. /əˈtrɪbjʊt/ 歸因於	
bass	n. /ˈbæs/ 鱸魚	n. /ˈbes/ 男低音	
bow	n. /bo/ 弓	v. /baʊ/ 鞠躬	
buffet	n. /bəˈfe/ 自助餐	v. /ˈbʌfɪt/ 猛	
close	a. /klos/ 近的	v. /kloz/ 關閉	
content	n. /ˈkɑntɛnt/ 內容	a. /kənˈtɛnt/ 滿足的	
desert	n. /ˈdɛzɚt/ 沙漠	v. /dɪˈzɝt/ 遺棄	
dove	n. /dʌv/ 鴿	v. /dov/ 潛水（過去式）	
excuse	n. /ɪkˈskjus/ 藉口	v. /ɪkˈskjuz/ 原諒	

graduate	v. /ˋgrædʒʊet/ 畢業	n. /ˋgrædʒʊət/ 畢業生
house	n. /haʊs/ 住宅	v. /haʊz/ 住
lead	v. /lid/ 領導	n. /lɛd/ 鉛
live	v. /lɪv/ 活	a. /laɪv/ 現場的
minute	n. /ˋmɪnɪt/ 分鐘	a. /maɪˋnjut/ 細微的
moderate	a. /ˋmɑdərɪt/ 中等的	v. /ˋmɑdəˏret/ 仲裁主持
produce	v. /prəˋdjus/ 生產	n. /ˋprɑdjus/ 農產品
refuse	v. /rɪˋfjuz/ 拒絕	n. /ˋrɛfjus/ 垃圾
resume	n. /ˋrɛzəme/ 履歷	v. /rɪˋzjum/ 重新
row	n. /ro/ 一排	n. /raʊ/ 吵架
sow	v. /so/ 播種	n. /saʊ/ 母豬
tear	n. /tɪr/ 眼淚	v. /tɛr/ 撕裂
wind	n. /wɪnd/ 風	v. /waɪnd/ 繞

同音異義字

　　還有一種同音異義字（homophone），音一樣，意思卻不一樣，如 allowed/aloud, aural/oral, bare/bear, board/bored, chord/cord, currant/current, dear/deer, died/dyed, grate/great, hear/here, holy/holey, idle/idol, meat/meet, rose/rows, venous/Venus, wood/would, they're/their/there, you're/you, it's/its, who's/whose，對我們來說，也麻煩。

　　中文由於是單音節，同音異義字更多如牛毛，一個音就可能有幾十個異義字，如：意、義、易、議、亦、益、異、藝、億、憶、譯、疫、液…。而且，中文不但有同音異義字，也有同音異義詞，如：由於和魷魚、枇杷和琵琶、請客和頃刻、悲劇和杯具、引擎和隱情、手勢和首飾、會話和繪畫等。

9.5　流行字詞

　　本節列出一些近年來流行的字詞，包括疾病衛生、一般生活、新興科技、環保綠能、政經社會等各類型，如下：

1. 疾病衛生：

Covid-19（2019 冠狀病毒）相關字詞：

airborne transmission（空氣傳播）、community infection（社區感染）、confirmed case（確診病例）、contact tracing（追蹤接觸者）、contract（染病）、corona（王冠 - 源自拉丁文）、curfew（宵禁）、death toll（死亡人數）、droplet（飛沫）、elbow bump（碰肘禮）、epidemic（流行病）、face mask（口罩）、flatten the curve（壓平曲線→ 減緩疫情）、fomite（傳染源）、furlough（無薪休假）、hand sanitizer（消毒洗手液）、helpline（求助諮詢熱線）、herd immunity（群體免疫）、home isolation（居家隔離）、incubation period（潛伏期）、hoard（囤積）、lockdown（封鎖）、novel coronavirus（新型冠狀病毒）、outbreak（爆發）、pandemic（大流行）、person-to-person transmission（人傳人）、recession（經濟衰退）、self-isolation（自我隔離）、self-quarantine（自我檢疫）、shelter in place（就地避疫）、social distancing（社交距離）、stay-at-home order（居家禁足令）、super-spreader（超級傳播者）、symptom（症狀）、travel history（旅遊史）、vaccine（疫苗）、ventilator（呼吸器）、virus（病毒）

一些其他的重大疾病

Avian flu（禽流感）、Cholera（霍亂）、Dengue fever（登革熱）、Ebola（伊波拉）、Hepatitis（肝炎）、Malaria（瘧疾）、Measles（麻疹）、Meningitis（腦膜炎）、Microcephaly（小頭症）、Pneumonia（肺炎）、Smallpox（天花）、Swine fever（豬瘟）、Zika（茲卡）

2. 網路：

cybersecurity（網路安全）、emoji（表情符號）、flash mob（快閃族）、go viral（爆紅）、meme（網紅的影視圖片等）、netiquette（網儀）、netizen（網民）、phishing（網路釣魚）、phubber（低頭族）、troll（惡意留言攻擊）、selfie（自拍）、SMS（Short Message Service）、spam（垃圾郵件）、text（發短信）、webinar（網上研討會）

3. 科技：

AI（人工智慧）、Big Data（大數據）、chatbot（聊天機器人）、

cloud computing（雲端運算），DL（Deep Learning 深度學習），drone（無人機），hologram（立體投影），IoT（Internet of Things），self-driving cars（自駕車）

4. 娛樂：

binge watch（追劇），bling bling（珠光寶氣），cosplay（角色扮演），lip sync（對嘴假唱），paparazzi（狗仔隊），rap music（饒舌樂），reality show（真人秀），remix（混音），streaming（串流）

5. 運動：

bungee jumping（高空彈跳），fidget spinner（指尖陀螺），glamping（豪華露營），hoverboard（懸浮滑板），Paralympics（殘奧會），parkour（跑酷），planking（撐體仆街）

6. 環保：

eco-friendly（環保的），carbon footprint（碳足跡），climate change（氣候變遷），dust storm（or sandstorm 沙塵暴），El Nino（聖嬰），melting glaciers（融化的冰河），global warming（全球暖化），greenhouse effect（溫室效應），heat wave（熱浪），La Nina（反聖嬰）

7. 健康：

carb（carbohydrate 碳水化合物），clone（複製品），cord blood（臍帶血），euthanasia（安樂死），in vitro（試管／體外），stem cell（幹細胞），trans fat（反式脂肪）

8. 社會：

digital divide（數位落差），discrimination（歧視），disadvantaged（弱勢），glass ceiling effect（玻璃天花板效應），LGBTQ（lesbian, gay, bisexual, transexual, queer），slash generation（斜槓世代），telecom fraud ring（電信詐騙集團）

9. 經濟：

austerity（撙節），Bitcoin（比特幣），bailout（紓困），block chain（區塊鍊），crowdfunding（群資），crowdsourcing（群眾外包），cryptocurrency（加密貨幣），economic sanctions（經濟制裁），FinTech（金融科技），gig economy（零工經濟），globalization（全球化），QE（quantitative easing 量化寬鬆），shale oil（頁岩油），sharing economy（分享經濟），startups（新創公司），sweatshop（血汗工廠），trade war（貿易戰），unicorn company（獨角獸公司），venture capital（創業投資）

10. 政治：

Al Qaeda（蓋達），alt-right（另類右派），Brexit（英國脫歐），boycott（抵制），denuclearization（denuke 無核化），embargo（禁運），grassroots（草根基層），hegemony（霸權），impeachment（彈劾），Jihad（聖戰），political outsiders（or amateurs 政治素人），populism（民粹主義），post-truth（後真相），Shia（什葉派），Sunni（遜尼派），Taliban（塔利班）

11. 性別

傳統英文有許多地方偏重用男性來概括兩性，這已不合時宜，現代英文在描述總稱性的字詞時，則流行用中性以示尊重性別，如：

總稱性的字詞	中性
chairman	chair, chairperson
mailman	mail carrier, postal worker
manpower	personnel, staff
policeman	police officer
salesman	salesperson, sales associate
weatherman	forecaster, meteorologist

12. 其他：

bully（霸凌），burkini（布基尼），cupping（拔罐），facekini（臉基尼），homebody（宅男），hype cycle（成熟度曲線），human trafficking（人口販運），karma（因果報應），lean in（挺身向前），

like（按讚），locavore（在地食物者），photobomb（搶鏡頭），
plugged in（跟上潮流），swag（自信、酷），urban mining（城市採礦）

※ 練習題 – 混淆字詞　（請參考【附錄 2】的解答）

（　　）1. 保母 (a) babysitter　(b) babysister
（　　）2. 榜樣 (a) road model　(b) role model
（　　）3. 保鏢 (a) body guard　(b) buddy guard
（　　）4. 好友 (a) body　(b) buddy
（　　）5. 毛巾 (a) towel　(b) tower
（　　）6. 恭喜 (a) congratulation　(b) congratulations
（　　）7. 車道 (a) lane　(b) line
（　　）8. 跑車 (a) sport car　(b) sports car
（　　）9. 昏迷 (a) coma　(b) comma
（　　）10. 總部 (a) headquarter　(b) headquarters
（　　）11. 點心 (a) snack　(b) snake
（　　）12. 關稅 (a) custom　(b) customs
（　　）13. 濃茶 (a) strong tea　(b) thick tea
（　　）14. 大風 (a) big wind　(b) strong wind
（　　）15. 煞車 (a) brake　(b) break
（　　）16. 評價 (a) access　(b) assess
（　　）17. 小島 (a) isle　(b) aisle
（　　）18. 寬度 (a) breath　(b) breadth
（　　）19. 出口 (a) exit　(b) exist
（　　）20. 菜單 (a) manual　(b) menu
（　　）21. 小館 (a) diner　(b) dinner
（　　）22. 帆布 (a) canvass　(b) canvas
（　　）23. 過敏 (a) allergic　(b) sensitive
（　　）24. 讚美 (a) complement　(b) compliment
（　　）25. 前言 (a) foreword　(b) forward
（　　）26. 貴賓 (a) honor guest　(b) honored guest

（　　） 27. 春假 (a) spring break　(b) spring brake

（　　） 28. 套房 (a) suit　(b) suite

（　　） 29. 祈禱 (a) pray　(b) prey

（　　） 30. 文具 (a) stationary　(b) stationery

（　　） 31. 房客 (a) tenant　(b) tenet

（　　） 32. 快艇 (a) airship　(b) hydroplane

（　　） 33. 月蝕 (a) eclipse　(b) ellipse

（　　） 34. 閃電 (a) lighting　(b) lightning

（　　） 35. 兼職 (a) moonlight　(b) moonshine

（　　） 36. 禁食 (a) fete　(b) fast

（　　） 37. 嘲笑 (a) taunt　(b) taut

（　　） 38. 幻覺 (a) allusion　(b) illusion

（　　） 39. 掃帚 (a) broom　(b) bloom

（　　） 40. 變形 (a) transfer　(b) transform

（　　） 41. 想家 (a) homesick　(b) home sick

（　　） 42. 暗示 (a) infer　(b) imply

（　　） 43. 經由 (a) via　(b) vie

（　　） 44. 雕像 (a) statute　(b) statue

（　　） 45. 琺瑯 (a) enamel　(b) enamor

（　　） 46. 屍體 (a) corps　(b) corpse

（　　） 47. 觀點 (a) perspective　(b) prospective

（　　） 48. 忠告 (a) council　(b) counsel

（　　） 49. 市集 (a) bazaar　(b) bizarre

（　　） 50. 同意 (a) ascent　(b) assent

（　　） 51. 人魚線 (a) Apollo's belt　(b)mermaid line

（　　） 52. 業務員 (a) sales　(b) salesperson

（　　） 53. 聖誕歌 (a) carol　(b) coral

（　　） 54. 聖誕節 (a) X'mas　(b) Xmas

（　　） 55. 運動鞋 (a) sneakers　(b) snickers

（　　） 56. 兩門車 (a) coup　(b) coupe

（　　） 57. 調味醬 (a) sauce　(b) source

（　　） 58. 葡萄園 (a) vinegar　(b) vinery

( ) 59. 嫉妒的 (a) green eyed　(b) red eyed

( ) 60. 非法的 (a) elicit　(b) illicit

( ) 61. 喉嚨痛 (a) sore throat　(b) sour throat

( ) 62. 不同意 (a) descent　(b) dissent

( ) 63. 老套的 (a) stock　(b) stuff

( ) 64. 湖人隊 (a) Laker　(b) Lakers

( ) 65. 大猩猩 (a) gorilla　(b) guerrilla

( ) 66. 調色板 (a) palate　(b) palette

( ) 67. 在旁邊 (a) beside　(b) besides

( ) 68. 古典的 (a) classic　(b) classical

( ) 69. 巨觀的 (a) macroscopic　(b) microscopic

( ) 70. 紀錄片 (a) document　(b) documentary

( ) 71. 同理心 (a) empathy　(b) sympathy

( ) 72. 機上盒 (a) setup box　(b) set-top box

( ) 73. 藥處方 (a) prescription　(b) proscription

( ) 74. 謹慎的 (a) discrete　(b) discreet

( ) 75. 頁岩油 (a) shale oil　(b) shell oil

( ) 76. 我煩了 (a) I'm boring　(b) I'm bored

( ) 77. 樸克王牌 (a) trump　(b) trumpet

( ) 78. 多個女婿 (a) son-in laws　(b) sons-in-law

( ) 79. 中學校長 (a) principal　(b) principle

( ) 80. 即將發生 (a) eminent　(b) imminent

( ) 81. 口音腔調 (a) accent　(b) ascent

( ) 82. 公司團體 (a) cooperation　(b) corporation

( ) 83. 舉個例子 (a) e.g.　(b) i.e.

( ) 84. 繼續進行 (a) precede　(b) proceed

( ) 85. 他們自己 (a) themselves　(b) their selves

( ) 86. 金剛鸚鵡 (a) Macao　(b) macaw

( ) 87. 下流笑話 (a) blue joke (b) yellow joke

( ) 88. 降低成本 (a) cost down　(b) reduce costs

( ) 89. 股票慘跌 (a) tank　(b) stock

( ) 90. 傳染媒介 (a) epidemic　(b) vector

( ) 91. 便利商店 (a) convenience store　(b) convenient store

( ) 92. 先進課程 (a) advance course　(b) advanced course

( ) 93. 預先付款 (a) advance payment　(b) advanced payment

( ) 94. 平行會議 (a) parallel sections　(b) parallel sessions

( ) 95. 現場轉播 (a) live broadcast　(b) life broadcast

( ) 96. 退休的人 (a) retire person　(b) retired person

( ) 97. 地方性疾病 (a) endemic　(b) pandemic

( ) 98. 會議論文集 (a) proceeding　(b) proceedings

( ) 99. 陸海空三軍 (a) armed forces　(b) arm forces

( ) 100. 有歷史重要性的 (a) historical　(b) historic

( ) 101. Even when Hanikezi's not wearing _____ , she's very beautiful.

　　　(a) makeup　(b) make up

( ) 102. Welcome _____ flight ABC123 to Buenos Aires.

　　　(a) abroad　(b) aboard

( ) 103. Is there an extra charge at the hotel for Internet _____ ?

　　　(a) access　(b) assess

( ) 104. He _____ a lot of knowledge in school.

　　　(a) learned　(b) acquired

( ) 105. It is hard to _____ this story for children.

　　　(a) adapt　(b) adopt

( ) 106. She served as an _____ to the former president.

　　　(a) aid　(b) aide

( ) 107. The bride walked down the _____ to the altar.

　　　(a) aisle　(b) isle

( ) 108. Without naming names, he criticized his opponents by _____ .

　　　(a) illusion　(b) allusion

( ) 109. Private cars are banned from the city on _____ days.

　　　(a) alternate　(b) alternative

( ) 110. An opportunity _____ and he decided to take the job.

　　　(a) rose　(b) arose

( ) 111. It is _____ who is the greatest golf player ever?

　　　(a) arguable　(b) argumentative

( ) 112. He is famous for inventing visual and _____ effects.

(a) oral　(b) aural

( ) 113. Don't stand on that old chair, it cannot _____ your weight.

(a) bear　(b) bare

( ) 114. There was no one in the room _____ Sonny and Cher.

(a) beside　(b) besides

( ) 115. The church's _____ law forbids remarriage of divorced persons.

(a) canon　(b) cannon

( ) 116. The judge _____ the driver but did not fine him.

(a) censored　(b) censured

( ) 117. "Stop this _____ nonsense at once!" his mom shouted furiously.

(a) childish　(b) childlike

( ) 118. The opening _____ of "A Hard Day's Night" is well known.

(a) cord　(b) chord

( ) 119. Strong red wine _____ steak, lamb, and barbeque.

(a) complements (b) compliments

( ) 120. The reports _____ his courageous actions.

(a) command　(b) commend

( ) 121. He is a trusted _____ of the president.

(a) confidant　(b) confident

( ) 122. Members must _____ to a strict dress code.

(a) confirm　(b) conform

( ) 123. Energy _____ reduces your fuel bills and helps the environment.

(a) conservation　(b) reservation

( ) 124. A _____ declaration form must be filled out.

(a) custom　(b) customs

( ) 125. Cheese and other _____ products do not agree with me.

(a) dairy　(b) diary

( ) 126. They were very _____ about the romance.

(a) discrete　(b) discreet

( ) 127. Zebras' black and white stripes make them instantly _____ .

(a) distinguishable　(b) distinguished

(　) 128. The crops died during the _____ .

      (a) draught   (b) drought

(　) 129. What are the most _____ cars on the market today?

      (a) economical   (b) economic

(　) 130. What are the negative _____ of computers on our society?

      (a) affects   (b) effects

(　) 131. _____ is putting yourself in the shoes of another.

      (a) Empathy   (b) Sympathy

(　) 132. He has no time to run _____ for me.

      (a) errant   (b) errands

(　) 133. The girl dressed in red is his _____ .

      (a) fiancee   (b) fiance

(　) 134. It's tough to _____ from your homeland to a new country.

      (a) immigrate   (b) emigrate

(　) 135. He forgot to attach a stamp to the _____ .

      (a) envelope   (b) envelop

(　) 136. The school has an _____ playing field

      (a) intensive   (b) extensive

(　) 137. Black rhinos are on the brink of _____ .

      (a) extinction   (b) distinction

(　) 138. The criminal was found guilty and _____ to death.

      (a) hung   (b) hanged

(　) 139. In Greek mythology, the Amazons were warriors and _____ .

      (a) heroines   (b) heroins

(　) 140. It's great to see so many people here on this _____ occasion.

      (a) historical   (b) historic

(　) 141. The telecom fraud ring has set up many _____ call centers.

      (a) illicit   (b) elicit

(　) 142. Ma was an innovative and _____ CEO.

      (a) imaginary   (b) imaginative

(　) 143. Can you _____ his accent?

      (a) imitate   (b) intimate

( ) 144. What is the best way to _____ a girl on the first date?

(a) express　(b) impress

( ) 145. Old people are _____ to look back on the past.

(a) inclined　(b) declined

( ) 146. He _____ from her silence that she was angry.

(a) implied　(b) inferred

( ) 147. The jury's role is to decide the guilt or _____ of the defendant.

(a) innocence　(b) ignorance

( ) 148. Listen, someone _____ at your door.

(a) knocks　(b) is knocking

( ) 149. Bill _____ some money to me.

(a) lent　(b) borrowed

( ) 150. I had no sooner _____ down than the cell phone rang.

(a) laid　(b) lain

( ) 151. The _____ part of his life was spent in Malaysia.

(a) latter　(b) later

( ) 152. The badminton game was broadcast _____ .

(a) lively　(b) live

( ) 153. She smiled _____ .

(a) lovingly　(b) lovely

( ) 154. He looked so _____ in his uniform.

(a) man　(b) manly

( ) 155. _____ I didn't treat you quite as good as I should have.

(a) Maybe　(b) May be

( ) 156. The team is struggling on the court because of a lack of _____ .

(a) moral　(b) morale

( ) 157. We are much _____ for your help.

(a) obliged　(b) obligated

( ) 158. I will walk _____ your house after school.

(a) passed　(b) past

( ) 159. My study of English _____ to this day!

(a) persists　(b) insists

(   ) 160. We wish you a _____ journey.

           (a) pleased   (b) pleasant

(   ) 161. The drug is very _____ but causes undesirable side effects.

           (a) potent   (b) patent

(   ) 162. Take this _____ to your pharmacy.

           (a) proscription   (b) prescription

(   ) 163. I support your strategy because of its underlying _____ .

           (a) principle v(b) principal

(   ) 164. He was _____ for drunk driving.

           (a) persecuted   (b) prosecuted

(   ) 165. A social worker is appointed to interview the _____ adopters.

           (a) prospective   (b) perspective

(   ) 166. It takes a long time to make a large _____ .

           (a) quality   (b) quantity

(   ) 167. Learning English _____ patience and persistence.

           (a) requires   (b) requests

(   ) 168. Natural _____ are not limitless.

           (a) sources   (b) resources

(   ) 169. She tried to explain the scientific _____ behind her work.

           (a) rationale   (b) rational

(   ) 170. There is a _____ for whoever returns my laptop.

           (a) award   (b) reward

(   ) 171. He _____ his hand to ask a question.

           (a) raised   (b) rose

(   ) 172. This conference has organized a successful Q&A _____ .

           (a) section   (b) session

(   ) 173. He found a job of _____ wool from sheep.

           (a) shearing   (b) sheering

(   ) 174. We should go out to eat _____ next week.

           (a) some time   (b) sometime

(   ) 175. A: Is Saeed there?   B: Who's _____ ?

           (a) speaking   (b) talking

(　) 176. _____ cars in traffic jams cause a great deal of pollution.
　　　　(a) Stationery　(b) Stationary

(　) 177. The right arm of the _____ of Liberty is 42 feet long.
　　　　(a) Statue　(b) Statute

(　) 178. We booked a _____ for 3 nights for this trip.
　　　　(a) suit　(b) suite

(　) 179. I just _____ my credit card and signed the credit slip.
　　　　(a) swiped　(b) wiped

(　) 180. She didn't _____ her right in this matter.
　　　　(a) wave　(b) waive

Part 4

 其他篇

CHAPTER 10　英式與美式的差異

英式與美式英文在語文的表現上有很多不一樣的地方，以下分別簡述字彙、文法、發音的差異。當然，即使在美國或英國，各自都可能有很多種表現方式，這裡是指一般的狀況。

10.1　字彙的差異

僅舉些常用字詞的美式與英式的不同：

美式	英式	
airplane	aeroplane	飛機
aluminum	aluminium	鋁
apartment	flat	公寓
baggage	luggage	行李
bar	pub	酒吧
bathroom (restroom)	toilet	廁所
buck	quid	美元英鎊
bus	coach	長途客運
can	tin	罐頭
candy	sweets	糖果
cell phone	mobile phone	手機
chips	crisps	洋芋片
cookie	biscuit	餅乾
corn	maize	玉米
diaper	nappy	尿布

eggplant	aubergine	茄子
elevator	lift	電梯
eraser	rubber	橡皮擦
fall	autumn	秋天
faucet	tap	水龍頭
first floor	ground floor	一樓
football	American football	美式足球
french fries	chips	炸薯條
gas	petrol	汽油
hood	bonnet	車引擎蓋
jump rope	skipping rope	跳繩
line	queue	排隊
mailbox	postbox	郵箱
math	maths	數學
mom	mum	媽媽
muffler	silencer	車滅音器
one-way	single（ticket）	單程
overpass	flyover	高架
pants	trousers	褲子
parking lot	car park	停車場
round-trip	return（ticket）	來回
sidewalk	pavement	人行道
sneakers	trainers	運動鞋
soccer	football	足球
stroller	pram	嬰兒車
subway	tube, underground	地鐵
sweater	jumper	毛衣
theater	cinema	電影院
tire	tyre	輪胎
trash, garbage	rubbish	垃圾
trash can	bin	垃圾箱
truck	lorry	卡車

trunk	boot	車行李箱
vacation	holiday	放假
zip code	post code	郵遞區號

holiday 在美國指的是政府或宗教上的節日，如：Labor Day, Christmas 等，vacation 則是度假。而英國一律用 holiday。

2016 年 4 月，美國前總統歐巴馬訪問英國，幫英國前首相 David Cameron 向英國人呼籲留在歐盟，他說，如果英國脫歐（Brexit），日後在與美國談判貿易協定時，將排在隊伍後頭（the back of the queue），這句話引起脫歐派反彈，並質疑他的講稿是由英國政府執筆代寫的，因為 queue 是英式用法，美國人應該不會如此說，會說 line 才對。

有些字有細微的差異，如：

美式多用	英式多用
afterward	afterwards
apologize	apologise
around	round
among	amongst
catalog	catalogue
center	centre
check	cheque
color	colour
defense	defence
dreamed	dreamed / dreamt
fiber	fibre
gray	grey
humor	humour
inquire	enquire
learned	learned / learnt
license	licence
mold	mould
parlor	parlour
program	programme

theater	theatre
toward	towards
traveled	travelled

在幾十萬的英文單字中，僅有 dreamt 這個字以 mt 結尾；發音是 /drɛmt/。美式用 dreamed，英式用 dreamt 或 dreamed。類似單字如 burned /burnt, leaned/leant, learned/learnt, smelled/smelt, spelled/spelt, spilled/spilt, spoiled/spoilt 等。

動詞單字以 l 結尾時，如 travel，美式用 traveled 與 traveling（一個 l），英式則用 travelled 與 travelling（兩個 l），相似的例子如 cancel, counsel, libel, marvel, peril 等，這些單字的重音都在第一音節。但是，有些單字如 control（重音在第二音節），美國人也是 controlled, controlling（兩個 l），類似的例子如 excel, patrol 等。

在英文中有幾個英文單字的結尾，在美國是 er，而在英國是 re，例如：美式 center, fiber, liter, luster, theater，相對的英式為：centre, fibre, litre, lustre, theatre。但是，要注意：兩種寫法的發音是相同的，例如，center 或 centre 都唸 /sɛntɚ/。

有些副詞，如 afterward(s), backward(s), forward(s), inward(s), outward(s), upward(s) 等，美式以 ward 為主，英式以 wards 為主。suffix 的 ward(s) 表示方向。

在較為正式的信件中，Sincerely yours 是美式的結尾方式之一，而英式英語則用 Yours sincerely。

10.2 文法的差異

文法方面的差異包括：

1. 集體名詞（audience, class, band, family, staff, team 等）美式通常用單數動詞，而英國人單數與多數動詞都有。

2. 對於剛剛發生的事情，美國人喜歡用過去式，英國人則喜歡用完成式，如 I already ate（美式）和 I've already eaten（英式）。

3. 美國人說：I have a sister. He doesn't have pets；英國人則說：I have

got a sister. He hasn't got pets。

4. 英式口語較喜歡用附帶問句，如 You like me, don't you?

5. 英國人常用助動詞 shall 表示第一人稱的未來式，如 I shall go home now，美式則通常說 I will go home now，事實上，shall 這個字在現代美式英文中已漸趨於消逝。

6. 標點符號的差異：（a）美式用 Oxford comma（詳見【7.2】），英式則否。（b）美式將逗號與句號均置於引號之內（詳見【7.4】），英式則置於引號之外。（c）美式的引句用双引號（詳見【7.4】），如引句中又有引句，則用單引號；英式則相反。

10.3 發音的差異

首先要再次聲明，本書所說的美國音或英國音，即使在美國或英國，都可能有多種差異，這裡是指一般的發音。

在發音方式的比較上，美式較放鬆，嘴巴張得較大。英式則相反，多用唇，較緊繃，嘴巴張得較小。

子音的最大的差別應該是 /r/ 了。美式基本上在任何情況都會清楚地發 /r/，英式則常不發 /r/，對比非常明顯。原則上，英式：

1. /r/ 後面跟著子音	→不發 /r/，如 Charlie, park
2. /r/ 後面跟著母音	→要發 /r/，如 origin, grass

有的單字字尾是 r，也不發 /r/，如 bar, car。此規則也適用於連音，four apricots, four avocados, four olives 中要發 /r/，因為後面是母音；four cucumbers, four durians, four guavas 中則不發 /r/。

複合母音字母 ar, er, ir, or, ur 等的美式發音通常是 /ɚ/ 或 /ɝ/；英式發音則都趨向 /ə/。

KK 音標有 3 個双母音 diphthongs：/aɪ/, /aʊ/, /ɔɪ/；英式音標則通常有 8 個雙母音：/aɪ/, /aʊ/, /ɔɪ/, /əʊ/, /ɛɪ/, /ɪə/, /ɛə/, /ʊə/，其中，/əʊ/ 相當於 KK 音標的 /o/，/ɛɪ/ 相當於 KK 音標的 /e/。

當字母 a 的發音在 /æ/ 與 /ɑ/ 之間時，美國趨向 /æ/，而英國人趨向 /ɑ/，如 advantage, after, answer, ask, bath, can't, cast, class, command, dance, example, fast, half, glass, last, laugh, past, task。

　　當字母 o 的發音在 /ɑ/ 與 /ɔ/ 之間時，美國人趨向 /ɑ/，而英國人趨向 /ɔ/。像是 Harry Potter，英國人發音近似 /ˋpɔtə/，而美國人發 /ˋpɑtɚ/。其他如 coffee, cop, hot, job, lot, rob, top。

　　還有，當字母 u 的發音在 /u/ 與 /ju/ 之間時，美式趨向 /u/，而英式傾向 /ju/，多了一個 /j/ 音，例如：attitude, costume, coupon, due, duke, duty, nuclear, nude, nuke, opportunity, produce, puma, presume, reduce, student, super, tube, Tuesday, tune 等。

　　下表是英美發音不同的一些日常的例子：

	美式	英式
address　n.	/ˋædrɛs/（或 /əˋdrɛs/）	/əˋdrɛs/
Amazon	/ˋæməzɑn/	/ˋæməzən/
apparatus	/æpəˋrætəs/	/æpəˋretəs/
banana	/bəˋnænə/	/bəˋnɑnə/
comrade	/ˋkɑmræd/	/ˋkɑmred/
either	/ˋiðɚ/（或 /ˋaɪðɚ/）	/ˋaɪðɚ/（或 /ˋiðɚ/）
erase	/ɪˋres/	/ɪˋrez/
figure	/ˋfɪgjɚ/	/ˋfɪgə/
leisure	/ˋliʒɚ/	/ˋlɛʒə/
lieutenant	/luˋtɛnənt/	/lɛfˋtɛnənt/
niche	/nɪtʃ/	/nɪʃ/
patent	/ˋpætənt/	/ˋpetənt/
resume　v.	/rɪˋzum/	/rɪˋzjum/
resume　n.	/ˋrɛzəme/	/ˋrɛzjume/
route	/rut/ 或 /raʊt/	/rut/
schedule	/ˋskɛdʒʊl/	/ˋʃɛdjul/
status	/ˋstetəs/（或 /ˋstætəs/）	/ˋstetəs/
tomato	/təˋmeto/	/təˋmato/
vitamin	/ˋvaɪtəmɪn/	/ˋvɪtəmɪn/
z	/zi/	/zɛd/

　　另外，有些單字在美國與英國的重音位置也不相同（也可能連帶地影

響到其他發音），舉幾個例子如：

	美式	英式
advertisement	/ædvɚ`taɪzmənt/	/əd`vətɪzmənt/
ballet	/bæ`le/	/`bæle/
brochure	/bro`ʃʊr/	/`brəʊʃə/
centrifugal	/sɛn`trɪfjʊgəl/	/sɛntrɪ`fjʊgəl/
controversy	/`kɑntrovɚsi/	/kən`trɒvəsi/
garage	/gə`rɑʒ/	/`gærɪʒ/
kilometer	/kɪ`lɑmətɚ/	/`kɪləmitə/
laboratory	/`læbrətori/	/lə`bɒrət(ə)ri/
moustache	/`mʌstæʃ/	/mə`staʃ/
renaissance	/`rɛnəsɑns/	/rə`nesəns/
vacate	/`veket/	/ve`ket/

　　當單字的結尾是 ary 時，美國人唸 /ɛri/，而英國人常省略其中的 /ɛ/ 音，如 military：美式 /`mɪlə<u>tɛri</u>/，英式 /`mɪlɪ<u>tri</u>/；secretary：美式 /`sɛkrə<u>tɛri</u>/，英式 /`sɛkrə<u>tri</u>/。

　　在結尾是 ile 的單字中，美國人較常唸 /əl/，而英國人唸 /aɪl/，如：agile, ductile, fertile, fragile, hostile, missile, mobile, sterile, versatile, volatile ⋯⋯。

　　英文屬於印歐語系下的日耳曼語族（Germanic），在它發展成長的過程中，不斷受到許多其他語言的影響，而英文也不斷地融合吸收。據統計，英文單字約有 28% 源自法文（也屬於印歐語系），可見法文對英文字彙的影響巨大，本章將簡略其詳。

　　西元 1066 年，法國諾曼地公爵（Duke of Normandy）進攻英國，大敗英軍，從而成為英王威廉一世（William the Conqueror）。往後的 3 百年，法語成為政府、法庭與文化的官方語言，英文倒成了下層階級人民的通用語言。所幸，這兩種語言是並行的，而且，由於英文淪為下層，不受高級知識分子的重視，反而造成英文的文法鬆綁，由複雜的古文法（Old English 時期，約西元 450 年～ 1100 年）轉向較簡單的文法（Middle English 時期，約西元 1100 年～ 1500 年）。

　　由於這段時間的法語統治，即使時至今日的 Modern English（約始於西元 1500 年以及莎士比亞的創作時期），英文仍處處可見法文的影子，大量的單字由法文演變而來，或是源自拉丁經由法文的傳介進入英文。

　　法文對英文的影響最大的是字彙，而領域多屬於行政、法律、文化、時尚、飲食等方面，這是因為威廉一世時期統治階級與上層社會都使用法語，慢慢滲入了英文中。

　　有許多的法文單字和英文極相像，我們可以輕鬆地看得懂它們的大意，但不幸的是，它們讀音幾乎都是完全不同的，極少可以用英語去模仿的！這種情形類似我們認得出許多日文單字的意涵，但是讀不出。

　　許多源於法文的單字都已經幾乎完全融入英文了，或以英文的形式進入一些美國的字典中。例如：

法文	英文	中譯
absorber	absorb	吸收
activité	activity	活動
administration	administration	管理
appartement	apartment	公寓
attention	attention	注意
ballet	ballet	芭蕾舞
calendrier	calendar	日曆
culturel	cultural	文化
déjà vu	deja vu	似曾有過經驗
divorce	divorce	離婚
entrepreneur	entrepreneur	企業家
esprit	esprit	精神
fiancé	fiance	未婚夫
faux pas	faux pas	失禮
garage	garage	車庫
genre	genre	文藝作品之類型
gouvernement	government	政府
juge	judge	法官
lingerie	lingerie	女性內衣
Renaissance	Renaissance	文藝復興
rendez-vous	rendezvous	約會
résumé	resume	履歷
vis-à-vis	vis-a-vis	相對於

　　對我們來說，英文受法文影響的一個好處是，透過英文與法文的相關性，可以較容易地看懂或猜到成百上千法文單字的意思。下表是一些日常單字，去法國旅遊時可能會遇到：

法文	英文	中譯
à la carte	a la carte	單點菜色
art	art	藝術
bacon	bacon	培根

banque	bank	銀行
bon appétit	bon appetit	請享用
bon voyage	bon voyage	一路平安
bouef	beef	牛肉
bagages	baggage	行李
café	cafe	小餐廳
chauffeur	chauffeur	汽車司機
chocolat	chocolate	巧克力
comédie	comedy	喜劇
conciergerie	concierge	門房
croissant	croissant	可頌麵包
cuisine	cuisine	烹飪
danse	dance	舞蹈
fruit	fruit	水果
hôtel	hotel	飯店
menu	nenu	菜單
mouton	mutton	羊肉
musique	music	音樂
non	no	不
opéra	opera	歌劇
photo	photo	照片
papier	paper	紙
sandwich	sandwich	三明治
souvenir	souvenir	紀念品
taxe	tax	稅
théâtre	theater	劇院
toilette	toilet	廁所
train	train	火車
véhicule	vehicle	車輛
vitamin	vitamin	維他命
zoo	zoo	動物園

有時要小心同樣的字在兩種語言中的意思不一樣，例如：法文 entrée 是前菜（第一道菜，如：沙拉），而英文 entree 則是主菜。法文的主菜是 plat。

　　portmanteau，這個單字也來自法文，而法文拼法略微不同：portemanteau。在現代英文中的意思是組合字或是旅行皮箱；在法文中則是吊衣架（英文的 coat rack）。

　　即使與英文拼法完全一樣的單字，讀音也是完全不同，以 opera 為例，這個字在英文及法文是一樣的，但字母 r 在法文中的發音「近似」英文中的 /h/，法文的 opera 聽起來像「歐培哈」。

　　但也偶有讀音類似英文的字詞，如果你去法國觀光，不幸遇到扒手，你可以大叫「pickpocket!」，這個單字在法文與英文中不但拼法一樣，讀音也近似。

　　上述的英文知識的好處，也適用於其他一些歐洲國家，尤其是除法文外，影響英文的另兩大語言：德文及拉丁文。

　　到德國旅遊也可以看懂或猜出一些德國字。另外，雖然拉丁文早已沒落，但因為在古代，拉丁語隨著羅馬帝國的勢力擴張而廣泛流傳於歐洲各地，至今，很多歐洲語言都還有許多拉丁語文的影子。甚至隨著歐洲國家 15 世紀以來的殖民與擴張，也將對語文的影響帶到了世界上其他不少國家。

Appendix
➡ 附錄

　　19 世紀後期，有一些西方的語言學家發願要設計一套音標符號將世界上所有語言的發音都囊括在內，作為「書面溝通」的標準，他們以拉丁字母為基礎，發展出一套國際標準的發音符號系統叫做 IPA（International Phonetic Alphabet），我們翻成國際音標，是現今普世語言最通用的音標系統。

　　這套國際標準 IPA 會有不定期的修訂，最新的修訂共有 107 字母（letters）、52 個音調符號（diacritics）和 4 個韻律標示（prosodic marks），後兩者通常是字母上下（或周圍）附加的小記號，協助標示此音標發音需做的其他變化等。

　　英文有許多不同的音標系統，我們最熟悉的是：DJ 音標與 KK 音標。DJ 是英國人 Daniel Jones 根據 IPA 發展出較反應英國發音的系統；KK 則是美國人 John Samuel Kenyon 及 Thomas A. Knott 大體根據 IPA 設計出的較反應美國發音的系統。

　　但是，絕大多數美國人是不知道什麼是 DJ 音標，什麼是 KK 音標的！可能只有語言學家或對語言有興趣的人知道，一般人對音標的認知端看用的是哪一本字典而定，因為每一本英美字典都有它自己的音標符號系統，每一本的符號設計都可能略有不同，甚至於音標符號的數目，也不見得一樣，相關的問題有些複雜，不在本書討論的範圍之內。

　　一般來說，英國字典多參照 IPA 國際標準設計，美國字典則不走國際標準（只有少數例外，KK 音標是其中之一，它基本上與 IPA 國際標準相符），幾乎每一本都有自創的一些不同的音標符號，使用時要很小心，必須先花些時間弄清楚你所用的字典每個符號代表的發音，否則會搞得很混亂。如果直接用聽的當然最好，但對我們來說，可能會有困難度，有時還是要看到音標，才確定是哪個音。

簡單地說，本書在發音的說明上，採用了華人較熟悉的、代表美式英語之一的 KK 音標（Kenyon and Knott phonetic symbols），用 KK 的 41 個符號來表示英語的發音。要特別聲明，並不是要大家學 KK 音標，只是以大家較熟知的 KK 音標來做為學習上的解析與說明。

KK 音標的 41 個符號標示如下：

單母音　14 個

/æ/	b<u>a</u>g, c<u>a</u>t, d<u>a</u>d, f<u>a</u>t
/e/	c<u>a</u>ke, l<u>a</u>ke, m<u>a</u>ke, n<u>a</u>me
/ɑ/	f<u>a</u>ther, h<u>o</u>t, n<u>o</u>t, t<u>o</u>p
/ɛ/	b<u>e</u>d, l<u>e</u>d, t<u>e</u>n, w<u>e</u>t
/i/	<u>e</u>ven, m<u>ee</u>t, l<u>ea</u>d, t<u>ea</u>
/ɪ/	f<u>i</u>t, k<u>i</u>ck, h<u>i</u>t, p<u>i</u>g, s<u>i</u>t
/o/	b<u>oa</u>t, g<u>o</u>, l<u>o</u>w, n<u>o</u>
/ɔ/	c<u>a</u>ll, c<u>au</u>se, b<u>a</u>ll, s<u>a</u>lt
/u/	f<u>oo</u>l, n<u>oo</u>dle, t<u>oo</u>, wh<u>o</u>
/ʊ/	b<u>oo</u>k, f<u>u</u>ll, g<u>oo</u>d, w<u>ou</u>ld
/ʌ/	b<u>u</u>t, c<u>u</u>t, l<u>u</u>ck, <u>u</u>p
/ə/	<u>a</u>go, <u>a</u>gent, an<u>i</u>mal, c<u>o</u>mmercial, foc<u>u</u>s
/ɚ/	calend<u>ar</u>, may<u>or</u>, summ<u>er</u>, und<u>er</u>
/ɝ/	b<u>ir</u>d, n<u>ur</u>se, p<u>er</u>son, w<u>or</u>k

双母音　3 個

/aɪ/	f<u>igh</u>t, <u>i</u>ce, h<u>igh</u>, l<u>i</u>ke
/ɔɪ/	b<u>oy</u>, c<u>oi</u>n, <u>oi</u>l, t<u>oy</u>
/aʊ/	ab<u>ou</u>t, h<u>ow</u>, n<u>ow</u>, <u>ou</u>t

有聲子音　15 個

/b/	a<u>b</u>out, <u>b</u>ag, ca<u>b</u>, jo<u>b</u>
/d/	<u>d</u>ate, <u>d</u>og, ma<u>d</u>, un<u>d</u>er
/g/	Au<u>g</u>ust, e<u>gg</u>, <u>g</u>ate, le<u>g</u>

/l/	call, late, leg, tall
/m/	mother, aim
/n/	nose, can
/ŋ/	ring
/r/	rat, cross
/v/	vote, love
/w/	way
/z/	zoo, haze
/ð/	the, this
/dʒ/	geometry
/ʒ/	azure, leisure
/j/	yes

無聲子音　9 個

/f/	forget, laugh
/h/	have, home
/k/	kite, look
/p/	pole, Alps
/s/	sale
/t/	tale
/θ/	thin
/ʃ/	she, cash, Chicago, Michigan
/tʃ/	check, lunch

APPENDIX 2

習題解答

1.8 練習題

發音

1. (a)	2. (b)	3. (b)	4. (a)	5. (b)	6. (b)	7. (a)	8. (b)	9. (b)	10. (a)
11. (b)	12. (b)	13. (a)	14. (b)	15. (b)	16. (a)	17. (b)	18. (b)	19. (a)	20. (b)
21. (b)	22. (a)	23. (b)	24. (b)	25. (a)	26. (b)	27. (b)	28. (a)	29. (b)	30. (b)
31. (a)	32. (b)	33. (b)	34. (a)	35. (b)	36. (b)	37. (a)	38. (b)	39. (b)	40. (a)
41. (b)	42. (b)	43. (a)	44. (b)	45. (b)					

3.1.12 練習題

動詞

1. (a)	2. (a)	3. (b)	4. (b)	5. (c)	6. (c)	7. (a)	8. (a)	9. (b)	10. (b)
11. (c)	12. (c)	13. (a)	14. (a)	15. (b)	16. (b)	17. (c)	18. (c)	19. (a)	20. (a)
21. (b)	22. (b)	23. (c)	24. (c)	25. (a)	26. (a)	27. (b)	28. (b)	29. (c)	30. (c)
31. (a)	32. (a)	33. (b)	34. (b)	35. (c)	36. (c)	37. (a)	38. (a)	39. (b)	40. (b)
41. (c)	42. (c)	43. (a)	44. (a)	45. (b)	46. (b)	47. (c)	48. (c)	49. (a)	50. (a)
51. (b)	52. (b)	53. (c)	54. (c)	55. (a)	56. (a)	57. (b)	58. (b)	59. (c)	60. (c)
61. (a)	62. (a)	63. (b)	64. (b)	65. (c)	66. (c)	67. (a)	68. (a)	69. (b)	70. (b)
71. (c)	72. (c)	73. (a)	74. (a)	75. (b)	76. (b)	77. (c)	78. (c)	79. (a)	80. (a)

3.3.5 練習題

名詞與代名詞

1. (c)	2. (a)	3. (b)	4. (c)	5. (a)	6. (b)	7. (c)	8. (a)	9. (b)	10. (c)
11. (a)	12. (b)	13. (c)	14. (a)	15. (b)	16. (c)	17. (a)	18. (b)	19. (c)	20. (a)
21. (b)	22. (c)	23. (a)	24. (b)	25. (c)	26. (a)	27. (b)	28. (c)	29. (a)	30. (b)
31. (c)	32. (a)	33. (b)	34. (c)	35. (a)	36. (b)	37. (c)	38. (a)	39. (b)	40. (c)

3.5.5 練習題

形容詞與副詞

1. (a)	2. (a)	3. (a)	4. (b)	5. (b)	6. (b)	7. (a)	8. (a)	9. (a)	10. (b)
11. (b)	12. (b)	13. (a)	14. (a)	15. (a)	16. (b)	17. (b)	18. (b)	19. (a)	20. (a)
21. (a)	22. (b)	23. (b)	24. (b)	25. (a)	26. (a)	27. (a)	28. (b)	29. (b)	30. (b)
31. (a)	32. (a)	33. (a)	34. (b)	35. (b)	36. (b)	37. (a)	38. (a)	39. (a)	40. (b)
41. (b)	42. (b)	43. (a)	44. (a)	45. (a)	46. (b)	47. (b)	48. (b)	49. (a)	50. (a)
51. (a)	52. (b)	53. (b)							

3.6.5 練習題

連接詞

1. (a)	2. (b)	3. (c)	4. (a)	5. (b)	6. (c)	7. (a)	8. (b)	9. (c)	10. (a)
11. (b)	12. (c)	13. (a)	14. (b)	15. (c)					

3.7.6 練習題

介系詞

1. (a)	2. (b)	3. (a)	4. (b)	5. (b)	6. (c)	7. (b)	8. (c)	9. (c)	10. (a)
11. (c)	12. (a)	13. (a)	14. (b)	15. (a)	16. (b)	17. (b)	18. (c)	19. (b)	20. (c)
21. (c)	22. (a)	23. (c)	24. (a)	25. (a)	26. (b)	27. (a)	28. (b)	29. (b)	30. (c)
31. (b)	32. (c)	33. (c)	34. (a)	35. (c)	36. (a)	37. (a)	38. (b)	39. (a)	40. (b)
41. (b)	42. (c)	43. (b)	44. (c)	45. (c)	46. (a)	47. (c)	48. (a)	49. (a)	50. (b)

4.3　練習題

句子種類

1. (a)	2. (b)	3. (c)	4. (a)	5. (b)	6. (c)	7. (a)	8. (b)	9. (c)	10. (a)
11. (b)	12. (c)	13. (a)	14. (b)	15. (c)					

辨別是否可省略 who, which, that, whose:

1. (b)	2. (b)	3. (a)	4. (a)	5. (b)	6. (b)	7. (a)	8. (a)	9. (b)	10. (b)
11. (a)	12. (a)								

6.12　練習題

綜合題

1. (a)	2. (b)	3. (b)	4. (a)	5. (b)	6. (b)	7. (a)	8. (b)	9. (b)	10. (a)
11. (b)	12. (b)	13. (a)	14. (b)	15. (b)	16. (a)	17. (b)	18. (b)	19. (a)	20. (b)
21. (b)	22. (a)	23. (b)	24. (b)	25. (a)	26. (b)	27. (b)	28. (a)	29. (b)	30. (b)
31. (a)	32. (b)	33. (b)	34. (a)	35. (b)	36. (b)	37. (a)	38. (b)	39. (b)	40. (a)
41. (b)	42. (b)	43. (a)	44. (b)	45. (b)	46. (a)	47. (b)	48. (b)	49. (a)	50. (b)
51. (b)	52. (a)	53. (b)	54. (b)	55. (a)	56. (b)	57. (b)	58. (a)	59. (b)	60. (b)

9.6　練習題

混淆字詞

單數題的解答為 (a)

双數題的解答為 (b)

一本突破中式英文盲點：掌握華人學英語發音．文法．字彙關鍵 / 張西亞作 .-- 初版 .-- 臺北市：時報文化，2020.04

面；　　　公分 .-- (Studying；31)

ISBN 978-957-13-8167-1(平裝)

1. 英語 2. 學習方法

805.1　　　　　　　　　　　　　　　　　　　　　　　　　　　　109004391

ISBN 978-957-13-8167-1

Printed in Taiwan

STUDYING31

一本突破中式英文盲點：掌握華人學英語發音・文法・字彙關鍵

作者　張西亞 | 校訂　Daniel Mark McMahon、吳娟 | 圖片提供　張西亞 | 特約編輯　劉綺文 | 副主編　謝翠鈺 | 行銷企劃　江季勳 | 封面設計　李宜芝 | 美術編輯　SHRTING WU | 董事長　趙政岷 | 出版者　時報文化出版企業股份有限公司　108019 台北市和平西路三段 240 號 7 樓　發行專線―(02)2306-6842　讀者服務專線―0800-231-705・(02)2304-7103　讀者服務傳真―(02)2304-6858　郵撥―19344724 時報文化出版公司　信箱―10899 台北華江橋郵局第九九信箱　時報悅讀網―http://www.readingtimes.com.tw | 法律顧問　理律法律事務所　陳長文律師、李念祖律師 | 印刷　勁達印刷有限公司 | 初版一刷　2020 年 4 月 24 日 | 初版四刷　2022 年 9 月 16 日 | 定價　新台幣 400 元 | 缺頁或破損的書，請寄回更換

時報文化出版公司成立於 1975 年，並於 1999 年股票上櫃公開發行，
於 2008 年脫離中時集團非屬旺中，以「尊重智慧與創意的文化事業」為信念。